JUN 15

Mistress OF Melody

D0556944

ANTHEA LAWSON

Fiddlehead Press

~ **Novels** ~

Sonata for a Scoundrel
Passionate
All He Desires

~ **Collections** ~

Kisses & Rogues: Four Regency Stories

~ **Short Stories & Novelettes** ~

Five Wicked Kisses
Maid for Scandal
The Piano Tutor
The Worth of Rubies
To Wed the Earl

Mistress OF Melody

MUSIC OF THE HEART BOOK 2

ANTHEA LAWSON

Cover models, Period Images and Hot Damn. Used with
licensed permission. Cover design, Kim Killion at The Killion
Group.

Edited by Laurie Temple, copy editing by Arran at Editing720.

Discover more at anthealawson.com, and please join Anthea's
new release mailing list at *www.tinyletter.com/AntheaLawson*.
Anthea also writes award-winning YA urban fantasy as Anthea
Sharp.

QUALITY CONTROL: We care about producing error-free
books. If you find a typo or formatting problem, send a note to
anthea@anthealawson.com so that the error may be corrected.

ISBN-13: 978-1-68013-061-4
ISBN-10: 1-68013-061-7

DEDICATION

To my husband, Lawson—my partner in music, and in life.
I love you.

CHAPTER ONE

Miss Lovell Enthralls!
To our surprise, the oft-talked-of Gypsy Violinist does not disappoint.
Last week at Lord B____'s, the dark-haired beauty played so eloquently
that listeners were moved to tears. If given the opportunity to hear Miss
Lovell perform, the Tattler advises you to attend!
-Tilly's Mayfair Tattler, June 11, 1839

Jessamyn Lovell, Gypsy Violinist. London's newest musical sensation.

Criminal.

Fear beat through Jessa in a fierce, uncontrolled rhythm. It would ruin her if she could not contain it. Her violin felt unwieldy in her hand, her bow arm lacking grace, but the audience in the opulent drawing room did not seem to notice. The lords and ladies in the front row watched her perform with every evidence of pleasure, though the melody of the *csardas* sounded raw and clumsy to her ears.

Breathe. Play. She leaned into the music, forcing her fingers to travel the well-remembered tune. A flurry of notes here, a smooth arc of the bow there. The air grew thick with heat and perfume and avid gazes. There was no room for failure.

Her guardian, Mr. Burke, hovered near the exit, waiting to slip away under cover of her performance. She could not bear to watch him.

Jessa closed her eyes and increased the tempo, pushing the melody higher. The metal tang of panic flavored her mouth. She flung herself into the tune, away from any knowledge of her guardian's activities, away from the horrible possibility of discovery. Headlong into the bright notes, her bow at last speeding obediently beneath her hand, the neck of her violin no longer cold and unyielding.

In memory, firelight flickered over laughing faces, the scent of smoke and spices wafted through twilight. She was safe, inside the haven of her music. Her pulse steadied, submitting to the tune, and she opened her eyes.

Now the audience was truly hers. She could feel the stillness in the air, the quiet breath of their rapt attention. Her body swayed as she relaxed and let the melody take hold. Each performance was different—this was the way of the music. Tonight she followed it into a minor turning, the wistful phrases spilling from her instrument. A yearning for home. A loved one, lost.

A woman in the second row brought her kerchief to her eyes. At the side of the room, someone crossed their arms impatiently, distracting Jessa. Whoever it was, they were not under the spell of her music. She lifted her gaze to the far wall, timing the motion with a sweep of her bow.

There. A tall, broad-shouldered figure poised near the door. He was watching her, his eyes glinting in the dimness. His scrutiny was tangible, the weight of his stare heavy against her skin.

Fear flared again. Who was he? Why did he stare at her so intently?

A moment later, he ducked out of the room, lamplight gleaming on his golden hair, and her throat went dry with anxiety. What if he discovered Mr. Burke prowling the hostess's mansion?

But enough. She could not think such a thing, not if she were to keep the audience spellbound. For her sister's sake— for both of them—she must play, and she must play perfectly. Holding fast to the bright threads of melody, Jessa poured herself into the music, finally bringing the *csardas* to a wild and whirling close.

"Bravo!" The front row of listeners surged to their feet, and the rest of the room followed.

Jessa tucked her violin beneath her arm and curtsied, forcing herself to appear calm. Had her guardian returned to the drawing room? Her breath came a little easier when she straightened and saw him. They were undiscovered. This time.

Servants hurried to relight the lamps, and her hostess, the Marchioness of Cowden, came bustling up.

"That was marvelous," she said, laying a ring-studded hand on Jessa's shoulder. Her self-satisfaction was palpable. "How lucky we are to have you perform for us, Miss Lovell."

Jessa all but heard the woman's thoughts—how the marchioness would be regarded as perfectly *au courant* for hosting a musicale featuring the fashionable Gypsy Violinist. And it was true: Miss Lovell did not play for just anyone. Her guardian made sure of that. He had zealously cultivated her reputation and mystique.

If only the patrons knew the true reason they were chosen to host her performances. Not, as they thought, for their musical tastes, but for the size of their bank accounts and the accessibility of their grand houses.

Until yesterday, she had thought it was her talent that moved Mr. Burke to so assiduously promote her concerts. She

4 ~ ANTHEA LAWSON

swallowed bitterness. To her horror, she'd discovered it was instead self-serving cleverness and greed that had launched her musical career. She had no doubt her guardian bribed the tastemakers among the newspapers and scandal sheets to bolster her growing celebrity as the Gypsy Violinist.

"Lady Cowden, I must beg an introduction to our talented performer of the evening."

The low voice came from behind Jessa, and she shivered, like the surface of a still pond stirred by a rising wind. She turned to find a tall, tawny-haired man watching her with guarded gray eyes. She was mortally certain it was the same gentleman she had seen slipping out of the room earlier.

The marchioness clapped her hands together. "Certainly, my lord!" She gave Jessa a superior look. "Miss Lovell, you have the great good fortune to make the acquaintance of one of the most upstanding members of the *ton*. Let me present you to the Earl of Silverton."

"Charmed." The earl made her a shallow bow. He did not look particularly charmed, despite his insistence on an introduction.

Jessa gripped the solid wood of her violin, and did not offer her hand. Far better to keep her distance. The suspicions she saw lurking in his eyes were dangerous.

"Lord Silverton." She dipped her head, so he could read no trace of fear on her face. "I am honored. Please excuse me, I must put away my instrument."

His hand was at her elbow before she could escape him. "I believe your violin case is in the parlor? Allow me to accompany you."

She sent one wild glance into the crowd, hoping to catch her guardian's eye. He had his back to her and seemed in deep conversation with a rotund gentlemen, no doubt determining if the man's large girth was an indication of even deeper pockets.

The marchioness was no help, either; she had turned away to greet another guest. Jessa had no choice but to go with Lord Silverton.

The earl closed the parlor door behind them, then stood blocking the way, arms crossed. Trying to keep her hands from shaking, she tucked her violin away. She covered it with the colorful scarf she kept in the case—a constant, bittersweet reminder of her past.

"Miss Lovell." The earl's tone was cool. "I find it curious that your uncle did not attend the majority your performance."

Jessa latched the case closed. Mr. Burke was her cousin once removed, but there was no point in telling the earl. Her guardian preferred to style himself as her uncle, arguing it made for a better presentation, and she did not have reason enough to dispute it. But she never, ever, called him *uncle*.

"Mr. Burke has heard me play so often…" She lifted one shoulder in a mock shrug.

She must brazen out the conversation, and then exit the parlor as quickly as possible. The earl certainly could have no real proof of anything untoward.

"So often that he must take to wandering about his host's home?"

She kept her tone calm, though her throat was tight. "No doubt he was looking for the convenience. Now you must pardon me, my lord. I'm sure the marchioness—"

"Really, Miss Lovell, do you think me a fool?" With two steps, he reached her. He took her chin in one strong hand and raised it, forcing her to look into his face.

Their gazes collided, and she was certain he could hear the panicked rhythm of her heart. He was tall and overwhelmingly near. Too close, too male, too suspicious.

"What are you and Mr. Burke up to?" he demanded.

"Nothing whatsoever. Now unhand me, sir!" She took

refuge in anger. "If this is the sort of behavior Lady Cowden approves of in her guests, I am shocked."

He released her chin, only to take her hand in his. It was not a hard grip, but there was enough strength in it to warn her she could not pull away from him easily.

"I did not mean to frighten you." His tone was not gentle. She doubted he meant it to be.

In truth, there was nothing gentle about the Earl of Silverton. He seemed fitted to his title—clad in a cold metal of respectability. *Upstanding*, the marchioness had called him. No doubt he thought himself honorable for questioning her. She would give nothing away.

She gave a quick shake of her head and felt a ringlet slip free to brush her cheek. "I am not frightened."

He pressed his lips together. A pity, for they were the only soft thing about him—full and well molded. Now he looked every inch the avenging knight. She forced herself to stand straight under his scrutiny. The pressure of his hand on hers was constant, and she was acutely aware of the heat emanating from his broad chest. He was so near she could see the pulse beating in his neck, could almost taste his scent. Cedar and smoke and a bare whisper of musk.

"It's a curious thing, Miss Lovell." His gaze had not left her face. "Upon close inspection you look nothing like your uncle."

"He is actually more of a cousin," she said. "No doubt he is looking for me even now. My absence will be remarked."

"Very well." He lifted his free hand toward her cheek, and she caught her breath. She had not thought he had followed her into the parlor with scandalous intent.

Instead of touching her face, he took her loosened curl between his fingers. He stared at it a moment, as if to determine whether jet black were her natural color, then tucked it up into her coiffure.

Of course. There could be no appearance of impropriety, no stray curls to suggest anything untoward had occurred in the parlor. Jessa wrenched her gaze from his lips.

"If you decide you have something to confide, here is my card." He finally released her hand to reach into the pocket of his waistcoat. "You may find me at Trevethwick House."

She studied the card, hoping he could not see the miniscule tremble in her fingertips. His name was boldly engraved across the rich, heavy paper. *Morgan Trevethwick, Earl of Silverton.* Without comment, she tucked it into her reticule.

"Good evening, my lord."

Inclining her head with a confidence she did not feel, Jessa caught up her violin case and swept past him. Unfortunately, the thick gold carpet muffled the annoyed tap of her shoes. She was certain nothing could make her seek out the earl. Indeed, she prayed never to set eyes on him again.

***

Morgan Trevethwick, the Earl of Silverton, folded his arms and watched the infuriating Miss Lovell fling the door open and stalk away. Her back was as shapely as her front, the patterned satin of her gown accenting her curves, her angry stride serving to show the outline of hip and thigh. Her black curls bounced indignantly above her ears. Had he secured that wayward strand well enough?

Once, he had been adept at restoring tousled coiffures, but that was long ago. Another lifetime, in fact. He had been a different man than the one who now stood in Lady Cowden's parlor.

A purely unwanted desire pierced through him as he recalled the black silk of Miss Lovell's hair sliding between his fingers. Her sinfully lush mouth, those almond-shaped eyes full of smoky promises.

But not for him.

He tightened his hands into fists, then strode out to take his leave from his hostess. It was clear he would get nothing more tonight from Miss Lovell, or her devious guardian.

The meeting tomorrow at Scotland Yard promised to be nothing but frustration.

CHAPTER TWO

Last week, an argument outside a house of ill repute ended in a brawl with the constables. Rumor places a few young men of the ton at the center of the fight, though the police declined to name any of the participants.
-The London Engager, June 12

The bells of Whitehall struck noon as Morgan stepped through the back entrance to Commissioner Rowan's office, shutting out the hubbub of the London streets. He'd prefer to be noticed by as few people as possible, despite the commissioner's promises of silence. The Silverton family name was at stake. He would take no chances.

Damn, he wanted this business over with. He had little patience for being a tool in this particular game, but Rowan had given him no choice.

The junior constable on duty nodded to him as he passed the man's desk. "Commissioner is expecting you, milord. Go on in."

The moment Morgan entered the room, which smelled faintly of pickled herring, Rowan motioned for him to close the door.

"Afternoon, Lord Silverton." The commissioner stood from behind his paper-piled desk and gave Morgan a cursory nod. "I assume you were at the performance last night, as planned. What did you find?"

Rowan was never one to waste time with courtesies, and Morgan was glad of it. The sooner he could depart Scotland Yard, the better. The very air tasted of spoiled secrets.

"Yes, I attended the concert." Morgan pulled one of the wooden armchairs up to the commissioner's desk. "It seems you were right in your suspicions. I caught Mr. Burke prowling the hallways of Lady Cowden's house last night."

"Good, good." Rowan sat again and began scribbling notes. "Did you see him enter any private rooms? Take anything?"

"I did not." If only it had been that easy.

"Damn. You'll have to keep watching him. Did you question the girl?"

"Yes." The memory of Miss Lovell's full lips and dark, exotic eyes sent another traitorous jolt through Morgan. It was only lust. He wrestled it back down, into the black pit where all the vices in his soul were prisoned.

"And?" The commissioner tossed down his pen. "Good God, man. Mr. Burke is the best lead we have. I know you're helping us under duress, but we must catch this blackmailer. Our clients among the *ton* are unhappy enough with the force. Allowing criminal elements like this mysterious Mr. Z to wreak havoc… we can't let it continue." Rowan ran his hand over his thinning hair. "And no need to scowl at me. It's not my fault your cousin Geordie got taken up for breaking the peace."

Damn Geordie for that. And damn himself for thinking this mess could be cleared up quickly, without undue attention. Nothing in his life had ever been that simple.

It was high time he had a talk with the boy. Morgan had

been letting him run too freely. As the earl, he'd worked long and hard to restore the family name, and he refused to let the taint in their bloodline ruin it again. Especially as, currently, Geordie was the presumptive heir to the Silverton title.

"Miss Lovell revealed nothing," Morgan said. Hidden by his palm, his thumb smoothed the metal of the earl's signet ring clasped around his finger. "Though I've no doubt her uncle was up to no good, poking about the Cowdens' hallways. I'm doing what I can."

"Well, do more. We can't press charges for 'wandering about a house.' For all we know, Burke was out taking a piss."

"That's what he claimed."

Burke was certainly clever. The blackmailer had been at work for nearly two months, leaving almost no trail behind. But he or his beguiling niece would make a misstep—and Morgan would be there to catch them when they did.

Rowan curled his fingers into a fist and tapped his desk. "We're having him followed, but you're our man inside. When's the next concert?"

"Next Thursday, I believe. At Lord Dearborn's."

"You'll be there." It was not a question. "Report back on Friday next—the usual time. I hope you'll have more for us then, my lord. Both myself and Sir Peel would like evidence. And, of course, to remove your cousin's name from this brawling incident."

So did he. Already a whiff of Geordie's misconduct had reached the papers.

And, privately, Morgan had to admit that even without the threat of family exposure hanging over the Silverton name, he wanted to help apprehend Mr. Z—this vulture gorging on the carrion of Society's misconduct. Such vermin should not be allowed to go freely about the streets of London.

***

Nearly a week later, Morgan leaned against the pale blue wall of Lady Dearborn's salon, and waited.

Waited for the lights to dim. Waited for the stunningly talented Miss Lovell to appear. Waited for her uncle to slip out of the room—as he knew the man would. This time, Morgan planned to catch the fellow. Those shifty eyes had belied his protestations of innocence at the last performance, but Morgan could smell the lies coming off his skin.

Tonight he must uncover the proof Rowan needed, the hard evidence. It could not be coincidence that Mr. Z was blackmailing several families where Miss Lovell had performed. But not *all* of them. And not every victim had hosted a musicale by the celebrated violinist.

Despite himself, Morgan felt a twinge of sympathy for Rowan and Scotland Yard. The man had not said precisely how many members of the *ton* had fallen victim to the blackmailer, but certainly it was enough to make his job quite uncomfortable until the villain was caught.

Yet another reason to live an exemplary life. Morgan's indiscretions were over a decade old—ashes and dust that would not fuel any scandals.

"Silverton!" A dark-haired gentleman approached, his voice lifted in surprise. "Haven't seen you about for ages. How have you been keeping?"

"Bandon." Morgan nodded a greeting. Viscount Bandon had once counted among his circle of friends. "Well enough."

He was hardly going to detail his difficulties since their days at Oxford. Not to Bandon—or anyone. Certainly most people knew of the accident that had taken his brother's life, and inexorably altered the course of his own—but the stringent path he had trodden ever since was not a matter for discussion.

The viscount raised a brow and surveyed the gathering. "Hard to think this is where we've ended up, after all our adventures. Stuffed in a room with the stodgiest members of society. A musicale at Deadly Dull Dearborn's." He affected a shudder, then dipped into his pocket and brought out a silver flask. He tipped it toward Morgan. "Care for a drink?"

"No." He never touched hard alcohol. Not after that night.

The viscount took a long swallow, then glanced at the front of the room. "At least the daughter is no hardship to look at. Too bad she's such a stickler for propriety. I'd like to steal a kiss from that one."

"She is too good for you." Morgan spoke the words mildly, but threaded them with steel.

Though he was not acquainted with the lady in question, he had made it a point never to allow ungentlemanly comments to pass him by. Constant vigilance was the only way to hold on to decency. One slip could turn an entire life astray.

Bandon gave him a level look. "So it's true, you've turned yawningly respectable. Unless you've got your sights on the girl yourself? I'll leave you the field, Trev. A pity, though." He shook his head, then took another swallow from the flask.

Trev. Morgan felt the name lodge under his skin like a sliver. His old name, from his old life.

"It's Silverton," he said. His dead brother's title. It had taken him years to feel comfortable wearing it.

"Good Lord, man. You needn't take yourself so seriously. I've told you I'll stand clear, if you want Lady Anne." He nodded, and Morgan followed his gaze to the bright-haired young lady in the front row.

Lord Dearborn's daughter. He hadn't considered that particular girl. He hadn't considered *any* particular girls, though he had every intention of starting a list of properly eligible young ladies. Marriage, after all, was the next step in the preservation of the earldom. Especially as his cousin, who was currently next in line for the title, had evidently inherited the family's wild streak.

In one thing, at least, Bandon was correct. Lady Anne was a lovely girl; cream-skinned and golden-haired, with wide blue eyes that held no knowledge of the darker shadows that lurked in men's hearts. Eminently suitable.

The lights dimmed, and he heard the viscount draw in a breath, then expel it in a low hiss. "Damn—now there's a woman. Keep your Society misses. I'll take the likes of *her* any day."

Morgan looked to the head of the room, where Miss Lovell had just entered. Her black hair gleamed in the lamplight, and the red silk gown she wore showed an indecent amount of bosom. Or precisely the right amount, if one's tastes ran toward titillation. Her dark-eyed beauty was of a different brand altogether than the proper misses seated in the audience, and he understood Bandon's fascination.

He'd wager that every man in the room had felt his blood heat the instant Miss Lovell stepped inside. Her lush lips begged for kisses. Her body curved in places that made a man's hands tighten with desire.

And then she lifted her violin and played, and the spell was cast over everyone, man and woman alike. The rich notes flew out from the instrument—runs and trills and harmonies. As before, Miss Lovell played without printed music. She knew the tunes intimately, and she moved with a natural, unconscious grace as she played. Her body swayed, she leaned and breathed, and the listeners breathed with her.

It was only after long minutes had passed that Morgan realized he'd missed his chance. Swallowing a curse, he tore his gaze from her and scanned the audience. Damnation. Her uncle was gone, slipped away while the niece kept the listeners distracted.

At least the rapt audience made Morgan's own exit easy. No one paid him any mind as he eased his way to the door. He paused and glanced once more at the performer.

She was watching him. It was a subtle scrutiny, with her lashes lowered over her eyes, her bow arcing deftly over the strings, but still he knew. He could see it in the way the black wings of her brows drew together, the tightening at the corners of her soft lips.

The memory of touching her jolted through him. He had held her hand tightly in his. He had felt the impossible silk of her hair. He had very nearly caressed her cheek and tugged her against him for an illicit kiss.

Arousal and self-disgust warred in him, and Morgan turned abruptly and strode from the salon. The music followed him, a scattering of notes like a barely-felt caress.

Where was that damned uncle of hers?

Morgan stalked through the halls. He halted at the private wing and surveyed the closed doors. At Lady Cowden's he had caught Mr. Burke skulking near the family quarters, but there was no sign of him here. After waiting several minutes, Morgan heaved a breath and turned back toward the salon.

The sound of a door closing, the faint movement of rain-scented air against his cheek—he pivoted and followed his intuition down a shadowed corridor. Empty, it led to an exterior door. He eased it open, quieting his breath. The pitter of summer rain on leaves, the flare and acrid stench of a phosphor match, then the glow of a cheroot. Morgan stepped outside, narrowing his eyes against the darkness until he could make out the figure of a man standing beneath a nearby elm. As he had thought, it was Miss Lovell's uncle.

"Mr. Burke," he said. "Again you absent yourself from

your niece's concert."

The man blew out a nearly invisible stream of smoke. "Lord Silverton. May I say the same for you? Odd behavior for a music lover."

"I never claimed to be an aficionado." Indeed, until he had heard Miss Lovell play, Morgan had not been overly fond of the solo violin.

"I warn you, my lord, if you keep seeking me out because you wish to do more than simply *listen* to my niece, I don't do that kind of business. She's not available for activities beyond concertizing."

Morgan blinked. Of course—Mr. Burke was probably approached all too often by men desirous of furthering their acquaintance with Miss Lovell. At least, whatever else the fellow was up to, he wasn't selling her favors.

"Miss Lovell is quite talented," Morgan said. "How long has she been in London?"

"Long enough for people to know musical brilliance when they hear it." Mr. Burke straightened and took another pull of his cheroot. "Would you be interested in hosting a musicale yourself, Lord Silverton? The fees are not exorbitant, if I may speak bluntly."

Host a concert at Trevethwick House? It was a mad thought. Yet what better way to keep Mr. Burke under surveillance than during a performance at Morgan's own home? He had to have *something* to give to the commissioner at their meeting tomorrow, and so far he'd failed to garner any evidence for Scotland Yard.

"How much?" If Mr. Burke was going to descend to the level of commerce, Morgan would meet him there.

Mr. Burke eyed him, as though calculating the cost of his fine wool coat, the weight of the sapphire set in his signet ring. "Three hundred pounds."

"And when is Miss Lovell free to perform?" Good God, was he really thinking of hosting a social event? He'd have to enlist his aunt's help, of course. Bachelor earls did not hold musicales.

On the other hand, perhaps he *would* make up that list of young ladies and instruct his aunt to see that they were invited. He needed a plausible reason to host the event. If the mamas of the *ton* saw it as a signal—well, perhaps they had the right of it.

"My niece will be able to play for you..." Mr. Burke pressed his thin lips together a moment. "In a fortnight. If that is acceptable, my lord."

"It will do." Two weeks should be enough time for his aunt to send invitations and attend to whatever other details were necessary. "Will Miss Lovell be performing before that time?"

"She's been asked to play before Queen Victoria next week." The man's voice was sharp with pride.

The queen. It would fortify Miss Lovell's reputation as a performer of the first order, and make Morgan's job that much more difficult. Still, if Peel wanted the girl and her uncle watched, he could wangle Morgan an invitation to court. Or do it himself. No doubt the former prime minister was welcome at the new queen's functions.

Morgan gave Mr. Burke a tight smile. "Very well—a concert at Trevethwick House in a fortnight. Where shall I call upon you to finalize the details?"

"I'll send you a contract, my lord. You can have your solicitor look it over, but I assure you everything will be properly set out." Mr. Burke dropped his cheroot and ground it under his heel. "The musicale must be nearly over. Good evening."

"Oh, I'll come with you." Morgan fell into step beside the

man as he turned back to the house. Mr. Burke would not escape him again tonight.

CHAPTER THREE

"**D**amn the man!" As soon as Jessa and her guardian stepped through the front door of Mr. Burke's home, he threw his coat to the floor and began pacing in tight, angry circles. "How am I to do my work when he watches every step?"

Keeping out of his way, Jessa edged toward the stairs. She could guess which man he meant. The Earl of Silverton, though she knew better than to speak that name aloud. After four months beneath Mr. Burke's roof, she had learned that the slightest things could send her bitter, unpredictable relative into a spiral of rage.

He whirled on Jessa, and she froze. "Did you tell Lord Silverton anything? I saw him with you after the performance at Cowden's."

"No! I swear it—"

"You're in this up to your neck too, girl. If I'm arrested, don't think I'll hesitate to name you as an accomplice. And where would that leave your precious idiot of a sister? Bedlam, that's where."

She swallowed hard. "I'll never say a word."

That horrible morning when she had discovered Mr. Burke's schemes was stamped in her memory. And though the marks of the cane switch had faded from Louisa's back, the echo of her screams still sounded in Jessa's nightmares.

Mr. Burke had gone out, leaving a half-composed letter upon his desk. Curious, Jessa had read it, her blood turning cold as she understood what she was seeing.

It was a blackmail note, threatening to reveal secrets about one of the patrons she had recently performed for. Hands trembling, Jessa had sifted through the desk and found more correspondence—all with members of the *ton* who had hosted the Gypsy Violinist.

Her guardian had returned, then, and seen her surrounded by the evidence of his perfidy. Foolishly, she had told him she'd go to the constables.

"Let me show you another letter," he'd said, rummaging in the bottom of the desk drawer. "This is merely a copy, you understand. Should anything happen to me—anything at all— immediate action will be taken."

Jessa had read it, icy despair seeping through her. The letter committed Louisa to the worst lunatic asylum in London.

"You can't," she'd said.

"Of course I can. I'm your guardian. And I'll prove that lesson to you over and over, until you believe it." His voice had been hard and angry. "Tell your sister I'll be paying her a visit. With the switch."

"No—please." Jessa had gone to her knees. "Beat me instead."

He'd looked down at her, his eyes hard as brown pebbles. "You have a performance on the morrow. I'm afraid your sister will be paying the price of your prying into my affairs. Don't do it again."

Despite her tears and pleas, he had not relented. Indeed, he had given her a rough punch to the stomach when she'd tried to block the door of their bedroom, then locked her outside while he striped Louisa's back.

Jessa swallowed down the bile that rose at the memory.

"Remember who it was that took you in after your father died and his filthy people turned their backs on you. You owe me, Jessamyn. Don't forget it." He glared at her, no sympathy in his expression.

"Yes, sir." She dipped her head, fingers clenched around the handle of her violin case.

Defiance would only earn her a painful blow to her back or ribs—something that would not show. And perhaps a backhand across the face for Louisa, since it did not matter if she sported a bruise upon her cheek.

Indeed, Mr. Burke seemed to enjoy the obvious signs of his abuse. The only protection she and Louisa had was the shield of Jessa's obedience.

There was no point in arguing, either. Mr. Burke wanted to believe that he had taken Jessa and her sister in after the Romani threw them out, but the truth was that she'd made the choice to go with him.

Her stomach clenched. Agreeing to live under Mr. Burke's guardianship had seemed the better path, when the alternative was a forced alliance to a dour Rom man three times her age. Now, however, she feared she had made the worse choice.

"You play before Queen Victoria next week, girl."

Jessa nodded. Before, the thought had filled her with anxiety, but now it would be a relief to perform without the terror that her guardian would be discovered. Buckingham Palace was too closely guarded for even Mr. Burke to contemplate prowling.

"And after that," he said, "I've spoken with the Earl of Silverton about a musicale at his mansion. The man is well heeled enough—and it would serve him right for prying into my business."

"Sir. Do you think that's wise?"

He narrowed his eyes. "Your fame is hardly going to last out the Season. The *ton* is fickle, always looking for the newest sensation. Gypsy Violinist today, Spanish Dancer tomorrow. I take the opportunities as they come. And it's still not enough for you to repay me. My brother inherited an empty title and a tower of debts—all on account of your mother."

It was his constant refrain, and there was nothing she could do to deny it. No matter that the debt had been accrued before she was born.

Her mother, Mr. Burke's cousin, had abandoned the single Season her poor yet genteel family had managed for her, dashing their hopes for a rise in their fortunes. And bankrupting the family in the process. The Burkes had spent thousands of pounds on gowns and gloves and jewels, only to have their beautiful daughter run off with the darkly handsome half-blood Gypsy who had been hired on as a stable hand.

Perhaps the young Miss Burke had not realized how close to financial ruin her family had been. Perhaps she had not thought she would be disinherited. Perhaps she had only known that she had lost her heart and must follow where it led.

Jessa kept her gaze on the dingy wooden floorboards. She and Louisa should not have to pay for her mother's folly, but Mr. Burke demanded it.

Night after night, Jessa lay awake, casting about for a way to be free of him, but her thoughts inevitably ended up chasing round and round, like a cur after its own tail. They had no resources. Mr. Burke had confiscated the few coins she'd managed to scrape together while with the Rom.

Still, she had seen a few shillings in his desk. If the opportunity ever presented itself, she and Louisa would flee.

And go where? She was wise enough to realize they could not survive on the streets. Perhaps the Rom would take them back. She swallowed back bile at the thought of wedding old Pietro. But to keep Louisa safe, she would.

Mr. Burke waved his hand. "Go. I want you to practice for the next five days until your fingers are numb. You must perform flawlessly before the queen."

"I will."

It was the only easy thing about her life now. If she could, she would live inside the music, crawl into the notes and never come out. Except that Louisa needed her. No doubt her sister was lying awake upstairs, waiting for her safe return. Jessa hurried up the cold, unlit stairwell.

Light trickled from beneath the door of the bedroom she and her sister shared. Jessa stepped quietly inside, in case Louisa was asleep, but when she turned from shutting the door she found her sister watching her with large, dark eyes.

"Jessie. I heard him shouting at you."

"It's all right, love."

Jessa set her violin case in the corner, then slipped her cape off and hung it in the wardrobe. Every item of clothing Mr. Burke bought was another tally on the endless debt he felt she owed. The one time she had torn her skirt, Louisa had been given a fierce blow in punishment. Since then, Jessa had taken the utmost care with the possessions he had provided.

She sat on the narrow bed that faced her sister's.

"Who is the Silver Lord?" Louisa asked in her soft, childlike voice. "Is he a prince from a fairytale?"

Jessa shook her head at the memory of Lord Silverton's cold demeanor, the threat in his eyes. "No."

There were no princes. Only men, with all their flaws and pettiness. Even her father, who had seemed perfect in her childish eyes, had been a foolish, selfish fellow. Would he still have eloped with Jessa's mother had he known that tragedy and hardship would be his daughters' only inheritance?

She let out a sigh, and Louisa reached over and patted her hand. It was a sweet gesture, and Jessa smiled at her sister.

"Shall I tell you a story?" she asked, reaching to smooth Louisa's dark brown hair from her forehead. "The golden apples and the princess?"

It was a favorite—one she had heard herself as a child around the Gypsy campfires.

Yearning flashed through her. With their father's untimely death, the carefree life of a Rom was closed to her. It was a life Louisa had barely known. If only their father had not been thrown by a half-wild stallion, her sister would have been cared for there, and respected for her curious, childlike wisdom.

But without family to stand for them, Jessa could choose to wed whoever would have her, or take her sister and leave. They were three-quarters *gadje*—non-Romani. Too much outsiders for the clan to offer them a home. And yet too Gypsy to be accepted into the Society their mother had abandoned.

Louisa sat up in bed and folded her arms around her knees. "I want the Three Wishes tonight. Do you think we can find a fairy and win three wishes from her, Jessie? I would wish Mama were still alive. And I would wish for the Silver Lord to be a handsome prince for you. And I would wish we lived in a beautiful castle all together, with plenty to eat and lovely gowns to wear."

Tears pricked the back of Jessa's throat. "Those are very good wishes, indeed."

Alas, they had no chance whatsoever of coming true.

***

The butler took Morgan's hat and gloves, then showed him into Aunt Agatha's parlor. It smelled of lemon oil, overlaid with some curious foreign spice that made his nose twitch. He paced to the mantel, the top of which was cluttered with curios. But these were not the usual porcelain shepherds and vases. No, of course not. Aunt Agatha would never display anything so conventional. Instead, these were carvings of wood, of ivory, of green-streaked stone. Each one depicted a human form. Naked. Some of them were even embracing.

He let out an aggravated breath. A pity he had no other female relatives to help in this endeavor.

"Morgan! Whatever brings you out to Surrey?" Aunt Agatha paused in the doorway, no doubt so that Morgan could admire the effect of her emerald silk turban. A white ostrich plume waved from the center, adding height to the already absurd headpiece. "Not that I'm displeased to see you, of course. Tea? Brandy?"

"It's eleven in the morning, aunt. Don't you think brandy is a bit extreme?"

She swept into the room. "That depends on *why* you are here. If it is to complain about Geordie again, then brandy is certainly in order."

"My complaints aren't idle. I'd prefer you kept your son on a tighter rein."

Geordie had always been a bit spoiled, having been born later in life to his aunt and her now-deceased husband. But there were limits.

She peered down her thin nose at him. "Geordie is sensible enough to behave well enough on his own. Besides, young men need to kick up their heels. Goodness knows you and your brother did—"

"And look where that ended." Morgan kept his temper leashed. His youthful indiscretions had not been his aunt's fault. Still, she needed to understand the seriousness of the situation. "I'd rather not have to haul your son out of a ditch."

Morgan closed his eyes briefly against the memory of his

brother's body being pulled out of the broken curricle, illuminated by torches that sputtered in the night rain.

"Oh, dear." She paused, then sank down on a gaily striped chaise. "He hasn't been racing, has he?"

"Not that, no."

"Gambling?"

"He hasn't the taste for it." Nor the ability. Thank God the boy kept clear of that particular vice.

"Dueling?" She whispered the word, her face pale.

"No." Blast it, he'd have to tell her—though he'd leave out the fact that the incident had happened outside the seediest brothel in Piccadilly. "He was in a brawl, and taken up for disturbing the peace. Apparently he broke a constable's nose."

Aunt Agatha rose and went to the ornately carved sideboard. "He didn't tell me of this." Her hands trembled slightly as she poured brandy into a glass, then took a gulp. "Is he... is he in jail?"

"Of course not. He sent word to me, and I posted a surety for his good behavior." All told, Geordie had spent less than two hours in the London jail—but it had been enough to shake the boy. Morgan hoped.

"Then all's well." She drained her glass and turned to Morgan. "I shall have a talk with him."

"Good. I've spoken with him already, but perhaps he will listen to you." And all was *not* well. Not with the charges still hanging over Geordie's head as insurance for Morgan's assistance in the damned Mr. Z case.

"Thank you for coming to tell me the truth," his aunt said.

"There is one other thing." Morgan picked up one of the inappropriate carvings, then set it hastily back down, and turned to his aunt. "I would like your... advice."

His aunt's eyebrows rose dramatically. "Goodness, Morgan. And here I thought you had your entire life well in hand." There was an acerbic edge to her voice. Aunt Agatha made no secret of the fact she did not approve of his rigidly controlled existence. But she did not understand that he had no choice.

Morgan paced before the hearth, his footsteps muffled by the garish red and orange carpet. "I've decided it's time to find a wife."

"Of course you have." The plume in her turban waved wildly as she nodded. "And have you anyone in mind for this singular honor?"

"I've a list."

"A list." She let out an unladylike snort. "No doubt it consists of the most boring and insipid females the *ton* has to offer. Do you plan to go down it, name by name, until someone will have you?"

He halted. "I'm not such a poor catch, Aunt. I doubt I will need to ask more than one."

"Then you had better choose well. It wouldn't do for the upright Earl of Silverton to make a bad match." She set her finger to her chin. "Though it all depends on how one defines a bad match. Some would say love—"

"I'm going to host a musicale at Trevethwick House."

He could not stand to hear her lectures on the importance of love. Emotions had no place in it. Just because she had enjoyed a deliriously happy marriage until her husband's death, she thought everyone should embrace such maudlin sentiments.

"You are?" She blinked up at him. "Well. A musicale. How unlikely."

"I need your help." The words scraped out of him.

A slow smile eased across Aunt Agatha's face. "Yes. You do, don't you? Goodness, but this will be amusing!"

"The aim is not amusement. It is a suitable engagement."

"I'll have to come up to Town. I'll stay with you at Trevethwick House—it's only sensible. Have you a date planned for this musicale?"

"The third of July."

Her expression of satisfaction faded. "That's a mere thirteen days away! Morgan, you can't be serious."

"I have every faith you'll manage to make it a splendid event, Aunt. Shall I expect you in London tomorrow?"

She pursed her lips. "Of course you may expect me. We will begin with the musicians. I wonder if Sir Thomas Moore—"

"I've already arranged for Miss Lovell, the Gypsy Violinist, to perform. She's rather the sensation about town." Though he hoped she would wear a less revealing gown. He could not afford to be distracted again. Especially not under his own roof.

"Excellent. I've read about Miss Lovell, and would very much like to hear her play. She seems quite the thing." Eyes narrowing, Aunt Agatha tipped her head. The plume in her turban quivered with the movement. "Have you attended any of her performances, Morgan?"

"Yes."

"And did you enjoy them? Is Miss Lovell as lovely as the scandal sheets say?"

Good Lord, his aunt was like a hound scenting a fox. Morgan rose. "I suppose she is lovely enough." Exotic-eyed and hair like black silk. "I must be going. I'll let the housekeeper know you'll arrive tomorrow."

Aunt Agatha folded her arms. "You won't be able to run away from me when I'm staying at Trevethwick House. And I believe the musicale will be quite diverting. I'm eager to meet this Gypsy Violinist of yours."

"She's not mine." And she never would be. Miss Lovell was perilously tempting, but she was a temptation he could refuse.

No matter the rough heat that filled the coldness he'd so carefully cultivated inside. No matter how unruly desire scorched through the bounds of his dreams until he woke, gasping, the echo of wild melodies pulsing through him, leaving him full of hot lust.

It was nothing that taking a wife could not cure. In the meantime, he would silently endure, and conduct himself properly. No wanton-eyed Gypsy lass could make him stray from the path he had set himself.

CHAPTER FOUR

Esteemed Earl Seeks A Wife?
News has reached the Tattler that Lord Silverton will be holding a
musicale, to feature London's newest sensation, the Gypsy Violinist Miss
Lovell. The bachelor lord is rumored to be inviting an array of Society's
most accomplished Eligibles. Watch for your invitations, ladies!
-Tilly's Mayfair Tattler, June 18

Jessa carried her violin case through the halls of
Buckingham Palace and tried not to stare. Since she'd begun
performing for the *ton*, she had seen wealth and ostentation
aplenty, but nothing rivaled the palace. The chandeliers glowed
brilliantly, the carpet underfoot was lush and thick, and the very
air itself seemed scented with royalty—a perfume of luxury and
privilege that saturated her senses.

The liveried footman led Mr. Burke and herself to a side
room, where she could warm up and make ready for her
performance before the queen. As soon as the servant left, her
guardian gave her a baleful look. It seemed that being
surrounded by so much wealth he could not touch had put him
in one of his blacker moods.

"Hurry up, girl. You must be ready when the queen sends
for you. I'll not have you shaming me."

Jessa dipped her head and busied herself with her violin: sweeping fine rosin dust off the gleaming wood, tightening her bow, carefully tuning her strings. She turned away from her guardian and played a lilting set of notes. The Fairy Glen waltz, to begin. Surely the young queen would favor such a sweet tune.

A servant cleared his throat from the doorway. "Her Majesty will hear you now, Miss Lovell. Please follow me to the Music Room."

Jessa tucked her instrument under her arm, then shot her uncle a quick glance.

"Go on," he said.

The footman did not move from the threshold. "Yourself as well, sir."

He gestured for Jessa and Mr. Burke to precede him out of the room, as if he suspected they were the sort that would make off with the silver candlesticks atop the mantel if left to themselves for too long. A wise fellow, indeed.

Eyes narrowed, her uncle stalked past Jessa, displeasure clear in the set of his shoulders. The footman nodded, closed the door behind them, then stepped forward to lead the way. His knee breeches and powdered hair made her feel as though they had slipped into the previous century, yet the formality was perfectly suited to the grand passageway they were traversing. The servant paused before a pair of wide doors and spoke, low-voiced, to another man—presumably the lord steward, who was resplendent in scarlet livery and carried a white staff.

At the steward's nod, the footman pulled open the doors, and Jessa's mouth went suddenly dry.

She, Jessamyn Lovell, who had grown up in the poorest area of Oxford, daughter of an ailing lace-maker and a gypsy stableman—*she* was being presented to the queen! Oh, but she must remember every moment so she could recount it all perfectly for Louisa.

At the far side of the domed room sat Queen Victoria. She wore a cream satin gown covered in lace and bows, cut low upon her shoulders, and the looped braids of her glossy brown hair were caught up at the back of her head in an elegant bun. Her face was round and regal, and her eyes were serious as she watched Jessa approach.

The lord steward tapped his staff upon the floor and announced, "Miss Lovell, the Gypsy Violinist. Mr. Burke. You may approach the queen."

Jessa stepped forward, the crystal gasoliers a blur of light, calling forth the sparkle of gems from nearly every neck and finger of the assembled court. When she was a few paces from the queen, the steward lifted his hand in a signal to halt. Jessa dropped into the most gracious curtsy she could manage with her violin tucked beneath her elbow. From the corner of her eye, she saw her guardian make a deep, precise bow. When she lifted her head, the queen gave her a faint smile.

"We are pleased that you have come to play for us, Miss Lovell."

"Your Majesty—it gives me great honor to perform for you and your court." Jessa took a steadying breath, then set her violin on her shoulder and looked to the steward. At his curt nod, she began.

It was such a blessed relief to play without fear, to pour herself into the music without watching the shadows. She had chosen a medley of tunes, beginning with the waltz, then moving into more spirited melodies. This was, like almost everything she played, music made for dancing. It always felt a bit odd to perform to a room full of still and silent listeners. She counted as a victory every foot she set to tapping, every lady's fan that waved in time to the beat. If these proper lords and ladies would not leap to their feet and kick their heels up in a wild mazurka, at least she made them dance inside. The thought made her smile.

There was one gentleman off to the side, unmoving and alert. She slanted him a look along with a flurry of notes—an invitation to enter the music—but her fingers nearly faltered when she met his cold gray gaze. The Earl of Silverton.

Her joy curled in upon itself like a flower exposed to frost.

There was something predatory in his eyes, as though she were a bird and he a cat, waiting for her to take flight so that he could pounce. Her guardian might claim she had made a conquest of the gentleman, but she did not see admiration in his eyes. Suspicion, certainly, and a rigid control that she did not think any music could unbend.

With a deep breath, she pulled her attention away from the earl, and back into the music. Her final tune was a scattering of sparks against a star-dappled sky, and she made her bow rock and dance over the strings, remembering.

The scent of wood smoke, the bonfire gilding the trunks of the trees, the bright gazes of the children as they sat, barefoot, listening to the music and the tales. That sense of the world in perfect balance, with everything as it should be.

Jessa brought the tune to a close, her focus now on the queen. Victoria's expression was wistful, her eyes filled with a yearning for simpler times. Of course, the queen must carry burdens even heavier than Jessa's own.

"Thank you," Queen Victoria said.

"Your majesty." Jessa dipped into a low curtsy, barely hearing the applause of the court. She hoped she'd helped the queen forget her troubles—if only for a short while.

The queen beckoned her forward. She unpinned a pearl and diamond brooch from her dress, and held it out to Jessa.

"A small token of my thanks," she said.

"I am deeply honored." Jessa took the brooch from the queen's gloved fingers, then bowed again.

Louisa would be so delighted to hold a pin that the queen herself had been wearing! When Jessa straightened, the members of the court had already turned back to their gossiping, and the queen's attention had shifted to an older gentleman who seemed to be an advisor.

The servant who had shown Jessa into the Music Room hovered at her elbow, ready to escort her from the royal presence. So quickly did her moment of glory evaporate.

Mr. Burke scowled and stalked after her as the servant led them back to the waiting room.

"Where's our pay?" he asked the servant as the liveried man turned to go.

A look of distaste crossed the man's face. "I have no doubt your compensation will be arriving shortly. Good day."

"Lackey," Mr. Burke muttered, even before the door was shut.

Jessa made no comment, instead busying herself with tucking her violin and bow away. The bright Rom scarf brushed softly against her fingers. Who would have thought that it—and she—would be here, inside the palace? It almost seemed a dream: the opulent carpet beneath her feet, the glittering chandeliers, the richly painted artwork decorating the walls. Yet she would trade anything for the perfect summers of her childhood, traveling the dusty roads and sheltering in the forests with her father's clan.

With a rueful twist of her mouth, she snicked the latches shut.

Her guardian grasped her shoulder and pulled her to face him. "The queen did not like your performance."

Jessa stared at him—his expression pinched with anger, the violence coming off him in hot waves.

"But… she did, sir. I am sure of it. She even gave me a token."

"As to that." Mr. Burke held out his hand. "A pretty enough trinket. I can put it to some use."

"Please. May I keep it?" She hated to beg, but she could not bear for him to rob her and Louisa of this small joy.

"No." His tone was implacable.

He stared at her, his eyes like dried molasses, until she reluctantly gave him the brooch. Her heart pricked as he tucked it away in his pocket. Another treasure, gone.

"The queen gives such tokens to everyone," he said. "It means nothing. Why did you choose sad songs to play?" His voice lifted on the rising tide of his temper. "You are trying to thwart me, aren't you? Attempting to undo your fame?"

He lifted his free hand, and she wrenched away, stumbling over the gilded table leg. The blow landed short, the punishing slap he had intended just clipping the side of her jaw. It stung, but not as fiercely as landing directly on her cheek would have.

"No! I am doing everything you say. I swear it." She backed away, furiously trying to think of the words that might placate him. "You know I would not jeopardize Louisa—"

"Perhaps you'd obey better if your sister truly *was* locked away." There was an ugly, exultant note in his voice. He lunged and caught her arm. "What do you say to that?"

"I say release Miss Lovell. Immediately." The cold voice came from the threshold.

The Earl of Silverton stood there, one hand on the open door. Though his voice was controlled, fire sparked in his eyes.

"My lord." Mr. Burke did not let go of Jessa. "No need to involve yourself, I assure you. My niece is sometimes in need of a firm hand."

The earl's gaze slid to Jessa's face. From the slight narrowing of his eyes, she was certain he noted the marks of her guardian's slap against her skin.

"Miss Lovell." Lord Silverton inclined his head toward Jessa. "May I escort you home? I would not like to see any... harm befall you."

"Look here!" Mr. Burke let go of her arm and set his fists on his hips. "That's completely unnecessary. You're meddling in our business, Lord Silverton. It's a family matter. Far beneath your notice."

"Nevertheless." The earl took three strides into the room, his presence dominating the space. "Then I shall wait with you until you depart from the palace."

Her guardian sputtered, but there was nothing he could do. Despite herself, Jessa let out a soft breath of relief. Her fingers crept to her jaw, where her skin still smarted.

The earl caught her gaze, and she was trapped there, falling into the chilly pools of his eyes. Cool, yes, but not entirely without sympathy. Of course, he was a gentleman. It was no doubt against his code to condone violence against women— although she had heard that many men of the *ton* proclaimed one set of values in public, while demonstrating quite another in private.

But despite the spark of genuine concern in his expression, there was no assistance he might give her. Beyond standing sentinel so that Mr. Burke would not abuse her, which was help enough. She mustered up a grateful smile, then perched on a nearby settee.

The earl remained standing, hands folded behind his back. His coat of silvery gray flattered his broad shoulders, and the white linen at his neck served to emphasize the gleaming gold of his hair. The line of his lips was uncompromising, as if he seldom smiled. His eyes met hers and he raised one fair brow.

Heat crept into her cheeks. Indeed, she had been staring at him overlong. Jessa dropped her gaze to her hands. What did he think of her, if he thought of her at all? Was it only chivalry that kept him there, a guard against her guardian's rough violence?

She peeked up through her eyelashes, to find him still regarding her. She knew that men found her attractive, though most of them wore their lustful thoughts plain on their faces. The Earl of Silverton did not. The predatory look was gone from his eyes, and now he watched her as one might assess an unfamiliar creature, waiting to see if it would take flight, or attack, or simply return to grazing upon a nearby bush.

"Mr. Burke, Miss Lovell." The servant reappeared in the doorway. "And Lord Silverton," he added smoothly.

Then he paused, looking to the earl.

"I am merely keeping the queen's guests company," the earl said. "Pay me no mind."

The servant nodded, and held out a thin leather wallet to Mr. Burke. "Your payment, drawn upon the Bank of England. I shall see you out now."

Mr. Burke took the wallet, checked the contents, then grunted in approval.

"Fetch your things, girl," he said.

Beneath the earl's watchful gaze, Jessa rose, donned her pelisse, and picked up her violin case. She wanted to thank him, but that would only earn her guardian's wrath. Instead, she met the earl's eyes as they passed, hoping her expression might convey her gratitude. She did not trust the man, but he had saved her from more blows. At least temporarily.

He inclined his head, ever so slightly. As she followed Mr. Burke into the wide hallway, she felt the earl's gaze upon her back. She did not know any longer what he was—enemy, ally, or something of both.

***

Morgan watched Miss Jessamyn Lovell follow her uncle down the wide hallways of Buckingham Palace. She held her head high, uncowed by the wealth and gentility displayed on all sides.

The constable had told him the Burke family was of minor nobility, but that Miss Lovell had been raised primarily in the slums of Oxford, and sometimes in Gypsy encampments. Her self-possession was remarkable.

The uncle, however... Morgan curled his hands into fists at the thought of the red mark on Miss Lovell's jaw. Had he entered the room a moment earlier, instead of sharing a brief word with Sir Peel, Morgan could have prevented Mr. Burke from striking her. As it was, he'd barely restrained himself from collaring the man and giving him a few blows in return.

But fighting in the public rooms of the palace would achieve nothing except a return to the notoriety he had spent a decade trying to erase. So he had mastered himself, but his dislike for Mr. Burke was now a hot coal inside his chest. He regretted scheduling the musicale, regretted that he must continue to deal with a man he despised.

Yet the entire point of hiring Miss Lovell was to bring her uncle to the justice he so richly deserved. Morgan would do well to keep himself fixed on that ultimate goal.

And his aunt was even now waiting to consult with him further. Clenching his jaw, he turned on his heel and departed the palace. He did not know which was worse—the plethora of useless details she insisted he make decisions upon, or the fact that she treated him as an errant schoolboy instead of the Earl of Silverton.

Some twenty minutes later, when he strode into Trevethwick House, she pounced upon him.

"Morgan!" No doubt she had been lying in wait,

anticipating his return.

"Yes, Aunt?" He hoped the weary coolness of his tone would deflect her, though it never had in the past.

She threaded her arm through his and towed him toward the drawing room. "The replies are coming in. I'm sure you'll want to look them over."

He most assuredly did not, but Aunt Agatha had him in her grasp, and there was no escape. She pushed him into one of the armchairs set beside the hearth, then bustled to the small desk and returned with a handful of envelopes.

"The first acceptance to arrive is from Lord and Lady Dearborn. I recall you mentioned that their daughter, Anne, was a lovely girl. And a likely prospect."

"Perhaps I did." He dimly recalled her yellow hair and sweet expression, but the features were hazy.

Damn, the face scribed all too clearly in his memory was that of dark-haired Miss Lovell. Who was a most unsuitable prospect—unless one were thinking of a single lamp burning at midnight, and the heat of her lips beneath his, and how soft her skin might feel under his hands...

His aunt rapped him across the knuckles with her sandalwood fan. The sting of it recalled him to the task.

"Enough woolgathering, my boy. Heavens, how you manage to run an earldom, I cannot fathom." Aunt Agatha thrust three envelopes at him. "In addition, the Adderlys and the Cornells would be pleased to attend. I hear that Honoria Adderly is well spoken, and Mary Cornell is reputed to be a clever thing."

"Very good." He could muster not one whit of enthusiasm.

She gave him an impatient look. "I declare, you must do better than that if you hope to woo any of these young ladies. A smile, at least. You used to turn heads with your smiles."

That had been when his life was a perfect platter of delights laid before him. In the folly of youth, he had thought it would last forever. Now, the present smothered him, and the future was a dark fog he must travel into. There was nothing for him to smile about.

"Enough." He stood. "I trust you to make further decisions as to whether the canapés should contain chicken salad or liver pate, and if the decorations should be lavender or violet. Just keep me informed which families are attending."

"My dear, I know this is difficult for you." His aunt rose and patted his arm. "But once you fix upon the right lady, everything will seem brighter."

He sincerely doubted it, and wished his aunt would cease clinging to her romantic notions. Despite the fact she knew he had little interest in any of the invited young women, she could not help but weave fancies that he would suddenly, precipitously, tumble into love with one of them.

More likely that the sun would begin to spin backwards across the sky than Morgan would lose his well-guarded heart to any woman.

CHAPTER FIVE

The ride back to Mr. Burke's home from Buckingham Palace was full of taut silence. The hired hack swayed roughly over the cobbles, and Jessa stared determinedly out the window. Soot smudged the rooftops, and clouds dimmed the sun, matching the grimness of her mood. The smell of burning offal stung her nose, and she braced herself on the worn leather seat as the hack turned a corner, the carriage creaking. The lopsided rhythm of the wheels matched her worried heartbeat.

Covertly, she glanced across at Mr. Burke. His legs were crossed, his face set in its usual sour expression. He drummed his fingers on the seat, as if lost in thought. She feared what those thoughts might be.

Would he truly take Louisa away and lock her up in an asylum? His threats were not idle—he'd taken pains to demonstrate as much to her in the past. Which meant that she and her sister were not safe.

A bitter laugh rose in her throat. What a fool she'd been, to think her relative's house was any sort of haven. She must come up with a plan to protect Louisa. Somehow.

As soon as they entered the front door, the hinges groaning as if in pain, Jessa hurried toward the stairs.

"Not so fast." Mr. Burke caught her arm. "What are you up to with Silverton?"

His fingers closed hard, creasing the fabric of her pelisse, and his eyes bored into hers.

"Nothing," she said.

He gave her a shake. "Don't lie to me. I've seen how he looks at you. Do you think to run away and find a different protector?"

"Of course not." But his words whirled about in her head like sparks. Could she, in fact, do that very thing?

"Don't deceive yourself, missy." He laughed in her face. "A man like that would tire of you within the week. And he certainly wouldn't take in that idiot sister of yours. Whatever you're plotting, it won't succeed."

She wanted to dash the sneer from his face. She wanted to gather her meager possessions and make a dramatic exit, taking Louisa with her. But the truth of his words cut deep. They truly had nowhere to turn.

Jessa raised her chin and pulled out of her guardian's grasp. "I am well aware that Louisa and I depend upon you. Good night, sir."

Mr. Burke folded his arms and scowled, but at least he made no further move toward violence. The skin between her shoulder blades prickling, she turned her back on him, lit a candle, and ascended the stairs.

Louisa stirred sleepily in her bed as Jessa entered. The candle flame flickered in the draft from the closing door.

"Did you see the queen?" Louisa asked, bringing one hand up to shade her eyes from the light.

"I did—and will tell you all about her, and the palace, on the morrow."

"And the Silver Lord, he was there too?"

"Yes."

Louisa smiled. "I knew he would be."

"Go back to sleep, duckling."

Jessa slipped out of her gown and carefully hung it in the wardrobe. She blew the candle out, and heard her sister burrow back under the covers.

Somehow she must disabuse Louisa of the notion that the Earl of Silverton was some kind of knight in shining armor. He was simply a man who intended to hire her to perform at a musicale. A man who, from all appearances, did not care overmuch for music. Or anything beyond his own reputation, if the gossip she had overheard was true.

At the edge of sleep, she could not help but conjure up his face. There had been a wordless sympathy between them when she left the palace. Ridiculous for her to think so, and yet, in that last gaze, she felt as though they had seen more deeply into one another's souls than either of them expected.

***

The sound of the bedroom door closing in the darkness woke Jessa. Had she forgotten to lock it?

Heart pounding, she sat up and strained to hear any sounds of movement from within the room. Nothing.

"Louisa?" she whispered.

She slipped carefully from between her covers, and reached for her sister. Tumbled sheets met her fingers, still slightly warm from her sister's body. But the bed was empty, except for Louisa's crumpled nightdress.

Either she was wandering the house unclothed, or for some incomprehensible reason she had dressed herself. To go outside?

Fear jolted through Jessa. She hurried to the window and pushed back the curtain. Moments later, she saw Louisa in her walking dress and cloak step out from their guardian's house and into the street.

"Louisa!" she hissed, but of course her sister could not hear her through the window.

Jessa dared not bang upon the glass, for fear of waking Mr. Burke. Desperately, she struggled to open the window, but the lock was jammed.

Outside, Louisa glanced up and down the street, her hesitation clear. Fog curled at the edges of the sparse streetlights, and the world lay in silence and shadow.

Jessa flung herself away from the window. Not bothering to dress, she grabbed her cloak from the wardrobe and slipped on the closest shoes to hand—a pair of red satin dancing slippers. Nearly trembling from the need for stealth and speed, she opened the bedroom door and crept as rapidly as possible down the hall.

Blessedly, her guardian's snores continued uninterrupted as she descended the stairs. She was careful to keep to the outer edges of the treads, where they would not creak. Gaining the bottom, she darted across the room to the front door. No time to light a lantern—which, in any case, would only draw unwanted attention. Flipping up the hood of her cloak, she carefully pulled the door just wide enough to slip outside. Thankfully, the hinges let out only the faintest protest.

The air was cool and clammy against her cheek, the cobbles slick beneath the thin soles of her slippers. They would be ruined, but she could not count the cost—not when Louisa was out wandering the streets well past midnight.

Where was her sister?

Jessa sent a desperate glance over the empty block. At the far end, she caught a glimpse of motion, the sway of a skirt turning the corner. Taking up the cloak in her fists, she dashed down the street.

The sound of her slippers slapping the cobbles echoed back faintly from the dark homes lining the block. A crumbling brick townhouse stood at the corner, and Jessa skidded around it, breath heaving in her lungs.

She nearly collapsed with relief when she saw her sister standing before a wrought iron fence some paces away.

"Louisa," she whispered urgently. "Come back."

"There you are." Louisa smiled at her, as if they were not shrouded in mist in the middle of the midnight street. "I hoped you would come."

"Come where?" Jessa hurried to her sister and took her hand, partially to reassure herself that Louisa was safe, and partially to keep her from darting off again.

"We're going on an adventure," Louisa said solemnly.

"I will gladly take you wherever you want. But not now. It is dark, and Mr. Burke—"

"We don't need to worry about *him*. Once we find the Silver Lord, everything will come out right." Louisa's eyes shone with perfect faith.

Oh, dear.

"Come back to the house, love." Jessa tugged her sister's hand. "Neither of us have the faintest idea how to find him."

"Goose. Of course I do." Louisa grinned, then fished in her pocket and pulled out a card. "It says so right here. Tref… Tarv…"

Jessa snatched the calling card from her sister. The Earl of Silverton's name was easy to read, even in the dim light. She did not bother asking how her sister had found the card. Louisa was trapped every day for hours in their bedroom. There was no use concealing anything from her, but Jessa had never thought her sister would take such precipitous action.

"Trevethwick House," she said. "But we cannot go there. It's the middle of the night."

She began leading Louisa back toward Mr. Burke's.

"Why not?" Her sister's steps slowed. "I want to find him *now.*"

"He…" Jessa thought furiously. If she could not keep Louisa from believing in fairytales, she would use them to her advantage. "By night, he is a ravening beast. If we appear unannounced on his doorstep, I fear he would devour us."

There. That should keep her sister from trying this particular folly again.

"Oh." Louisa began walking once more, her expression downcast. Then her face brightened. "We shall go tomorrow, then, in the afternoon!"

"It is not that simple. First, I must complete the quest."

She must find some way to convince her sister that the Earl of Silverton was not going to miraculously save them. There was no fairytale ending.

"What is the quest?" Louisa's voice was full of innocent belief.

"Well—in only a few days I will play a musicale there. If I am able to… recover a talisman from Trevethwick House, then the earl will have to grant us a boon."

The thought of that stern man ever being in her debt made her words seem all the more foolish, but Louisa squeezed her hand with excitement.

"What is the talisman?" she asked.

"Ah, that's the difficulty. I won't know it until I see it." Sufficiently vague. "My quest has very little chance of succeeding."

"You will, though." Louisa gave a satisfied nod. "And then we will go live in the castle."

Jessa let out an inaudible sigh as they approached Mr. Burke's door.

"Hush now," she said. "We mustn't wake him."

There was no explanation they could make that would satisfy their guardian, should he discover them creeping through the house.

The front door opened quietly, but as they shut it the hinges creaked loudly. The bar of the lock clunked when she slid it home, and Jessa froze, listening. Everything seemed quiet. Perhaps the noise of their entering had not been so very loud, after all.

Making their way carefully through the dimness, she and Louisa ascended the stairs. Louisa set her foot wrong, and the tread let out a groan.

"Go, go," Jessa whispered, giving her a little push. They were so close to safety.

Louisa hastened down the hallway, with Jessa right behind her. As she had feared, light bloomed from beneath their guardian's door. They had woken him.

Panic spiking through her chest, Jessa whipped off her cloak and thrust it at Louisa. Mr. Burke's door opened, his squinting face illuminated by the flickering light of a candle. She prayed he could not see them too clearly.

She shoved her sister into their room, then turned to face Mr. Burke.

"What's this?" he demanded, lifting the candle higher.

"Forgive us for waking you, sir," Jessa said. "Louisa was thirsty and our pitcher was empty, so I took her down to the kitchen for a cup of water."

Thank heavens she was still in her nightdress. Surreptitiously, she scooted her feet back, hoping the shift concealed the damp toes of her red satin slippers.

Mr. Burke scowled at her a long moment, then turned and scanned the hallway. Shadows danced and darted at the edges of the light, but of course there was nothing to be seen.

"I'll take a look in your room," he said. "You can't keep

secrets from me."

"Of course." Jessa turned into their bedroom.

She desperately hoped that Louisa had climbed back into her bed, and pulled the covers up to conceal the fact she was dressed. But with her sister, there was no guessing what she might think the proper action would be. As the circle of light fell across the threshold, Jessa knitted her fingers anxiously together.

The candle illuminated the lump of Louisa in her bed. The bedcovers were rather sharply pointed at the bottom, and Jessa prayed Mr. Burke would not be able to tell that Louisa was still wearing her boots. And that he would not notice the discarded cloak bundled in the corner behind the door.

"Yes?" Louisa blinked up at the candle flame.

Mr. Burke grunted, then turned on Jessa.

"Back to sleep—and don't disturb mine again, or you'll be sorry."

"We shan't. Our apologies, sir." She bowed her head, and kept it lowered until he had withdrawn. The light faded, leaving the bedroom in darkness.

"I wish we could have gone," Louisa whispered.

"Take off your shoes and dress," Jessa said. The aftermath of fear trembled through her, making her feel slightly ill.

They had been lucky. That time. But luck was almost never on her side.

She removed her slippers, then shoved them into the far recesses of the wardrobe. Water-marked and soiled with street dirt, they would be damning evidence if Mr. Burke discovered them.

Her sister rustled and grumbled, and Jessa went to help her, unknotting the tangled laces of her boots and unfastening the few buttons Louisa had managed to close on the dress. It was a wonder the thing hadn't fallen off while she was traipsing about the streets.

Setting her jaw, Jessa resolved to keep a closer eye on her sister.

"Good night," Louisa whispered, finally ready to crawl back beneath the sheets.

"Dream sweetly," Jessa said, though she knew her own dreams would be filled with darkness and fear, and a small room where the walls were steadily closing in.

CHAPTER SIX

While it is commendable to invite talented performers to Buckingham Palace, one must question the wisdom of Queen Victoria receiving such persons as the Gypsy Violinist into the inner sanctum of nobility. Such riffraff should not be looked upon kindly, and the young queen's advisors would do well to remember it.

-Parliamentary Procedural, July 1

Morgan twitched as his valet, Johnson, tied his neckcloth. Although it was not too tight, the strip of linen still felt as though it were choking him.

"Excellent, my lord," Johnson said, brushing imaginary lint off the earl's customary gray wool coat. "The young ladies will be quite impressed by your appearance this evening."

Morgan regarded himself in the glass. He did not think he looked impressive. No, that accolade was due to the title resting invisibly upon his shoulders. He looked... glum, perhaps. With effort, he forced a smile onto his lips, but it did not fit well, and so he dropped the charade. He would be as he had always been, these past years. Duty-bound.

"Have you any favorites?" Johnson asked.

"Not particularly." Morgan frowned at the man. Usually

his valet was quiet and competent.

As if sensing his master's disapproval, Johnson did not continue with further questions. Instead, he ran a comb through Morgan's thick blond hair, brushing it in a somewhat sideways style that was apparently all the rage among the young bucks.

"Enough." Morgan turned. "My aunt is expecting me downstairs."

Of course, she was not expecting him for another quarter-hour, but he was done with preparing. Tonight, he would select a young lady to begin to court. The woman who would become his countess and bear his heirs. The prospect filled him with resignation.

"Very good." Johnson bowed, comb clasped in one hand. "Good evening, my lord."

Morgan gave his valet a curt nod, then strode out of his dressing room. Despite his excuses, he was not quite ready to face Aunt Agatha and her bright-eyed expectations.

For the past five days, she'd been incessant in her desire to discuss—to death—the particulars of each of the young ladies they had invited to the musicale. One might think this was the prince's engagement ball from that dreadful French fairytale. But the fate of the realm did not rest on the outcome.

Just the fate of the earldom.

"My lord." One of the footmen hailed him as he descended the long, swooping staircase. "Mr. Burke and Miss Lovell have arrived. As per your instructions, they've been escorted to the yellow drawing room."

"Someone is with them, I presume?" He had given strict orders that the pair not be let out of sight until he had greeted them. He'd also informed all the servants, down to the scullery maid, to remain discreetly aware of Mr. Burke's whereabouts throughout the musicale.

"Yes, my lord. I believe Thaddeus has been attending them."

"Excellent."

Morgan nearly felt like smiling at the thought of the trap he had laid for Mr. Burke. A particularly juicy one that he anticipated would catch his prey, though it would take time to see the proof of that success.

Morgan lengthened his stride. His boot heels thudded over the polished parquet floor as he turned toward the drawing room.

"Morgan!" Aunt Agatha hurried to catch up with him. A shockingly scarlet plume waved from her ornately curled gray hair, and clashed with the lavender satin evening gown she wore. "I hear Miss Lovell is here. I must meet her at once."

Morgan halted and dutifully offered his arm. "Then I shall introduce you."

"I think the evening will be a success," she said as she hooked her arm through his. "Everyone who was invited will be here. I do miss throwing parties."

A pang went through Morgan. He ought to have invited his aunt up to London more frequently. Despite her uncomfortably flamboyant nature, she was family. And he was fond of her.

"Then we shall host a few more," he said, surprising himself.

"Well, of course we will. A courtship requires a number of events to come to a satisfying conclusion." She set a red-gloved finger to her cheek. "A picnic, next? Boating? Or perhaps—"

"I prefer to navigate the evening ahead before planning anything further," he said, holding open the drawing room door so that she might precede him.

Thaddeus, the head footman, stood sentinel beside the door. Morgan met his eyes, and the man gave an imperceptible nod. Good—his guests had been watched since the moment they'd set foot inside Trevethwick House.

At the head of the room, past the rows of chairs, Miss Lovell stood. This evening she wore a green gown, the bodice shaped to her curves before flowing into a sweeping skirt. She was bent over her violin case, running a brightly patterned scarf over the strings of her instrument.

"Lord Silverton." Mr. Burke rose from his seat in the front corner and made a punctual bow. His eyes flicked to Aunt Agatha.

"Allow me to present my aunt, Lady Agatha Fielding," Morgan said. "This is Mr. Burke, Miss Lovell's uncle."

"Delighted," Mr. Burke said, with a false-looking smile.

Aunt Agatha raised one brow. "Of the Trenton-on-Trombley Burkes? Isn't your elder brother Viscount Trenton?"

Strong emotion flashed through Mr. Burke's eyes. Morgan was aware of Miss Lovell freezing in place, her fingers tightening around the scrap of colorful fabric in her hand.

"Yes," Mr. Burke snapped.

Aunt Agatha gave a sharp nod. "Still in Italy, is he?"

"The last I heard." Mr. Burke's mouth pinched at the corners.

"That would make you Miss Lovell's cousin, then, not her uncle." Aunt Agatha leaned forward, peering at him with interest.

"Close enough to claim legal guardianship." Mr. Burke pivoted and beckoned to Miss Lovell. "Come and pay your regards to our host and hostess."

She carefully set the scarf down and moved forward. Without meeting Morgan's eyes, she dropped into a deep curtsy. His mouth went dry at the sight of her dark hair gently brushing her bare shoulders. Resolutely fixing his gaze on the top of her head, he waited for her to rise.

When she rose, her full lips were pressed together, her expression set. But whatever the undercurrents of the conversation between Mr. Burke and Aunt Agatha, Miss Lovell seemed willing to let it pass without further comment.

Morgan would have to ask his aunt about that, later. He would not have thought that Mr. Burke was so close to the title. The man evidenced a decided lack of good breeding.

There was a story there, if Morgan did not miss his guess. And who knew better than he the tragedies that could befall a noble house?

"We're delighted you've come to perform for us," Aunt Agatha said, her voice decidedly warmer as she addressed Miss Lovell.

"The pleasure is mine," the violinist said. "Please excuse me, however. I need to warm up and check the acoustics before your guests arrive."

"Of course." Aunt Agatha clapped her hands together, her scarlet gloves muting the sound. "I've been looking forward to the chance to hear you play."

Morgan escorted his aunt to a chair in the front row, but declined to take a seat himself. Not while Mr. Burke still hovered like a carrion bird.

After a moment or two more of preparation, Miss Lovell took up her violin and bow and walked to the center of the Turkish carpet. The evening light slanted in through the windows behind her, casting her in silhouette and picking fiery highlights from her dark hair. Morgan suspected she was looking at him, but it was impossible to tell.

She swept her instrument up to her shoulder, then took a breath and set the bow to the strings.

The piece started low, the notes at first distinct and even. Gradually, they sped, moving to a higher register. Miss Lovell's bow flashed back and forth, weaving the sound while her fingers spun the tune out. Faster, more insistent.

She began to sway slightly with unconscious grace, and Morgan realized he was drumming his fingers against his leg in time to the music. He did not bother stopping himself. It was his drawing room, his pounds going into Mr. Burke's pocket for this performance, and he had every right to some small enjoyment from it.

Aunt Agatha let out a sigh of contentment. He glanced down, to see that her eyes were bright, her lips curved in a satisfied smile. The echo of her younger self lay across her face—the girl with the joyful spirit, who had defied convention and married for love.

The notes swirled through the room, melding with the late sunbeams and stirring an unwelcome wistfulness in Morgan's chest. He let it settle there, burning as if he'd tossed back an entire glass of cognac.

It was the music. It was the dark-haired siren playing so sweetly, her eyes now closed. It was the weight of past regrets and might-have-beens.

When the ache became too much, he cleared his throat. Jessamyn Lovell opened her eyes and looked straight at him, and for a moment he felt as though she could see right into his soul. The man he had been, the man he was now, the man he'd once wanted to be—all quantified in a single look.

He did not enjoy the uncomfortable sensation that he'd somehow been found lacking. No half-Gypsy girl had the right to judge him, granddaughter of a viscount or no.

Slowly, she brought the music to a close, the notes swirling to rest like a flock of evening doves coming to roost. She stilled, the last phrase resonating in the quiet air of the drawing room.

"Oh, my." Aunt Agatha dabbed at her eyes with a kerchief edged in violet lace. "That was splendid. Simply wonderful.

Your reputation is well deserved, Miss Lovell."

"Thank you." Miss Lovell cradled her violin in her arms and bowed. "I'm pleased you enjoyed the music."

Her gaze flickered to Morgan, and he gave her a tight nod.

"Very good," he said. "Miss Lovell, Mr. Burke, you are welcome to wait in the adjoining parlor until the musicale commences. The servants will bring you some refreshment."

"Too kind of you." Mr. Burke sounded less than delighted.

"Aunt?" Morgan offered his hand. "Our guests will be arriving shortly."

"Of course." She tucked her now damp kerchief away, then rose and took his outstretched arm.

They were not a moment too soon. As they stepped out of the room, the thud of the doorknocker echoed through the hallway.

"Someone's arrived punctually," Morgan said, tamping down a twinge of dismay.

Good Lord, was he really going to choose a future wife this evening? His former self would have been aghast at the cold calculation of it, as if he were simply evaluating horses for breeding.

"I've a guess who it might be." Aunt Agatha glanced up at him. "Do remember that love can be built on a foundation of mutual respect and admiration. It can grow from a tiny seed into the finest of flowers, given the right conditions."

"Indeed." He did not actually agree with her, but it pleased her to think there was still hope of a love match for him, and he did not want to dim the happy light in her eyes.

"My lord," the butler said as they gained the entryway. "The Marquess of Dearborn and his family await you in the red room."

Aunt Agatha made a small sound of approval, and Morgan tried not to sigh. Truly, Lady Anne Percival was a lovely girl.

He could do worse.

"Very good," he said. "Show in our other guests as they arrive."

At the doorway to the red room he paused, and Aunt Agatha patted his hand.

"Courage, my dear," she said, then towed him forward.

"Lord Silverton!" Lady Dearborn hoisted herself off the scarlet-upholstered settee and hurried to greet him. "We are too, too delighted to attend your musicale this evening. Aren't we, Anne?" She pushed her daughter forward. "Allow me to introduce my darling girl."

Lady Anne Percival curtsied low. "Charmed to make your acquaintance," she said in a light voice.

Her blue satin dress matched her eyes, and her blonde hair was done up in a flurry of ringlets that bobbed about her face as she straightened. The look she gave him was hopeful, and a touch wary.

"My pleasure," Morgan said, bowing over her hand. "May I fetch you a glass of champagne?"

She blushed. "Certainly, my lord."

Goodness, she was young. At least she wasn't one of the simperers. Or the gigglers. He was afraid he'd invited a few of those, but Aunt Agatha had been adamant that he have a wide field from which to choose his potential bride.

Lord Dearborn was at the refreshment table. A bit of curried ham clung to his mustache as he greeted Morgan.

"Fine choice of entertainment tonight," Lord Dearborn said. "Miss Lovell has wide appeal. Heh. A pity my son couldn't be here."

Morgan well knew the appeal Lord Dearborn was speaking of, but hearing it put so bluntly made his lip curl in distaste. Certainly, those gentlemen who didn't care a whit about the music would sit and ogle the performer. He was just as glad

Dearborn's son was missing from the gathering, if that would have been the young man's sole purpose in coming.

"Indeed." Morgan was thankfully distracted by the new arrivals being ushered into the room.

He greeted Lady Adderly and her slightly gawky, long-toothed daughter, then the Cornell family with assorted daughters and girl cousins in tow. Soon the room filled with high-pitched conversation. Morgan moved to and fro between his guests, aware that at every turn speculative female gazes were fastened upon him.

One good thing about choosing a lady to court: he would no longer have to suffer their avaricious and grasping mamas.

At length, just when he felt he was going to suffocate, Aunt Agatha rose and clapped her hands. The noise had little effect, so she stripped off her scarlet gloves and tried again. Heads turned at the sharp sound, and the babble subsided.

"We're so pleased to have you all as our guests," she said. "If you would repair to the drawing room, it's time for the musical portion of the evening."

A dozen pairs of eyes fixed on Morgan, and there was a general surge in his direction. Belatedly, he realized that all the young women were going to vie for his escort. Whether by luck or by artifice, Lady Anne was standing nearest. Morgan quickly offered his arm.

"Allow me to show you in," he said.

A murmur of disappointment riffled through the room, and Lady Anne's eyes lit.

"I would be delighted." Her voice was high and breathy with excitement.

She settled her arm atop his and, under the approving gaze of Aunt Agatha, led her out of the red room. The rest of the guests followed. Out of the corner of his eye, Morgan was aware of jostling near the front of the group. He only hoped he would not be trampled to death | the halls of his own home.

The drawing room seemed f₂ Lady Anne did not cling to his limpet-like quality to her touch.

"Do you enjoy music?" he as₁ question.

"Very much, my lord! I play the p. told I have some skill at it. And you? composers?"

"The usuals." He racked his brain, tryin₅ a few names. "Beethoven and, of course, Mend₍

"Beethoven is a bear to play." She blushed. ' am too outspoken."

Feeling a great deal older than Lady Anne, he ₁ hand in reassurance. Fortunately, they had reached th double doors of the drawing room, and there was no need for stilted conversation. He escorted her to the front r₀

"Will this do?" he asked.

"Splendidly." She did not release his arm. "Do join me, my lord. And we must save a place for my mother."

Morgan glanced about, hoping his aunt might step in, but she merely smiled at him from the back of the room.

He had not considered this aspect of the evening. No, all his focus had been on ensnaring Mr. Burke. While for the young ladies present, all their attention had been bent on ensnaring him.

The belated realization crept over him that he would not be able to absent himself from the musicale, as he'd done at Miss Lovell's previous performances.

"It would be my pleasure to sit with you," he said to Lady Anne.

She took a seat and beamed up at him, patting the chair

stantly, three nearby young ladies collided in a
led dash for the seat on his other side. One of the
edged her cousin out and slid breathlessly into the
ave Morgan a rather horsey smile.
kind of you to invite us," she said. "I've heard such
things about the Gypsy Violinist. Is it true she's
n Italian principessa?"
don't believe so."
as Mr. Burke spreading such rumors, or had this gossip
hold on its own? In either case, he didn't care to add to
peculation.

"Yet it might be true." Miss Cornell's eyes shone with a
mantic light.

"I heard she's an orphan, plucked off the streets." Lady
Anne leaned forward and addressed Miss Cornell. "I have it on
the best authority."

Where had the Gypsy Violinist come from? And blast,
here he was thinking of her again, when his attention ought to
be on the assorted young ladies chatting and giggling in his
drawing room. Miss Lovell was altogether too interesting for
Morgan's peace of mind.

Aunt Agatha rose from her chair at the end of the row.
The guests quieted, voices fading to a low hum of anticipation.

"Ladies—and gentlemen." Morgan's aunt smiled at the
few male figures scattered about the room. "Without further
ado, let us welcome Miss Lovell to perform for us!"

A servant opened the door into the adjoining parlor. Miss
Lovell stood there, her violin tucked under one arm. In the
shadows behind, Mr. Burke hovered.

As she stepped into the drawing room to the patter of
applause, Morgan glanced at his head footman. Thaddeus
nodded, confirming he knew his duties for the evening: allow
Mr. Burke the run of the mansion and keep out of his way.

Morgan had intended to try and watch the fellow, but no matter. The bait was there, set out enticingly for Mr. Burke to snatch. Perhaps it was just as well Morgan was trapped in his drawing room. It would keep him from arousing his quarry's suspicions.

At the front of the room, Miss Lovell made a brief curtsy. Without a word of introduction, she tucked her violin beneath her chin and waited for quiet. The audience hushed, and into that silence, a long, sweet note blossomed.

Miss Lovell held the tone, the volume increasing until, with a sudden bow lift, she launched into a wild flurry of music. The sound made Morgan think of sparks flying up from a bonfire, the thrill of galloping his gray, Sterling, through the crisp morning air, the whip and spray of the sea crashing into stone.

Beside him, Miss Cornell tapped her fan against her leg in time with the music, while on his other side, he glimpsed Lady Anne's toes moving up and down. It was music that called the body into motion, but he could not imagine the steps of a cotillion set to such an insistent, pulsing beat.

The Gypsy Violinist, indeed. She publicly skirted the edge of something wild and tumultuous, from her sensuous curves and loosely coiffed black hair to the thrumming perturbation of her music. For now, Society was titillated by her.

What would Miss Jessamyn Lovell become once the ton's fascination with her faded? He did not want to contemplate her options. Not with a guardian so unwholesome as Mr. Burke.

Speaking of whom... Surreptitiously, Morgan scanned the drawing room. He was not surprised to find Mr. Burke absent. The man was a master of slipping away unnoticed.

A bright chord drew Morgan's attention back to the front of the room, where Miss Lovell brought her first piece to a triumphant resolution.

The applause was immediate, and Lady Anne turned to him, her eyes shining.

"How thrilling," she said. "Why, I nearly sprang up and began dancing."

Then she laughed, a slightly artificial sound meant to convey to Morgan that of course a true lady would do no such thing. A pity, but then, the spark of originality was snuffed out of the young ladies of quality at a young age. He shouldn't expect—or desire—anything different.

Miss Lovell bowed. "Thank you. I shall now play a ballade."

Lady Anne clasped her hands. "Oh, is it a love song?"

A shadow moved through the violinist's eyes. She hesitated a moment, then inclined her head. "I will say it is about love."

This time the tune wound about, spiraling up and down on the violin. Miss Lovell swayed gently in place, her brows slightly pulled together. She finished the lower phrase, then ascended, her fingers flicking against the strings to make a curious sobbing sound.

If this was a love song, it was not filled with happiness.

But then, was that not the truth of love?

As the yearning notes continued, Morgan could not avoid thinking of his brother. Jonathan Trevethwick, heir to the earldom—the perfect, merry, golden fellow, who had fancied himself invincible.

Until that fatal night, when the Trevethwick's lives had, quite literally, crashed down into misery. Morgan's chest burned with the memory. After Jonathan died, his father—already morose from Lady Silverton's wasting illness and recent death—seemed to give up altogether. He descended into such destructive vices that it was a relief when he passed on, leaving the bitter fragments of the title for Morgan to reassemble.

Miss Lovell began to play two strings at once, the notes folding into harmony, then a keening disharmony, then back into solace. Her expression was distant, as though she viewed a faraway land, and it seemed she poured her own wistful soul into the music.

On Morgan's right, Miss Cornell twisted her kerchief between her hands, and he heard a few discreet sniffles further back in the room. Anyone who had encountered loss could not help but be moved by the song unfurling from beneath the Gypsy Violinist's fingers.

Slowly, the music grew softer, fading like evening light over distant hills. Morgan listened, straining to follow the faint thread of sound, but he could not discern the moment it ceased.

Miss Lovell stood motionless, her arm extended with just the tip of her bow perched on the string. She looked like a pagan muse, some goddess of lost love and shadows. The drawing room was utterly still for the space of two heartbeats, and Morgan could hear the inevitable tick of time in that moment.

Time—moving forward and taking the world with it, whether or not the world wanted to go. There was no escape from the future.

Then the audience applauded. To his right, Miss Cornell brought her hands together vigorously, while on his left, Lady Anne was less enthusiastic.

"I don't think I much care for Gypsy love songs," she said, wrinkling her petite nose. "It was rather... rustic. Don't you think, my lord?"

"Love is not all sweet joy, Lady Anne." He knew he sounded stuffy. Old. But he could not play the foolish games of youth.

"Of course not. I only meant it seemed an odd choice.

Given the occasion." She blushed and sent him a look from beneath her lashes.

Ah yes, the supposedly romantic nature of his musicale, wherein he would choose a lady to court. It seemed Lady Anne fancied herself in love with him. An easy enough fancy to have, he supposed. He was titled and wealthy, and handsome enough—at least, he'd believed so in the past. He was not the type of man who beat his animals or his servants, or derived satisfaction from cruel and debauched behavior. Certainly, Dearborn's daughter could do worse than catch the Earl of Silverton.

He felt another set of eyes upon him, and glanced up to see Miss Lovell regarding him. Her gaze held far more depth than the guileless blue of Lady Anne, and he recognized what he saw there. Jessamyn Lovell knew sorrow, and tribulation, and a life dashed to pieces.

"We shall have one more tune," he said, "and then a break for refreshments."

Miss Lovell nodded. "As you wish, my lord."

Deliberately breaking the somber mood she had evoked earlier, she commenced with a sprightly bit of music. No minor notes or low sighing, just sprays of brightness underpinned with a whirling rhythm that set toes tapping again.

Miss Lovell's expression smoothed, the hint of a smile at one corner of her lush lips. When the tune ended, even Lady Anne applauded without reservation.

"That was delightful indeed," she said, turning to him. Her eyes shone with anticipation. "What a splendid evening, my lord. I can scarcely wait for what comes next."

Morgan's mouth went dry, his neckcloth feeling too tight once again.

"Excuse me a moment, Lady Anne." He raised the back of her gloved hand to his lips, then stood. "I'll be back shortly—

there's a matter I must attend to."

"Oh." She blinked up at him. "Of course, Lord Silverton. I fervently await your return."

As did all the young ladies and their mamas, judging by the eager looks cast his way as he strode from the drawing room.

Aunt Agatha followed him out, then grasped his arm once they had gained the hallway.

"Where are you going?" she asked.

"Can't a man move about his own house without being detained?"

"Tsk. You can't run away from this, Morgan. You know very well that tonight you'll need to declare for one of those young ladies." She sent a significant look at the drawing room door.

"I am fully aware of my duty," he said.

She pressed her lips together and shook her head. "If you persist in thinking it an unpleasant task, I fear for your future."

"I must see to a bit of business first," Morgan said. "And then, I shall make my selection. I promise."

CHAPTER SEVEN

Morgan pivoted to avoid the disappointment in his aunt's eyes, and headed down the hall toward his study. Before he commenced selecting a wife, he must speak with his head footman to see if his plan had borne fruit. Had Mr. Burke done as anticipated, or was the man waiting for the second half of the evening to reveal his criminal intent?

As Morgan passed the small parlor, a flash of green silk caught his attention. Quietly, he moved to the half-open door and stood there, watching Miss Lovell.

She paced before the hearth, then stopped, facing the mantel. Head tilted, she seemed to be studying the knick-knacks on display: a Venetian glass teardrop—clear, with a swirl of scarlet inside, a tiny cloisonné box inlaid with flowers, a carved enamel dragon from the Orient, and a brass statuette of a nymph clad in flowing scarves. A cobalt vase of yellow lilies completed the arrangement.

Carefully, Miss Lovell picked up the glass tear and held it to the light.

"A pleasant trinket, isn't it?" Morgan asked as he strode into the room. Anger hardened his voice. He'd thought better of her, but he supposed tainted blood would tell.

Miss Lovell let out a gasp and whirled to face him. The teardrop glinted between her fingers.

"Forgive me," she said, her voice a bit breathless. "I was just admiring—"

"Yes, I see that." He closed the distance between them and grasped her upraised hand, capturing both it and the glass she held. "Don't drop it, I pray. A pity to break the bauble when you only meant to steal it."

Color swept across her cheeks, and she stiffened. "I had no such intention!"

Morgan lifted one brow and leaned in close. He could smell the warmth of her skin, see the pulse beating in her neck, just below her jaw. The scent of lilies curled in the air about them.

Jessamyn Lovell stared up at him, wide-eyed, her full lips slightly parted. Without thinking, he bent his head and covered her mouth with his own. Heat raced over him, a lightning flash of long-pent desire scorching him down to the soles of his feet. All he could do was hold on to her, tasting her sweet lips, feeling her body sway into his.

Closer, closer—his free hand slipped around her back and pulled her against him. Her palm slid up over his shoulder, and he was lost in the fire. She fitted perfectly in his arms, and he wanted to lick his tongue into her mouth, trail kisses along that graceful neck and bare shoulder, cup her breasts and...

Damnation. He tore his mouth from hers and set her at arm's length.

Her chest rose and fell in deep exhalations, her cheeks flushed. "Lord Silverton, I am not the wanton you seem to think me."

His apology died on his lips at her protest.

"You appeared to enjoy my kiss well enough, Miss Lovell. No screams of maidenly outrage, no slap across the face."

Although she had not kissed like an experienced lover. Her lips had been willing, but unsure beneath his.

She glanced down at the hearth rug, then back up to him. "Would you prefer I make a scene in you parlor, sir? Especially on this evening, when it is rumored you are about to make some *well-bred* lady the object of your affections?"

Guilt put him on the defensive. "Are you trying to tell me you've never been kissed before, Miss Lovell?"

"I have been." Her eyes narrowed. "Not that it is any business of yours."

"Some fumbling Gypsy boy, I'd guess."

She clenched her hands, the glass teardrop still in her fist. "Make up your mind, sir. Either I am an experienced courtesan, or an unschooled country wench. I can hardly be both."

He was being unkind to her, it was true.

"I suspect you are neither a wanton nor a complete innocent." He softened his tone. "Like most women, you are far too complicated. And I behaved in a most ungentlemanly manner."

Ungentlemanly, but he could not be sorry that the feel of her lips still burned against his mouth. Though he was utterly displeased with himself, it was hardly fair to castigate her for his own failings.

"Indeed." Her tone was cool.

He held out his palm. "Give me the bauble."

She set the scarlet-streaked glass in his hand, then lifted her chin and met his gaze. "I had no intention of taking anything from you, Lord Silverton."

"Yet I stole a kiss from you." And what a catastrophic loss of control that had been.

She looked on the verge of replying, when Mr. Burke's

voice sounded in the hall. A moment later, he stepped into the parlor, followed by Thaddeus.

"There you are," Mr. Burke said, his gaze darting from Morgan to his niece. He smiled, but it was more a baring of teeth.

Morgan inclined his head. "I was just offering Miss Lovell this small trinket, in thanks for her fine performance so far."

He held the glass teardrop out to her.

"It's not necessary, my lord," she said, her eyes widening.

"Oh, take the thing." Mr. Burke stalked forward. "If a man offers you gewgaws, never turn him down."

He reached for the teardrop, and Miss Lovell quickly snatched it up before he could touch it.

"Thank you." She folded her fingers around the glass and gave Morgan a small curtsy.

"Morgan!" Aunt Agatha rushed into the room, the scarlet plume in her coiffure bobbing with agitation. "Whatever are you doing, lurking back here in the parlor? Your presence is required in the drawing room. With your eager guests."

Eager indeed. The time had come. In fact, it was for the best that he settle upon a suitable young lady. Someone who would keep his attention away from distractions like Miss Lovell. She had a kiss and a bauble from him, and that was one thing too many.

Though deep down he could not quite bring himself to regret either.

"Begin playing again in a quarter-hour," he told Miss Lovell.

He strode to the door, his aunt hovering behind him like an overlarge hummingbird. Just before he exited he raised a brow at the footman, who shook his head. So, Mr. Burke had not yet snapped up the bait. Well, he had another chance.

"Who will it be?" Aunt Agatha asked, threading her arm though his as they turned into the hallway.

Morgan set his jaw and remained silent. He'd hoped the choice would be clear, but he still was unable to fix upon one particular lady over another. Indecision pulsed uncomfortably at his temples.

"Oh heavens, you haven't decided?" Aunt Agatha halted, her expression aghast. "Morgan, you *must*. Surely one of the young ladies, Miss Adderly perhaps—"

"Her father has a regrettable habit of gambling."

"Then one of the Cornell girls—"

"Their brother was sent down from Oxford."

"No family is immune from some small misdeeds." Her tone held a sharp edge. "It's ridiculous to look for perfection from anyone. Even yourself."

"If I can't hold myself to the highest standards, how can I expect others to rise above their own awful humanity? Without that striving, all of Society would be lost."

"Then you'd best marry Lady Anne," she said tartly. "Lord Dearborn's reputation for dullness is well earned."

Morgan stared at the gold-figured wallpaper, attempting to master his seething emotions. This should not be so damnably difficult.

"You are correct," he said at last. "Dearborn's daughter is the least objectionable of the lot."

Aunt Agatha let out a gusty sigh and took his arm again. "I despair for you at times, Morgan, truly I do. Tell me, do you feel even the smallest spark of affection for Lady Anne?"

"I hardly know her."

"Attraction, then."

"Gentlemen do not discuss such things with ladies." He began marching down the hall, avoiding his aunt's gaze.

Certainly, Lady Anne was a pretty girl. And he'd proved

just moments ago that his baser urges were not buried as deep as he'd thought. He could imagine kissing her. Even if her hair was blonde instead of raven-wing black, and her eyes innocent blue, not dark and sorrow-tinged.

Enough. He would cease thinking of Miss Lovell.

Morgan squared his shoulders and strode through the drawing room doors. The chatter in the room rose a notch. Aunt Agatha gave his arm a squeeze, then stepped back.

Throat dry, he scanned the assembled guests. Hopeful gazes pricked his as he turned, looking for the particular bright shade of Lady Anne's hair. There she was, near the front of the room. Her eyes met his, and a pink blush colored her pale cheeks.

An anticipatory silence fell as he approached her. Into that quiet, he spoke.

"Lady Anne, will you allow me to call upon you tomorrow afternoon?"

"I…" Her voice squeaked upward, and she took a moment to gather herself. "Yes, my lord. That would please me very much."

"Excellent." He raised his voice. "I hope you are all ready for the second half of the musicale."

The room filled with speculative whispers and unhappy faces. He waited until Lady Anne sat, then once again took the chair next to her. On his other side, Miss Cornell gave him a glum look.

He should have delayed until the end of the evening to make his selection—but at least it was done. The hollowness he felt inside was simply that of a man following his duty. Nothing more. Ruthlessly, he tamped down the searing feeling that he'd made the wrong choice. As the Earl of Silverton, he had made the only one possible.

CHAPTER EIGHT

"Aha," Mr. Burke said from his station at the cracked-open parlor door, where he stood peering into Lord Silverton's drawing room. "It seems the gossips were correct."

"About what?" Jessa wiped the light dusting of rosin from her instrument and attempted to keep her voice even.

She felt as though the proof of the earl's kiss must blaze above her head, a scarlet sign visible to everyone. Yet neither her guardian nor the earl's aunt had seemed to notice anything amiss, despite the fact she was utterly marked by the experience.

Her lips still tingled with the memory of how his mouth had descended to hers, and a curious heat spread through her limbs at the recollection of his arm around her waist, pulling her tightly against his tall, well-muscled form.

It had not been her first kiss, true—but the earl's warm lips and firm embrace were worlds removed from Matteu's inexpert kisses and brief caresses. Indeed, she was a lifetime away from the sweet shadows beyond the lanterns where she and Matteu had first declared their undying love for one another. Undying—for the space of four days, until a different girl caught his fancy.

Just as well, for Jessa had been growing increasingly uncomfortable with his forays into intimacy. On their last night, she'd spoken sharply to him as he'd fumbled at her dress. The next evening, he had led Mirabelle into the shadows instead.

Had Matteu's kisses been like the one she'd just received, however, she might now be happily wed, with barefoot children tumbling about the camp.

Her heart tightened, and she blinked back sorrow for the lost past, and a future that was never hers.

"It would appear the earl has chosen a bride," Mr. Burke said.

Jessa's distress blazed higher at the words. Foolishness. One kiss meant nothing—at least, nothing to the earl. He was a peer of the realm, and she a part-Gypsy musician.

"Who is it?" she asked, gathering her instrument and coming to stand behind her guardian.

"Dearborn's daughter. She'll make a pretty bride. If only the gossips were not here, I could turn a penny on this information." He grunted. "They're ready. Play well, Jessamyn."

He meant play entrancingly, distractingly, so that he might go about his sordid business. Jessa glanced at the footman who had been shadowing Mr. Burke all evening. At least Lord Silverton was wise enough to oversee her guardian, but she had no doubt the footman would be given the slip in less than a quarter-hour.

Mr. Burke pushed open the door, and Jessa stepped into the drawing room. It felt like stepping into a foggy London twilight, the mood of the room was so gloomy. The lamps struggled against the shadows. In the entire audience, the only person who seemed to be smiling was Lady Anne.

Jessa darted a glance at the earl as the applause faded. His mouth was set in an uncompromising line, his eyes hard. For a moment, she pitied the yellow-haired young lady seated next to him.

Then Lady Anne patted his arm and gave him a look that was half infatuation, half greed, and Jessa found that she had, in fact, more sympathy for Lord Silverton than the young woman he had chosen to court. Admiration could so easily fade, and money was a poor substitute.

Regardless of her sympathies, her task was to lift the temper of the crowd, to push back the dimness. No matter how bleak or difficult it would be to cheer the room, the Gypsy Violinist always rose to the occasion.

She began quietly, in her favorite key of E Dorian. The minor notes acknowledged the unhappiness on the faces of most of the listeners. There was no point in throwing cheerful notes at them—not until she'd assuaged their melancholy. And yet the mode of the music held an unexpected upturn at the end of the scale, a stray beam of light breaking through dark clouds.

Slowly, Jessa coaxed the listeners forward, letting the music twine about them like some sweet fragrance, half forgotten. Autumn roses, or fresh-baked bread. *Yes*, the music whispered, *the world is full of disappointment, but hope remains.*

The melody beneath her fingers modulated as she began to add more sharps. First a brightness here, then another, until she had climbed into A major: the happiest of keys.

Her bow danced then, stitching arpeggios between the simple notes of the tune, until it was embroidered with silver, with gold. The earl leaned back, the line of his mouth easing, and she felt ridiculously satisfied at the sight.

But she would not think of his mouth.

Jessa closed her eyes and let the music fly through her, speaking of sunlight glimmering off water, the taste of ripe cherries, the chime of unfettered laughter. All the goodness the world held, the small moments of wonder that could keep a heart beating, moment to moment, even in the face of unutterable despair.

Up and up she played the tune, letting it climb like a bird in flight. A lark, high in the clear blue air, until at last it had flown beyond sight. With a deep breath, she let the last note ring, pure and true.

Stillness filled the room for a perfect moment. She smiled and opened her eyes, and applause surged like a wave upon the shore.

Even though not every face held pleasure, enough did. The earl had chosen his bride, but already the bitter shade of failure was fading from some of the audience. One auburn-haired young lady's eyes sparkled, as though she were thinking of the man she truly wished to marry. A matron in the second row leaned over to speak to her daughter, her face untroubled.

For the next half-hour, Jessa was careful not to let the music stray back into somberness. She performed a sprightly Irish melody popularized by Thomas Moore, and then one of Becker's recent waltzes for solo violin. Toes and fans tapped as she swooped through the elegant yet simple melody, dipping and turning as one might in the dance.

Not that she had ever waltzed, but the music was so evocative, she felt as though she knew the steps and twirls by heart.

At the close of the piece, she bowed and made to leave the room.

"Encore!" Lady Agatha cried.

The audience called their approval. It was not unexpected. Jessa was usually persuaded back for at least one tune at the close of her performances, if not more.

She inclined her head in agreement, and launched into a *sîrba*. The insistent beat was studded with triplets. In memory, she heard the stomp of hard-soled shoes, saw the swish of bright skirts as the dancers performed the flashing steps. It was best danced on a hard surface—the dusty floor of a barn, or hinged doors laid down for a makeshift stage, so that the rhythm of the feet could play counterpoint.

At the end, she was breathless from the pace. A strand of her hair clung to the side of her perspiration-damp neck as she bowed.

When she rose, her gaze met the earl's. The appreciation in his eyes warmed her even more than the generous applause. Her attention slipped to Lady Anne, who threaded her arm through the earl's with a proprietary expression.

Keeping the smile on her face, Jessa bowed again. The splinter pricking at her heart meant nothing.

"Thank you, all," she said. "It was a pleasure playing for you this evening."

The earl gave her a nod of dismissal, and she measured her steps back to the refuge of the small parlor.

As she entered, her guardian tucked a notebook into his pocket, then rose from the yellow-striped chair he'd been occupying.

"Another excellent performance." His voice was overfull of satisfaction, and Jessa's spirits sank at what that must mean.

Despite the watchful footman, her guardian had managed to ferret out some dark secret of the earl's. She swallowed a sigh. Why must every noble have a past littered with mistakes for Mr. Burke to hold over their heads?

And why was she so keenly disappointed that the Earl of Silverton had proved no exception?

"Pack up, girl," Mr. Burke said. "Time to go."

As the grim-faced footman showed them to the servants' entrance, Jessa caught a glimpse through the drawing room doorway of the Earl of Silverton. Lady Anne hung off his arm, her bright laughter punctuating the air.

He lifted his head, as if feeling Jessa's gaze. Their eyes met, then held for a heartbeat too long. Jessa's pulse beat against her throat.

Then he looked away and gave Lady Anne a tight smile.

"Come." Mr. Burke prodded Jessa's shoulder.

"Of course," she murmured.

The sounds of mirth faded as they followed the footman down the back hallway. Stepping out of Trevethwick House, she slipped her hand into the pocket of her pelisse, where she'd tucked the bauble the earl had given her. The glass was cool under her fingers, but warmed to her touch. She only hoped Mr. Burke would not take it from her, as he had the queen's token. It was a small trinket, but far more important than he might suspect.

It was an enchanted talisman, to keep her sister from wandering the night.

It was the perfect memory of a kiss.

***

"Well!" Aunt Agatha smiled brightly as the last of the carriages rattled away over the cobblestones. "A successful evening on all counts, I would say."

Morgan stood a moment longer at the open door, hoping the night air would clear his head. Unfortunately, there was no erasing the memory of kissing Jessamyn Lovell.

"Indeed," he said. "You were a fine hostess. Thank you for undertaking this event on my behalf."

"Pish." She gave him an affectionate swat on the arm. "Let the butler close the door—and do contrive to leave your moodiness outside. We can speak more comfortably over a glass of brandy. Well, brandy for me. You may have your usual water, you silly boy."

It was no use protesting his aunt's eccentricities, or explaining his own. Aunt Agatha knew well enough why he preferred water, or the occasional glass of lesser spirits. Letting the words dissolve on his tongue, he turned and followed her bobbing scarlet plume down to the study.

The fringe-shaded lamps pushed back the shadows, and a small fire warmed the room. Not that the evening was particularly chilly, but he'd noticed that Aunt Agatha often used a shawl even when he considered the air perfectly comfortable. Anticipating this conversation, he'd directed the servants to light the coals on the hearth.

As he strode past his desk, Morgan glanced at the tidy pile of papers he'd set there. They appeared undisturbed, but he knew that the contents had been carefully sifted by Mr. Burke. A slight smile curled the corners of his mouth. The clink of the brandy decanter against the glass was the sound of his plans falling into place.

"I'm glad you are satisfied with the outcome of this evening," Aunt Agatha said as she accepted the half-full glass of brandy he handed her.

"I am," he said. Though the prickling sensation inside his chest was more resignation than satisfaction.

"Lady Anne is a lovely girl. You'll come to love her in time, I'm certain of it. Once you've kissed her once or twice."

"Aunt—"

"Oh, sit down and don't play the prude with me." She waved her hand at him. "We both know it's true. Even though I suspect you haven't kissed a woman in far too long, you're a handsome young man. Establish a certain degree of intimacy, and the heart will soon follow."

Morgan took a swallow of cool water from his own glass, letting the liquid carry away the scorch of his all-too-recent kiss.

Though it was an indelicate subject, he hoped his aunt was right. Clearly a lack of female companionship had brought his baser urges to the fore, where they fastened on the nearest available woman. All he needed to do was transfer the focus of his desire from Jessamyn Lovell to Lady Anne. Simple enough.

"What will your first outing together be?" Aunt Agatha asked.

"Well, I intend to call upon her tomorrow," he said.

She released a gusty breath and sent her gaze up to the ceiling, as if searching for patience. "As I feared, you've given this courtship almost no thought. Really, Morgan, it's fortunate I've decided to remain here another month. You need a woman's guidance in this matter."

How like his aunt to invite herself to stay. Yet instead of being irritated by her presumption, he was obscurely glad of it. In truth, he was finding himself a bit at sea when it came to the wooing of a young lady of quality.

Much as he disliked giving up control, he had to admit that his aunt's input was necessary in this endeavor. The Earl of Silverton must carry out a successful courtship.

"Very well," he said. "What do you suggest?"

Aunt Agatha beamed at him. "I knew you'd see the sense in it. We shall have another gathering soon, perhaps a garden party. But first, you will invite Lady Anne to go riding in Hyde Park."

Morgan swallowed back his automatic refusal. Although he detested playing the *ton*'s games, his aunt's suggestion was sound. The obligatory parade of see-and-be-seen in the park would cement his intentions toward Lady Anne in the eyes of Society.

"Splendid," he said.

His aunt raised an eyebrow at his tone. "You need to muster up more enthusiasm than *that*, my boy. I declare, your first kiss with Lady Anne cannot come soon enough."

"Aunt." He gave her a repressive look.

"And don't forget to take flowers when you pay your call," she continued, uncowed. "Pink roses, with two white carnations and a spray of myrtle. That should do admirably. Not too forward, yet the meaning is clear enough."

"If you say so."

She patted his knee. "Trust me in this, Morgan. And now, I'm off to bed. Would you ring for my maid?"

He rose and jangled the bell pull. When Aunt Agatha's maid arrived, he kissed his aunt's cheek.

"Good night," he said. "Pleasant dreams."

"I believe they shall be filled with Gypsy melodies." She let out a contented sigh. "Such a delightful evening."

Morgan kept the frown off his face until she departed, then slumped back into his armchair and stared at the hearth flames. He feared his own dreams would be full of Miss Lovell's influence, as well. Black hair like silk, passion-filled eyes, and a lush mouth he wanted to kiss for days.

Once again he glanced at his desk. How soon until he received a blackmail letter from Mr. Z? He rather hoped it would arrive quickly. The sooner he was able to put Jessamyn Lovell out of his life, the better.

CHAPTER NINE

A happy day for Lady Anne Percival, Lord Dearborn's eldest daughter!
The lovely young lady appears to be the object of Lord Silverton's affections.
Alas, the unchosen hopefuls must turn their eyes to a new prospect.
Viscount Cottering, perhaps?
-Tilly's Mayfair Tattler, July 5

Jessa sat across from Louisa in the threadbare armchairs drawn before Mr. Burke's hearth. She was darning a hole in her stocking, while her sister stared dreamily into the flames. Louisa's mending lay abandoned on her lap, and the lamplight picked out the amber highlights in her dark brown braid.

"Six days!" Mr. Burke paced angrily back and forth. "Six days, and not a single inquiry for a performance. Jessamyn, your fame is fading."

She darted a glance at him. "It is the end of the Season. Surely that has some bearing."

"Yes—and you ought to be busier than ever. Parties, picnics, musicales." He halted and gave her a venomous look. "Did you play poorly at Lord Silverton's?"

"Of course not." She straightened her back. "Had you

been present, you would've heard the excellence of my performance." Especially how she had lifted the somber mood of the room, so that the event might not end in gloom and regret.

"There must be a reason. Perhaps you displeased his bride-to-be."

Jessa's needle slipped and she pricked her thumb, but dared make no sound. Surely the earl had not mentioned their kiss to anyone in Society? But what other explanation could there be? Heat, then chills coursed over her, and she set her darning aside.

"I'm certain more requests for performances will come in," she said, trying to keep her tone even, while her mind darted frantically.

"They had better," Mr. Burke's said. "If your run as the Gypsy Violinist has ended, I'll have to find a new financial solution for the burden the two of you represent. Luckily, I have a plan easily set in motion."

His gaze slipped from Jessa to the pensive form of Louisa, and the look on his face stopped Jessa's breath in her throat. He couldn't be thinking of using Louisa for something dreadful! Oh, but the cold trickle of premonition down her back knew that Mr. Burke had no scruples whatsoever.

Jessa drew in a shaky breath.

There was only one person she could think of to go to, one man who might provide her some assistance. And an explanation for why no more performances were forthcoming.

The Earl of Silverton. Surely he would not be entirely insensible to her pleas, especially if he'd contributed to the ruin of her career.

The rest of the evening wore away at an excruciating pace. Jessa dared not excuse them early from the parlor and risk raising Mr. Burke's suspicions. At last, the clock on the mantel chimed nine.

Louisa looked up. "The birds are chirping," she said.

"They're telling you it's time to make ready for bed," Jessa said. "Gather up your sewing."

She looked over at Mr. Burke, who had settled at his desk and was scribbling furiously, ink spattering from the pen.

"Good night, sir," she called.

He grunted acknowledgement and did not lift his head from his work. Jessa folded her newly darned stocking into her mending basket, lit a candle at the hearth, then led the way upstairs.

"Jessa," her sister said, as soon as the door closed. "Why don't we use the talisman? I am ready to leave here, and the Silver Lord owes us a boon. You said so."

Jessa set the candle on the bedside table, the single flame sending long fingers of shadow up into the corners of the room.

"I've told you before"—every evening since the musicale, in fact—"the talisman is too small for such a great favor as taking us under his roof."

"I was thinking, tonight. The fire dreamed me a story." Louisa began unbraiding her hair. "You must use the boon to get another talisman. Then another. The third one will be powerful enough to make everything come out right."

It made sense, in the odd logic of fairytales. And it would provide an excuse for what Jessa must do that night.

"You are right," she said. "I will go this very evening to the earl's."

"You will?" Louisa clasped her hands together. "Oh, be brave! Beware his beastly form."

Ah, yes—Jessa had nearly forgotten her fabrication that Lord Silverton transformed into a ravening beast after dark.

"The glass teardrop will protect me," she said. "But you must promise to stay here. It will not be safe for you."

Louisa nodded, her eyes wide. "Don't forget to find the second talisman. And hurry back."

"I'm not leaving yet, love. I must wait until Mr. Burke is fast asleep."

Indeed, it was well after midnight when Mr. Burke's snores finally resounded through the upper floor of the house. Louisa had long since fallen into slumber, her faith in her sister leaving her to dream untroubled.

Jessa had not bothered to don her nightdress, but spent the time perched on the edge of her bed, planning the best way to reach Trevethwick House.

She could not walk. Not only was it some distance from Westminster to Mayfair, but a woman alone at night was far too vulnerable. From the questionable residents of the neighborhood surrounding Mr. Burke's lodging to the drunken dandies of the *ton*, she would face danger on all sides.

The only solution was to take a hackney. And the only way to pay for the fare was the Venetian teardrop. She prayed it would be enough.

The fog-shrouded night air lay clammy against her skin as she stepped out of Mr. Burke's house. She glanced over her shoulder, but no lights kindled in the windows to signal that her absence had been detected.

Gathering her cloak tightly about herself, Jessa made her way down the street. It was only three blocks to a busier thoroughfare, and even at this late hour she could hear the clatter of carriage wheels over the stones.

Despite the prickling between her shoulder blades, she reached the busy street without incident, and within five minutes had hailed a hackney.

"Where to?" the driver asked, peering down at her from

his seat.

"Mayfair." Jessa gave him the address of Trevethwick House.

He grunted. "Show your fare."

Carefully, Jessa extended her gloved hand to reveal the teardrop resting in her palm.

"What's this?" The driver squinted at it.

"Enough to pay the fare ten times over," she answered. "Will you accept it?"

"Steal it, did you?" He shook his head. "Silly chit."

"No—it was given to me."

"By a stupid lordling, no doubt. Next time, make him pay for your favors in coin."

She did not argue with his assumption that she was a woman of light reputation. The circumstances spoke for themselves.

"Please?" She lifted her hand even higher.

The driver plucked the bauble from her palm, his grubby fingertips poking out of his fingerless gloves. He held it up a moment to the thin flame of the carriage lamp, then tucked it away.

"Get in." He nodded for her to enter the hackney. "I'll take you, but it's only enough for a single fare. Don't 'spect me to wait about while you do your business."

She climbed in quickly, before he could change his mind. Her heart raced with relief, then fear as a host of new challenges presented themselves. Still, she would risk everything to keep Louisa safe.

The interior of the carriage smelled dank, with an undertone of vomit. Jessa wrestled the window down and tried to calm the thoughts whirling through her mind. What if she arrived in Mayfair and could find no way to enter Trevethwick

House, or rouse the earl? What would she do, sleep under a rosebush in the garden?

Yes, then wait until dawn and tread the miles back to Mr. Burke's, hoping he would choose to lie abed that morning.

She threaded her fingers together and hoped desperately her errand would not meet with failure.

All too soon, the carriage halted before Trevethwick House. Jessa descended from the hackney. It was not too late—the driver might still return her to Westminster if she begged him.

But no. She shut the door on the dim, squalid refuge, then turned to face the earl's mansion. It looked enormous in the dark, and even more intimidating.

"Remember," the driver said. "Coin, this time."

He slapped the reins, and the carriage clattered away, leaving her standing alone on the cobbles. No light shone in the windows of the mansion, but she knew her way to the servants' entrance on the side. It would be too much to hope that door was unlocked, but she must try.

Dew wet her skirts as she made her way through the shadowy front garden and around the corner. A hawthorn bush snagged her cloak, and she stumbled painfully into a wrought iron bench. Shins stinging, she paused a moment to gather her bearings.

The house remained still and unlit. And, to her regret, the servants' entrance was bolted up tight.

Bitter disappointment squeezed her throat. She had wasted the glass teardrop, and come for nothing. What a hopeless fool.

Then light bloomed at the back of the mansion, shedding a soft glow over the rear lawn and garden. Jessa squeezed her eyes closed. When she opened them, the light remained. Carefully, she rounded the corner, to see that a room was illuminated. Someone was still awake. If it was a servant, might they let her in?

Pulse beating in her throat, she crept up to the light. The ground-floor windows were just at eye level. Fingers clinging to the sill, she rose on tiptoe to peek into the lit room.

It appeared to be a study. And—thank all the stars—the Earl of Silverton was within, seated at a wide desk. As she watched, he ran a hand through his hair. Instead of his usual mask of cool indifference, his face showed regret and weariness and frustration. It made him seem more human, and even more handsome.

Jessa knocked on the glass, and he lifted his head. She rapped again, and he stood, his gaze going to the window.

When he strode forward, she took a few steps back, so that he might see her in the light falling from the room. When he caught sight of her, his gaze hardened.

"Let me in," she whispered, exaggeratedly mouthing the words. As he continued to regard her, she added, "Please."

His mouth firmed into a line. He gave her a sharp nod, then pointed to his left.

Navigating around another mass of shrubbery, Jessa came to a patio with French doors leading into the mansion. She climbed over the small balustrade and watched as the earl's candle bobbed toward her through the darkened room.

He opened one of the doors and slipped out, then set his small lantern on the flagstones. The single flame cast his face in forbidding shadows, and sudden fear snagged her breath. Here she was—alone at midnight, and utterly at this man's mercy.

"Miss Lovell," he said, folding his arms, "what are you doing here?"

"I must know what you have been saying about me." She lifted her chin, trying to push back the knowledge of her own vulnerability. "Ever since I played your musicale, not a single person has approached Mr. Burke to schedule a new concert."

One of his brows lifted slightly. "I've nothing to do with that, I assure you."

"Haven't you?" She took a step toward him, righteous anger warming her. "I know how men gossip about their conquests, and how women listen to what is both said and unsaid. No one will want to hire me if it is suspected I am a seductress, leading gentlemen astray."

"Not a soul knows that we kissed." His gaze fell to her lips, and the memory of his embrace trembled through her. "Believe me, Miss Lovell, one kiss does not a seduction make. It is hardly worth troubling yourself over."

"Yet I am troubled. And my guardian even more so."

"Did he hit you again? Does he know of this indiscretion?" He stepped forward and took her chin, then gently turned her face to either side, inspecting it in the dim light.

His fingers were warm on her night-cooled skin, and she fought the urge to lean into the solid warmth of his body. Instead, she took his hand and drew it away from her face.

"No. Mr. Burke does not know we kissed. But I fear the lack of interest in my performances will drive him to some unpleasant action."

"Mr. Burke does not strike me as a particularly pleasant person to begin with. How did you come to be under his protection?"

Jessa swallowed and glanced away. Dew glistened on the shadowed lawn, and distant shouts of laughter drifted through the dark air.

"When my father died," she said, "there was no one else to take me and my younger sister in. He is one of our only relatives on our mother's side."

"The Gypsies would not keep you?"

"Do not call them that, they are the Rom. And no. Our

ties of blood were too weak."

"Too weak? Are you not half Gyps—Rom?"

She shook her head. "Father was. My sister and I are only quarter-blood. But none of that matters now. We are beholden to Mr. Burke."

The earl's lips firmed, and his hand tightened around hers. She had forgotten that their fingers were still clasped together.

"I will engage you for my upcoming garden party," he said. "And encourage my acquaintances to consider doing the same."

"Thank you." She hoped it would sufficiently placate Mr. Burke. "I must go."

She slipped her hand from his and turned away.

"Wait." He caught up the lantern and strode to her side. "I doubt you have a carriage waiting at the curb. How do you intend to return home?"

"I hired a hackney to bring me here." Let him think she would do the same again for her return journey.

"I'll escort you."

"My lord, that's completely unnecessary. It's late, and—"

"Precisely. This is no hour for a woman to be going about the streets." They rounded the corner of Trevethwick House, and he frowned. "Did the cab not wait?"

"I did not know how long I might be."

"I will take you home, then."

She shook her head. "It will hardly do my reputation any good for you to rouse your driver to convey me home after an illicit night visit. Do not concern yourself, sir."

"We shall ride." He gave her a close look. "Do you know how to ride, Miss Lovell?"

"I do."

And how she missed the nimble ponies of the clan, the

wild bareback rides across fields and over low stone walls. But that part of her life was gone—and had never truly been hers to begin with.

The earl regarded her a moment more. "A woman of surprises. Pull up your hood."

Jessa drew the cloth up about her face. It was essential she not be recognized. What the servants might think of their master taking a midnight ride with a mysterious woman was the earl's concern, not hers.

In the stables, the smell of hay and manure and warm animal wrapped about Jessa, more comforting than her cloak. She inhaled deeply, careful to keep her face concealed from the sleepy stable lad who sprang to assist them.

As soon as two horses were saddled, the earl gestured for her to take the chestnut. It did not surprise her that he would ride the larger gray.

The stablehand led her horse to the mounting block. Jessa tried not to frown as she glanced up at the sidesaddle. Her plain dark skirts were no riding habit, but voluminous enough that she could hook her leg about the high, curved pommel. How foolish the gentry were, with their notions of what was proper for a lady. She was far more accustomed to riding astride. Not that she imagined the earl would countenance her even suggesting it: he seemed such a rigid paragon of propriety.

Though she did find it ironically amusing that his honor demanded he ride with her through the streets of London in the dead of night. It reeked of illicit scandal.

A pity the only scandalous thing between them was a single kiss.

"Might I assist you?" Lord Silverton asked, coming to stand beside her.

She nodded and stepped onto the mounting block. One hand on the saddle, the other grasping her skirts, she set her foot into the low stirrup. The earl clasped her waist and boosted her up, the warm print of his hands lingering as she settled herself. It felt awkward to be perched all on one side of the horse, but secure enough.

Without a word, he adjusted her stirrup, then swung up onto his horse. The stable hand led Jessa's horse out, and she bit back her frustration. Truly, she was capable of guiding her mount out of the building—but the less she said that might reveal her identity, the better.

The fog still cast a haze over the night, but the moon had broken free of the clouds and was sending tilted silver light over the sleeping city. Jessa lifted her head, and her mount's ears pricked up when the lad handed her the reins.

"Come," the earl said, and urged his horse into the quiet street.

The clop of hooves over cobbles seemed loud in Jessa's ears, but the rumble of a carriage's metal-bound wheels would have been worse. Gas lamps shed pools of light, the illumination much more regularly spaced than in Mr. Burke's neighborhood. She leaned forward and let her mount draw even with the earl's. He glanced over at her.

"What is the gelding's name?" she asked, patting her mount's neck.

"Mayberry." There was a note of approval in his voice. "Tell me, Miss Lovell, where are we bound?"

"Westminster." It was not the poorest or most dangerous area of London, but shabby gentility was quickly giving way to less savory elements in certain quarters.

"We'll cut through Green Park and St. James's, then," he said.

She nodded. It would shorten the distance, and she felt safe enough in his company.

They rode past furled gardens and splendid townhouses. Some were dark and slumberous, while others shone with light and merriment, and likely would until dawn. What a strange life the *ton* led. And how odd that, had she a different father, she might even now be attending one of those parties. Not as a performer, but as a guest.

Two gentlemen emerged from a brightly lit mansion in front of them. One was singing loudly, though not terribly, and the other weaved back and forth. Whether he was dancing or simply stumbling on the cobbles, she could not determine.

"What ho!" The singer broke off and peered toward them. "Greetings, fellow travelers of the night."

"A lady of the night, to be sure," his companion said. "And could it be? Upon my word—the Earl of Silverton!"

"Can't be him. Silverton would never consort with a demimondaine."

Jessa sent the earl a wide-eyed glance. The two gentlemen might forget the encounter by morning. Or they might not.

"Can you keep your seat?" he asked in a low voice.

"Well enough." She gathered her reins, and felt her horse tense beneath her.

The earl spurred his mount forward, and Mayberry was quick to follow. They clattered past the men, and Jessa gritted her teeth against the jumbled trot. Then her horse strode out, falling into a canter, and she adapted to the smooth rocking motion. The drunken lords were left far behind.

Her hood fell back, and the wind against her face and hair was glorious. Despite herself, she laughed. For one perfect moment, all her cares were left behind.

They turned the corner, and the earl reined his mount back. Jessa regretfully slowed her own horse, until they were back to a walk.

"I don't think they recognized you," he said.

Belatedly, she pulled her hood back up. "They certainly knew you."

"No matter." His tone was terse. "You ride well, Miss Lovell."

"I miss it," she said, then bit her tongue. It was no use pining for things she would never have again.

Wild night rides and kisses from severe earls foremost among them.

***

Morgan covertly studied Jessamyn Lovell as they rode through the night-shrouded streets. She sat her horse confidently, despite being obviously unused to a sidesaddle. During their quick canter, she'd handled Mayberry well.

What a paradox she was. He wanted to demand if she was aware of her guardian's criminal pursuits, but that would tip his own hand too clearly.

And truly, how could she *not* be aware?

They turned into Green Park, and the horses' ears pricked up as their hooves met soil instead of stone. The memory of her spontaneous laughter echoed in his mind—so unlike the well-mannered titters of the young ladies of the *ton*.

He glanced ahead, to the silver-lit swath of the green, and the old wildness within him stirred. The green was completely empty, the sounds of Mayfair muffled behind hedges and walls.

Miss Lovell would not condemn him for unleashing the mad urge to gallop into the night. Indeed, he suspected she'd join him willingly. And he wanted to hear her laugh again.

"Ready?" he asked, relishing the startled glance she sent him.

"For what?"

"To ride."

Before she could respond, he sent Sterling forward. Trot, canter, then gallop, the fast gait keeping pace with his racing heartbeat. The moon shone down strongly, as if encouraging him to abandon all caution and dive into the lunacy of the night.

Behind him, he heard the thud of hooves—and then the sound he'd been listening for. Jessamyn Lovell's laughter was so full of delight that he could not help but smile in return, though he kept his face turned away.

Too soon, they reached the end of the green, where the trail narrowed and wound through the shrubbery. Morgan slowed his horse, and she drew up beside him, her dark hair disheveled, her eyes bright.

"Oh, that was wonderful. Mayberry has excellent gaits." She patted the horse's neck with her gloved hand, and he bobbed his head, as if in agreement.

Her cloak had blown back, and her chest rose and fell. The scent of roses on the nearby bushes filled the air. Their gazes met, held.

It was the damnable moonlight, the aftermath of the reckless gallop, the indisputably desirable woman before him, her lips still smiling. Everything conspired to make the kiss inevitable.

Sterling allowed his rider to guide him directly beside Mayberry. A good mount, he remained perfectly steady as Morgan leaned over and tasted Jessamyn's mouth.

She gasped slightly, and his tongue slipped between her lips. Hesitantly, she sent her own to meet his, and the heat of it jolted through him. More than anything, he wanted to take her down from the horse and lay her on the moon-swept ground, dew falling from the roses above while he—

With an oath, he pulled back. He was not so lost to

decency that he would ravish her here, in the middle of the green. Despite the fire scorching his blood and the insistent throb between his legs.

"My lord…" She stared at him, fingers twined in the reins. Mayberry snorted and sidled.

"My name is Morgan." He owed her that much, after twice taking liberties he should not have even contemplated.

Without further conversation, he led them out of the perilous park and back onto the streets. When they reached the outskirts of Westminster, he nodded for her to take the lead. Despite a few furtive lurkers in the shadows, they safely reached a long street lined with shabby, once-genteel row houses.

Miss Lovell halted. "It's the blue one, in the middle. Thank you for your escort."

Before he could move to assist her, she'd swung gracefully down from her horse and handed him the reins.

"Good evening," he said softly. It was the only thing he could say.

She straightened her cloak, pulled her hood forward, then turned and walked quickly down the street. When she reached the stoop, she glanced back. He lifted one hand, and Sterling shifted beneath him. Even after she had slipped inside and closed the door, Morgan waited.

No lights bloomed in the upstairs windows, no curtains stirred. Sterling whuffled impatiently. After long minutes, Morgan finally turned and, leading the second mount, rode away.

***

Jessa let out her breath, a faint fog on the windowpane, as

Lord Silverton departed. The feel of his kiss still tingled on her mouth, and she traced her lips with one finger.

"Jessie?" Louisa stirred in her bed. "Are you here?"

"Yes, love." She turned away from the window and went to sit on her own bed.

"Did you get the second talisman?"

If she told Louisa no, her sister would insist she return again to the earl's—and that was something Jessa would not do. Her heart and mind were already impossibly tangled whenever she thought of him. Better to keep as much distance as she could between herself and the Earl of Silverton.

"Well?" Louisa demanded. "What did the Silver Lord give you? A golden coin? A silken rose?"

Jessa should have at least plucked a flower from the earl's garden. She pinched the brow of her nose, thinking desperately. The dew dampening the bottom of her skirts would not satisfy, and she must never speak aloud the fact of their kiss. There was only one answer she could make.

"He told me his true name," she said.

"Ahh. That means he must help us whenever you say it."

"Perhaps." Jessa smoothed her sister's hair from her forehead. "Go back to sleep."

"But there will be one more talisman," Louisa murmured. "There are always three."

"Shh." Jessa began to hum an old lullaby.

She had no earthly idea how she was going to disabuse Louisa of her fairytale notions. But for now, they were safe.

When her sister's peaceful breaths showed she was asleep, Jessa removed her cloak and gown and stowed them in the back of the wardrobe. She would need to brush them well to ensure no stray horsehairs clung to the fabric. But that ride had been worth everything, bittersweet and stolen though it might be.

More secret still was the memory of the earl's kiss, the taste of his name on her lips as she fell into dreaming.

CHAPTER TEN

*Was Lord Silverton glimpsed in loose company late the other night?
Unreliable witnesses swear the upright earl was cavorting on horseback
through the streets of Mayfair, accompanied by a dubious female
companion. The Tattler can scarcely credit such a tale!*
-Tilly's Mayfair Tattler, July 8

Two days later, over their thin porridge, Mr. Burke announced they would have a visitor later that day.

"Make sure you're dressed nicely," he said, then pointed his spoon at Louisa. "Especially her."

"May I inquire who is coming to call?" Jessa asked, apprehension tightening her ribs. If it involved Louisa, she truly feared what their guardian intended.

"An acquaintance of mine, who might be able to help us out of our predicament." Mr. Burke smiled, showing too many teeth.

Oh, no. She glanced at Louisa, whose innocent expression only heightened Jessa's worry. Could her sister even comprehend what might befall her? The possible scenarios made Jessa shiver.

The rest of the morning crawled by. As instructed, Jessa helped Louisa dress in one of her two nice gowns—a pale blue silk that complimented her complexion. Despite the dread circling Jessa, she curled her sister's hair and helped her pin it up.

"Who is coming to visit us?" Louisa asked.

"I don't know." The words caught in Jessa's throat.

"I like this gown." Louisa smoothed the skirts with her palm. "It feels like water."

Jessa could not voice her usual promises about how one day she would buy Louisa a pretty dress in every color, and bonnets to match. Tales of a bright future were too quickly fading under the shadow of the present.

For a short while, she practiced her violin, but even the solace of music could not distract her. The notes were angular, the tone thin, and after an unsatisfying half an hour, she put her instrument away.

She and Louisa ended up waiting in the parlor, where Jessa pretended to read a novel, and her sister drew. Louisa had no talent for it, but her childish scrawls of flowers and oddly formed animals pleased her well enough, and kept her from asking Jessa any more unanswerable questions.

At last the sharp clack of the knocker resounded through the house. Jessa jumped up and set her novel aside, then helped her sister tidy away her drawing supplies.

"Remember," Jessa said, tucking up a stray curl of her sister's hair, "no matter what happens, I will protect you."

Her heart burned fiercely as she regarded her sister's sweet and trusting smile. Jessa did not know how she would shield Louisa from harm, only that she would.

But first, she must understand what danger approached. She led her sister to the settee and they perched there on the slightly prickly cushions, hands clasped.

Footsteps resounded down the hall, and Jessa could hear Mr. Burke's voice. He was using that oily tone he assumed when he was trying to ingratiate himself with the listener.

For one wild moment, Jessa imagined that perhaps it was Lord Silverton, come to offer his assistance. She shook the ridiculous notion from her head. He'd already said he would hire her for a garden party, and that was the full extent of his aid. Her and Louisa's plight meant nothing to him.

When the door opened, the man standing beside Mr. Burke bore no resemblance whatsoever to the earl. He was thin and stooped, and though he wore well-made clothes in fine fabrics, the colors did not suit him, making his skin appear sallow. His few strands of black hair lay combed across the top of his pink scalp, and his dark eyes were deep-sunk behind a long, thin nose.

"Here they are," Mr. Burke said. "The Misses Lovell, Jessamyn and Louisa, my wards. Girls, this is Sir Maurice Dabbage."

Jessa let go of Louisa's hand and gave the man a curtsy, which her sister emulated. "Pleased to meet you," she said.

Sir Dabbage peered down his nose at Louisa, and his nostrils flared. "I thought she would be younger."

Jessa took a half-step forward. "May I inquire, what is your interest in my sister?"

She did not like the look in the man's eyes as he watched Louisa, assessing her as though she were a horse he was considering purchasing.

"Let's not be hasty," Mr. Burke said. "Sit down, so we might all become better acquainted. Sir Dabbage, you'll find that, although a grown woman in appearance, Miss Louisa has still a very childlike mind."

Their guest frowned, but deigned to take a seat once Jessa and Louisa had perched again on the settee.

An awkward silence encased them. Jessa opened her mouth, but her guardian gave her a dark look and she closed it again.

"That's a pretty dress, Miss Louisa," Sir Dabbage said at last.

"Oh, it is," she said. "I think it's like wearing a bit of the sky after it rains. Except it is dry."

"Would you like more gowns, and jewelry to wear about that soft neck of yours?"

Louisa turned to Jessa, a question in her eyes.

"And why would you bestow such things upon my sister, sir?" Jessa asked, though the crawling sensation in her gut told her well enough.

"Now, now," Mr. Burke said. "Sir Dabbage is a banker, of some note." He laughed at his poor joke, and their guest managed a pinched smile. "Sadly, he is a widower, and is looking to remedy that situation."

Jessa shot her guardian an appalled look. "You can't mean to give Louisa to him!"

Mr. Burke stood and grasped Jessa's arm.

"Excuse us a moment," he said, then towed her to the far end of the room.

"You cannot wed her to that man. Or any man." Jessa wrenched herself from his grip. "My sister is completely innocent of the things that pass between a husband and wife."

"That is her appeal," Mr. Burke said. "Sir Dabbage has... particular tastes."

"I forbid it."

At this her guardian laughed, his stale breath washing over her. "You have no say in the matter. Unless you'd rather I gave him your sister *without* the benefit of matrimony?"

Jessa curled her fingers tightly into her palms. Oh, she wished she were a man so she might punch that amused smile off his face.

"I won't play for you any longer," she said. "I'll refuse all offers to perform."

"Since those have been in short supply lately, you may do as you wish. But your sister will marry Sir Dabbage."

"Why?" Jessa shot a glance to the other end of the parlor, where their guest leaned toward Louisa as a spider leans toward an unsuspecting fly.

"As I said, he's a banker. One whom I, unfortunately, owe a rather large sum of money. Luckily, he wants a young wife even more than the interest on his loans. We are hoping to reach a mutual agreement."

It was unsupportable, but she could not hope to dissuade her guardian from this course of action. Once he made up his mind, he never veered.

"Then I will go with her," Jessa said. She would find some way to protect Louisa. Even if it meant taking her sister's place in the marriage bed. She shivered at the notion.

"Oh, you're not to his taste," Mr. Burke said, as if reading her thoughts. "I'm looking for a man with more seasoned appetites to take you on."

"What?" She swayed, and whiteness flashed through her, rendering her incapable of thought. With one hand, she reached and steadied herself against the parlor wall. The flocked wallpaper was bumpy beneath her fingers.

"I can't afford to keep you both on any longer," he said. "I've gotten what I need from your performances, and I'm afraid your usefulness to me is nearly at an end. I'm only doing what any guardian would. It is my duty and responsibility to see you advantageously married."

Advantageous to himself, of course. What she and her sister thought of it mattered not.

They must flee.

She wanted to rage and scream. She wanted to empty the contents of her stomach over Mr. Burke's shoes. She wanted to run Mr. Dabbage through with a dagger.

But for now, she must appear resigned to this horrible plot. Clenching her teeth, Jessa bent her head.

"I understand," she said.

"Good. I knew you would. You've a sensible streak." Mr. Burke patted her shoulder, and she forced herself not to shudder away from his touch. "It won't be bad, if you cooperate. We'll find you a tall, blond fellow—you appear to be drawn to that sort."

He laughed, then strode over to rejoin Sir Dabbage and Louisa. Jessa hurried to follow, her stomach clenching.

"Well," Mr. Burke said, glancing at Louisa's pale hand caught in their guest's grasp. "You two seem to be getting on splendidly."

"Indeed. I think your niece will do quite well." Sir Dabbage looked Louisa up and down, then smiled, an expression that made his sunken eyes glitter unappealingly.

Louisa glanced up at Jessa. "He says I'm to come live with him and have all the lovely gowns and sweets that I desire. But you will be there, won't you?"

"Don't worry." Jessa laid her hand on her sister's shoulder.

"Excellent!" Mr. Burke rubbed his hands together. "Girls, you may go now. Sir Dabbage and I have a few details to finalize."

Their guest rose and, finally, released Louisa's hand.

"I look forward to our happy day," he said.

Louisa nodded, but Jessa was certain her sister had no notion of what the man actually meant. Head throbbing with panicked thoughts, Jessa led her sister from the room. She felt as though they were on a sinking ship, the frigid water rising about their ankles, and no land in sight.

CHAPTER ELEVEN

As the Season winds down, the Tattler eagerly awaits news of an announcement from the Earl of Silverton. Might we look forward to a late summer wedding?

-Tilly's Mayfair Tattler, July 10

"Lovely weather," Lady Anne said, peering up at Morgan from beneath the brim of her ribbon-festooned hat. "Don't you think it's a perfect day for an outing?"

She rode beside Morgan on a white mare with an easy, placid gait. Since they had met ten minutes ago at the gates of Hyde Park, Lady Anne had been much involved in greeting acquaintances and waving hellos. They'd stopped to exchange niceties with nearly a dozen other members of the *ton*, but at last had come to a less crowded area of the bridle path.

"Indeed, an excellent day for a ride," he said. Warm sunlight bathed the trees, and spangled the path ahead with dappled shadows and light. "Would you care for a trot?"

As if understanding his words, Sterling snorted and mouthed the bit. The horse was ready to do more than walk sedately about the park. As was Morgan.

"Oh, no, thank you," Lady Anne said. "I find the trot to

be quite jolting."

"A canter, then?"

She let out a nervous trill of laughter. "My brother broke his arm when he fell from a cantering horse. I'd rather not risk it."

"Then a gallop is straight out of the question, I suppose."

He tried not to let his disappointment show. Lady Anne was a trifle staid for someone of such young years, but truly, was that not what he desired in a wife? Someone sensible and cautious, without the wild streak that had led his family into ruin.

Certainly not someone who would race recklessly over the moonlit green, laughing.

"Now you are teasing me." She gave him a bright smile. "If you wish to gallop, and show off your excellent horsemanship, I would be delighted to watch."

"No, no. I will not abandon your charming company." Besides, the small wood they were riding through was hardly the proper terrain for a hard gallop.

"You are too kind." She said the words matter-of-factly. "Oh, look, what delightful flowers."

She pointed off the path, to where a spray of columbines grew. Morgan did not think them particularly fetching, but he understood they were meant to provide a distraction.

"Shall I pluck you one?" he offered, reining in Sterling.

"How lovely. I would like that above all things."

Morgan dismounted and handed her the reins. "I promise he will not move an inch."

Sterling watched Morgan step into the underbrush, his ears pricked forward, but true to his training, he remained still. The loam was springy under Morgan's boots, and birds flickered and sang in the branches overhead. He plucked a stem of the pale blue and white flowers, then returned to present it to Lady

Anne.

"Thank you," she said. "I believe it will look stunning tucked into my hatband. Would you?"

Before Morgan could protest, she leaned precariously down.

"Lady Anne, I truly don't—"

Too late. With a little cry she tumbled off the saddle, and into his arms. She clung to his shoulders and lifted her face to his, lips parted.

He hesitated, then, with a mental shrug, bent to kiss her. Her lips were sweet and soft beneath his, but no urgency ran through his veins, no fire spiraled upward from his belly. Kissing Lady Anne was pleasant, but that was all. He pressed her closer against him, hoping to spur a deeper reaction. Nothing but a faint stirring.

Surely, in time, it could become something more. Forcing back his disquiet, Morgan ended the kiss.

"Oh, my," Lady Anne said, blinking up at him. "I hope you do not think me too forward."

Color pinked her cheeks. Clearly the kiss had affected her far more than it had moved him. Curse it.

"I am only glad I was here to catch you," he said, letting go of her waist. "Are you steady now?"

"It was rather clumsy of me." She removed her hands from his shoulders and made a show of tucking the flowers into her hat. "Thank you for your assistance."

A more calculated clumsiness he had never seen, but he could not begrudge her. She'd chosen a secluded spot, at least. And if anyone had observed them embracing, well, he was set on marrying her anyway.

"It was my pleasure." More or less.

He assisted her in mounting her white mare again, and the two of them rode out of the wood, into the sunshine and social flurry along the Serpentine. Lady Anne sent him dreamy glances and shy smiles from time to time, and he supposed he was glad that she found him such an object of romantic interest—beyond his title and fortune, obviously.

She was pretty enough in both form and manners. He had made an excellent choice. Certainly the majority of Society matrons approved, judging by their manner when he and Lady Anne stopped to greet them, and the overloud whispers of what a lovely couple they made as they rode away.

Morgan straightened his shoulders. This grimness that settled like fine dust over him was what any man would feel at the thought of matrimony, nothing more.

***

Commissioner Rowan's office still smelled of pickled herring as Morgan took his usual chair. Across the desk from him, Rowan steepled his fingers and gave him a thoughtful look.

"You're sure Burke took the bait?" he asked.

"Quite." Morgan leaned back and folded his arms. "Although it could well be weeks until I'm contacted by Mr. Z. Don't you think it's time you removed all charges against Geordie?"

Rowan let out a gusty breath through his nostrils. "I suppose. You've done everything you can to help, I'll give you that. But I expect you to keep us apprised of anything else you discover about Burke, or his activities."

"Of course. There is one thing." Morgan kept his tone cool. "I understand he is not, in fact, Miss Lovell's uncle, but rather a cousin of some kind."

"True."

"What is the family's connection to the *ton*?"

He had planned to ask his aunt, but it would not do to show too much interest in Jessamyn Lovell when he was supposed to be courting Lady Anne. And Rowan would not find his questions odd, given that they were both involved in uncovering Burke's identity as Mr. Z.

The commissioner straightened a pile of papers on his desk. "As I recall, Miss Lovell's grandfather held the title of Viscount Trenton. No male heirs, and quite a scandal involving the daughter."

"She ran off with a Gypsy fellow, yes."

"Not only that, but the family fell into financial ruin. When the viscount died, the title passed to his brother's son, Phinneus Burke. I believe that gentleman removed to Italy, and is living there in poverty. Our Mr. Burke is the viscount's younger brother."

"So, he remained in London, and assumed guardianship of the disinherited daughter's children." Morgan leaned forward. "A convoluted tale."

"And not likely to end well for the Lovell girls, whether or not we manage to collar Mr. Burke. I wouldn't wish his guardianship upon a pigeon, let alone two young ladies."

A twinge of guilt went through Morgan, but truly, what else could he do to aid Miss Jessamyn Lovell? Nothing that would not compromise her reputation beyond repair. She'd been correct in thinking that no one would engage her for performances if she were considered a light woman.

Well, no one *respectable* would hire her. And her performances would be expected to consist of more than concertizing.

At least she would play at his garden party, and this time he'd offer her more than a glass bauble in extra compensation. Something useful, like a bag of coins, or jewelry she might be able to pawn in need.

He shifted, the chair uncomfortably hard. "Is there no other recourse for the Lovell sisters?"

"Short of running off to Naples and throwing themselves on the viscount's mercy?" Commissioner Rowan gave a rueful shake of his head. "It's a common story, Silverton. Girls fall into ruin daily. Even those with a better pedigree than the Lovells."

"What about places of refuge? The Magdalenes?"

"Better than the streets, I suppose." Rowan's mouth twisted, as if tasting something bitter. "I don't like the tales I hear of what happens behind those walls."

"Sir." The junior constable rapped on Rowan's closed door. "Dispatch for you."

"Come," Rowan called. He stood, his chair scraping against the floor. "Keep us abreast of things, Silverton."

"I shall. Good day."

Morgan donned his hat and strode out into the afternoon, squinting against the too-bright sunshine. He had cleared Geordie's name. Yet instead of relief, he felt only a grim resignation toward life. Duty and honor were damnable weights to carry about constantly on one's shoulders, and they would be his true companions until he died.

CHAPTER TWELVE

According to sources, the case involving the Piccadilly brothel brawl has been closed. No parties were charged, and it appears the constabulary is not interested in revealing further details.

-The London Engager, July 12

Jessa's spine prickled with fear as she and Louisa crept down the stairs, each carrying a valise. Their small store of jewelry weighed heavily in the pocket of her cloak. She had a few shillings as well, taken earlier that evening from Mr. Burke's desk.

If he caught them now, there would be no concealing the fact they were running away. But Sir Dabbage was coming on the morrow to take Louisa. Jessa desperately hoped that by waiting until the last moment, Mr. Burke's suspicions would be allayed—and that there would be no time for him to pursue and find them, or concoct a reasonable tale for Sir Dabbage.

The front door opened smoothly, thanks to the cooking oil she had been regularly applying to the hinges. They stepped out into the night, and the latch snicked shut behind them. She prayed she would never cross that threshold again.

Louisa opened her mouth, but Jessa waved her to silence.

Keeping to the shadows, she led her sister down the street. Unfortunately, no night fog shrouded their passage. Above, the sickle moon shone through the faint haze of soot, and a few stars struggled to stab through the darkness.

At last they reached the bustle of the busier streets. Jessa hailed a hackney, told the driver their destination, and handed up a precious shilling.

"Right-o," he said, as matter-of-factly as if he often transported young ladies about London in the dead of night. Which perhaps he did.

Jessa helped Louisa into the carriage, then settled next to her, tucking their valises beside their feet. The hackney lurched into motion, and she felt the tightness binding her ribs ease a notch. They were not safely away—not yet—but each turn of the wheel over cobbles carried them farther out of reach.

"Are you worried?" Louisa took Jessa's hand. "You are frowning."

Jessa attempted to smooth her expression. Dangers still loomed ahead, with no guarantee that they would find safe refuge.

"Perhaps we should have gone to find the clan," she said. Part of her wanted to flee London altogether.

"But you told me that is the first place Mr. Burke will look," Louisa said. "He would have found us there and taken us again. The Rom would not protect us."

Jessa gave her sister a reluctant nod. Louisa had the right of it. And Jessa's second thought, to find rough lodgings and play her violin on the street for money, was too perilous—and held the same lack of safety. Once he discovered they were gone, Mr. Burke would upend London to recover them.

There was only one answer.

Louisa squeezed her hand and leaned forward, nothing but excitement shining in her eyes. Of course, she was convinced they would receive a warm welcome and an immediate offer of shelter and safety. Jessa was far more realistic in her expectations.

The hackney wended through the streets. Each time they swayed around a corner, Jessa shot a glance behind them. Nobody seemed to be following; no telltale lamps shone at a steady distance, no furtive riders tailing them, or scuttling figures in the shadows. Still, fear lay dry and metallic against her tongue, as if she had licked a knife blade.

Knives, too, pricked in her stomach as the hackney drew up before the dark, imposing bulk of Trevethwick House.

Louisa hopped down, smiling, and Jessa had to grab her hand to keep her sister from marching up the walk to the front door. The hackney trundled away, and Jessa steered Louisa into the concealing shelter of the front hedge.

"We can't just knock at the door," Jessa said.

"Why not? There's a lamp lit—I can see the light."

Jessa clenched her teeth for a moment. Sometimes Louisa's lack of understanding was difficult to bear.

"Because it is the middle of the night. And rousing the butler would cause far too much gossip. People of our station should use the servants' entrance. It's more discreet."

"But you are the princess," Louisa said.

"Duckling, that's only in the stories you tell. I'm not truly a princess—you know that. Lord Silverton might not even take us in."

He was their last hope, however. And he was powerful enough to protect them from Mr. Burke until she could procure another situation for them. Perhaps as governess to some family of the lesser gentry. Although she had no references, and they must be willing to take Louisa as well, and…

She pulled her thoughts away from the many obstacles in

their way. One step at a time.

"We will go around to the back," Jessa said. "Follow me. Quietly."

To her disappointment, no light shone from the earl's study. The entire back of the house was quiet and still. Jessa halted beside the terrace and rubbed her temples. What should they do? Find a place to shelter until the servants began to stir? Wake the house and face the consequences?

The rustle of shrubbery made her turn. Her sister was gone, leaving her alone in the dark garden.

"Louisa? Louisa, where are you?"

She must have returned to the front, stubborn girl. Jessa grabbed her valise and ran down the garden path. She must stop her sister before she did something foolish.

Jessa rounded the house, in time to see Louisa rap at the front door. At least she used her gloved hand, and not the immense lion-headed knocker, which certainly would have woken the entire house.

"Stop," Jessa whispered urgently as she dashed up the steps.

She took Louisa by the arm, just as the front door opened. The thin, disapproving form of Lord Silverton's butler stood there. Behind him, Jessa saw the head footman, hair tousled with sleep, striding down the hall with a candlelit lantern.

"What do you want?" the butler demanded.

"We need to see the Silv—" Louisa began.

Jessa cut her sister off. "Is Lord Silverton available?"

"He is most decidedly not. Nor is he in the habit of taking up with street doxies. Begone, the both of you."

The butler began to close the door, but the footman stopped him.

"Wait. The dark-haired one looks familiar." The man squinted at her. "Is that Jessamyn Lovell?"

"Yes." Jessa shook her hood back. It was too late to do anything except brazen things out. "I apologize for the lateness of the hour, but might we speak with the earl?"

"Most irregular." The butler frowned at them. "No, you may not."

"But—"

"He has not arrived home for the night," the butler continued.

"Put them in the yellow parlor," the footman said. "Clearly they wouldn't be here except for some dire trouble. I'll keep watch on them."

The butler sniffed, but stepped back and opened the door. "I suppose you may wait."

He raised his eyebrows at Jessa's valise, but she did not feel any great need to explain it to him. Soon enough she'd be facing the earl, and must save all her resolve for that encounter.

"Come along, ladies." The footman led them down the hall, their candlelit reflections whispering in gilt-edged mirrors and the polished side of an oriental urn.

He ushered them into a sitting room that held as much furniture as Mr. Burke's entire house, and lit two lamps. The even light reflected off polished wood, warming the yellow and cream carpet covering the parquet floor. Louisa glanced longingly at the plush divan.

"May I sit down?" she asked.

"Certainly," the footman said.

Jessa wagered her sister would be asleep within five minutes.

"Thank you," she said to the man. "I'm sorry to put you to any trouble."

He gave her a sympathetic look. "I'd say you're in worse. The earl should be home within the hour."

"Where has he gone?" Louisa asked, then stifled a yawn.

"A party at Lord Dearborn's, I believe. Make yourselves comfortable. I'll be just outside."

Before they could ask him any more questions, he'd slipped out and shut the door behind him. At least he hadn't locked them in.

"I'm going to lie down," Louisa said. She kicked off her shoes, then settled down on the cushions.

Jessa found a lap robe folded on top on an ornately carved chest, and covered her sister. The cashmere was soft against her fingers, and for a moment she wished that she, too, could curl up and escape into sleep. But the agitation running through her would not allow it.

To the sounds of Louisa's gentle snores, Jessa paced and mustered her arguments. There were not many, beyond appealing to the earl's sense of honor and chivalry. Or... She paused, reluctant to admit there might be one other way.

She could appeal to the desire she had seen in his eyes.

The rumble of male voices in the hallway made her turn and face the door. She made herself lower her hands, though she wanted to keep her arms tightly folded across her chest. But that was not the best way to present herself.

The parlor door opened, and the Earl of Silverton stepped inside. The lamplight polished the golden highlights in his hair, but did little to soften his grim look.

"Miss Lovell. What are you doing here?" He closed the door, shutting out the hovering footman. "Thaddeus informs me you have also brought your sister?"

"Yes." She gestured to the slumbering form on the divan. "Please, my lord. We have no place else to go. Would you... take us in? It would only be for a short time, until I could find some employment."

His stern look did not change. "Did your guardian put you out on the street?"

"Ah… no. We left of our own accord."

"Then perhaps you ought to return of your own accord. Unless there is a compelling reason to keep away." In two strides he was before her. He set his fingers to her chin and tilted her face to the light. "Did he hit you again?"

"No. Not yet. Although he has beaten Louisa, in order to ensure my compliance."

"Then what brought you here?" He released her chin, but did not step away.

She could feel the heat of him, smell the echo of perfumes and perspiration from whatever event he had been attending.

"He means to marry my sister off."

The earl's mouth twisted. "Marriage is not so horrible a fate."

"You don't understand." She shot another glance at Louisa's sleeping form. "My sister is a simple girl, and very innocent. She does not have a great deal of comprehension about the workings of the world, though she is blessed with a merry spirit. I fear…" She swallowed back the dryness in her throat. "I fear the man our guardian will marry her to would like to break her innocence, and her spirit. In fact, I believe it is his chief aim."

She saw her own distaste mirrored in the earl's eyes, and was grateful for it.

"You cannot protect her from him," he said. "And so, you come to me."

"Yes." She smiled up at him, relief washing over her.

"I cannot take you in," he said, stepping back. "Surely there is somewhere else you might go."

"But…" Her relief curdled to panic, her heartbeat leaping into her throat. "There is nowhere else."

"There must be." He rubbed at his forehead. "Blast it. The hour is too late. You'll have to stay the night. I'll tell the butler to wake a maid to fix a room for you—but in the morning we must find a different solution."

At least he was not throwing them back out into the night.

"Thank you," she murmured, fighting back the tears that stung the corners of her eyes.

Perhaps once he met Louisa, he would see how charming she was, and how in need of protection. She clung to that hope, as she roused her sister and followed the sleepy maid up the stairs.

The girl showed them to a spacious suite, and turned down the bedcovers as if Jessa and her sister were true gentility.

"Wait." Jessa caught her arm as the maid turned to go. "Which room is the earl's?"

The girl gave her a saucy look. "Ah, so that's the way of it. Good luck in that direction, miss—his lordship's not one for taking up with light women."

"I know." But she must try.

Things were at a desperate pass. She did not bother to argue with the girl that she was not a "light woman." Not when she intended to behave like one that very night.

"His rooms are in the far corner, on the left. But don't say I didn't warn you when he turns you away."

"Thank you," Jessa said.

The maid left, and Jessa helped her sister get ready for bed. Once Louisa was tucked beneath the sheets, murmuring about the delightful size of the bed, Jessa removed her corset and donned her own nightdress.

"Rest, love," she said to her sister. "I must think on things a bit."

"Don't worry," Louisa said, her words softening into sleep. "The Silver Lord will take care of us."

If only Jessa could have such utter faith in the world.

Sleep beckoned as the coals on the hearth dimmed down

to embers, but it was easy enough to keep the drowsiness at bay. Jessa pulled a thin shawl around her shoulders and perched on one of the chairs near the fire. She tried not to think of what failure would mean.

Or even worse, success.

This was no light endeavor she was embarking upon. After tonight, she would be used goods, a soiled dove. Far less valuable as a wife. But she was destined to be used by a man, in any case.

Instead of fleeing to the Rom and having to accept whoever would take her, or staying with Mr. Burke and being given to a man not of her choosing, she could control this outcome. If she must lose her innocence, at least she could do so in a manner that was the most benefit to her and Louisa. And with a man who turned her blood to fire.

Yet the prospect still frightened her. To fortify her nerves, she let melody fill her mind—the sweet, dark tune of a love song distracting her fearful thoughts.

Finally, when a full hour had passed, she rose and slipped out of the room. Though the hallway was dark, a beam of moonlight shone from the window at the far end. Where Morgan's rooms were.

Jessa walked, bare feet silent on the carpet, toward that cool silver light. Her heart beat like a drum, pounding inside her chest. Outside his door, she hesitated, then carefully opened it. It swung open soundlessly. Swallowing past the dryness in her throat, she stepped inside. She stood in his sitting room, a few chairs and a writing desk illuminated by the moonlight sifting in between the half-closed draperies.

On the other side of the room, the door to his bedroom stood ajar. No light shone within.

She squeezed her eyes shut for a moment, and took a deep breath to steady herself. Now was not the time for the fear and anxiety curling about her. She would not be able to succeed if she crept into his room as a frightened young woman. And she must succeed.

She must be all temptation and heat. She must be irresistible.

Jessa paused with her hand on the doorframe and summoned up the memory of Morgan's kisses. That first one, so unexpected and searing, leaving her breathless at the feel of his hard body pressed against hers. And the second, after their night ride. The heat of his mouth, the flames he ignited low in her belly.

How would it feel, to have him make love to her?

She would know soon enough.

Softly she stepped to his bedside. The fitful moonlight revealed his sleeping form, and the deep breaths of his dreaming filled the air. He slept on his back, the rumpled bedclothes pushed aside to expose his bare chest and muscled arms.

She shoved down the panic skittering through her nerves, and made herself focus on him. Morgan. The passionate man she had sensed lurking beneath the cool façade of the earl. Reaching him was her only hope.

Moving carefully, so as not to wake him, she slid onto the bed. Her breath trembled in her lungs with fear, with desire. She lay beside him, propped up on one elbow, then lowered her face to his. Her lips brushed across his mouth, and a thrill ran through her.

Here she was, in the dark hours, slipping into Morgan's bed and risking everything on a kiss. It was foolhardy and exciting in equal measure.

He stirred, and she bent lower, tasting his lips, then letting her tongue slip out to trace the seam of his mouth. The heat of his body flared through her, as though she lay next to the banked coals of a hearth.

As she deepened the kiss, he let out a half-startled breath. Then his arms came around her and, before she could utter a word, he pulled her on top of him. Their mouths still fastened together, she lay upon his chest, nothing but the thin material of her nightdress between them. His hands pulled at the fabric, and she did not, could not, protest as he bared her legs.

His hands burned on the naked skin of her thighs as he caressed her, pushing her nightdress ever higher—past her hips and the curve of her waist, until the thin cotton was bunched beneath her breasts.

Sparks tingled in the wake of his touch, while his tongue slipped into her mouth and twined with hers. Her mind hazed with pleasure, with triumph. Despite her lack of experience in such matters, she was going to seduce the earl.

CHAPTER THIRTEEN

Morgan dreamed of his misspent youth—of soft, warm lips and heated skin, of the pressure of a woman's body next to his. Half awake, his groin throbbing, he pulled her atop him, his hands restlessly uncovering her nakedness.

The soft skin of her thighs, the sweet curve of her bottom, the swell of her hips. Lust scorched through him at the memory of his former lovers. It had been so long. Too long.

Wait.

His hands stilled, and the woman—the unmistakably *real* woman—lying over him murmured and wriggled gently. Almost, he let himself slip back into the pretense of dreaming, so that he could continue to stroke her body, continue to plunder her mouth with kisses. But no.

Heaving a frustrated breath, he tumbled her off him and propped himself on his side.

His pulse beat through him, insisting he pull her back into his embrace and spread her legs, plunge his aching cock inside her and take the release and pleasure he'd too long denied himself. Rigidly, he clamped down on that reckless desire, forced himself not to reach for her—whoever the girl might be.

"While it's a novel sensation, being woken thus in the

middle of the night, I'm afraid I'm going to have to ask you to leave," he said.

She drew in a breath to speak.

"Don't say anything." He lifted his hand to the shadowy shape of her face, and set his fingers over her lips.

Her full, moist lips.

"It's better I don't discover who you are," he said. "That way, I don't have to put you out on the street without employment or references. Now, go. I trust there will not be a repeat of this night."

She pulled his hand away from her mouth. "You think I'm one of your housemaids? I don't know whether to be flattered or insulted."

Damnation. She'd said too much, and he recognized her voice.

"Jessamyn Lovell, what the devil are you doing in my bed?"

Keep her here, a reckless part of him whispered. *Taste her again. Take her beneath you.*

With a groan, he sat up and lit the candle on his bedside table. The warm light showed her wide, dark eyes, her hair bound into a braid, her lips, parted and still reddened from his mouth. Her bared legs and the curve of her hip.

"I know you desire me," she said.

"That's beside the point." No matter what his body insisted. "Go back to your room."

She shook her head, sat up, and began undoing the ties at the front of her nightdress. For a moment, all he could do was watch as the lush hollow of her cleavage was revealed. Her nipples peaked against the thin fabric, and his mouth went dry at the thought of her breasts.

With a sharp movement, he caught her hands. "I don't know what you think you're doing—"

"You don't?" There was laughter in her voice. "I thought you were the experienced one."

"You need to leave. Now. You're my guest, and I do not abuse my hospitality in this manner."

"Even if your guest might wish it?"

His fingers tightened around hers. "I did not take you for a loose woman, Miss Lovell. Indeed, I thought you a virgin."

She flushed at that, and dropped her gaze. He released her hands, and she set them in her lap. After a moment, she spoke.

"I wish to become your mistress."

"I've no need of a mistress." The tightening between his legs argued otherwise, but he ignored it. "Now, out of my room, Miss Lovell."

She sighed and slipped off the bed. Then, before he could stop her, she shrugged off her nightdress. The flickering light played over her full breasts, her wide hips, and the dark triangle of hair between her legs.

"Put your clothing back on." He gripped the sheets, hard, to keep from reaching for her.

"I can't."

"For God's sake. You mean you won't."

He slid out of bed, on the opposite side of where she stood, aware that his drawers were tented with arousal. When he rounded the bed, her gaze fell on his erection. Her eyes widened, and then a small smile came to rest on her lips.

"Here." He bent and scooped up the nightdress, trying to ignore how close he was to her naked body, the scent of rosewater and the sea.

She did not take it, but instead began unbraiding her hair. Her fingers wove in and out of those long, dark tresses.

"Miss Lovell. I demand you get dressed and leave immediately. Or I will force you to."

He took a step forward, even as the thought of tussling

with her made his desire flare. He could pull the nightdress over her head and pinion her arms, holding her firmly against him. Pick her up and carry her down the hall. His body went taut.

"I shall scream," she said calmly. "Your aunt, my sister, the servants—everyone will rush in. That would be a bit of a scandal, don't you think?"

He grasped her by the shoulders, seeing the determination in her eyes. Her skin was deliciously smooth beneath his palms.

"Do you honestly believe your reputation could challenge mine?" he asked. "A Gypsy violinist against the Earl of Silverton?"

She stepped forward, her breasts brushing his bare chest, and he stifled a groan.

"Still, it would cause gossip," she said.

"And be your ruin," he said through gritted teeth. "You came to my bedroom, Miss Lovell. You will be the one found guilty—especially given my standing in Society. Is that truly what you want?"

Despite his strong worlds, he could not manage to release her. She stared up at him, and he saw the moment resolution turned to defeat, the spark fading from her eyes.

"Very well." Her voice was subdued. "I will leave. But first, you must kiss me once more. It's all I ask."

It was a devil's bargain, but he could not refuse it. Could not refuse her.

He slipped his hands up into the heavy silk of her unbound hair, and bent, fastening his mouth over hers. She let out a little sigh and parted her lips, and he drank, tasting her like the finest wine. Fire burned through him, intoxicating.

Only the thin cotton of his undergarment kept them from touching, skin on skin, the entire length of their bodies. He pressed her against him, one hand untangling from her hair to smooth down her back. His cock strained, eager to be free of its confines of cloth. The flimsy barrier of his drawers was the one thing keeping him from throwing her onto the bed and taking her.

Another moment more, and he would stop. As soon as his roving hand cupped her breast, his thumb caressing back and forth against her nipple.

She gasped and arched against him, and, drunk with the scent of her, he dipped his head and licked at the taut peak of her breast. Her fingers dug into his shoulders as he closed his mouth over her nipple. He wanted to taste her everywhere, wanted to spread her legs and put his tongue there.

Desire shuddered through him, and with the last of his shredded restraint, he forced himself to stop. She breathed heavily in his embrace, her eyes heavy-lidded, her hair spun about her like black silk.

Morgan squeezed his eyes shut. It was the only way to keep himself from kissing her again, and again. He let his arms fall to his sides, his fingers curled into fists.

"There. Your kiss. Now put your nightdress on."

He waited until he heard the rustle of cloth before opening his eyes. The garment covered her adequately, though the bodice was still half undone. His hands ached to caress her breasts again.

"Please," she said. "I beg your protection."

"And you thought seducing me would secure it?"

She met his gaze frankly. "If you took me as your mistress, yes."

"I don't keep a mistress." He made his tone hard, despite a tantalizing vision of her lying naked between his sheets. Under him. "And I have no intention of doing so."

"I had thought…" She wet her lips and glanced at the candle. The flame reflected, a point of gold in each eye.

"Thought you wanted me."

The proof of his craving was still making his drawers stand. "Miss Lovell. You are beautiful and desirable, there is no question of that. But I cannot take advantage of you."

She met his gaze and opened her mouth to speak, but he held up one hand.

"No," he said. "A woman in desperate circumstances is forced to actions she would not ordinarily take. I understand that. But I will not be a party to it."

"Then you will not help us?" She swallowed, distress clear in her expression.

"I took you in this evening, didn't I?" Did she have to make him out to be so heartless?

"But you are turning my sister and myself out again on the morrow."

"Perhaps." That had been his intent, but now he was not so certain.

Clearly things were more fraught for her than he had thought, if she was moved to such rashness as trying to seduce him in order to claim his protection.

"My guardian is dangerous," she said. "We are not safe from him—unless you agree to aid us."

"And do what? Ship you off to the Continent, out of his reach?"

"I'd hoped to reach an agreement with you." She sighed.

"Catching a powerful man's fancy is not a solution," he said forcefully, trying to make her believe the words.

What if she left Trevethwick House and set her sights on becoming someone else's mistress? His gut tightened unpleasantly at the thought. The next man she approached might not be gentleman enough to turn her down. He himself had barely managed it. Thank God his desire for her was finally ebbing to bearable levels.

Speaking of which… He snagged his dressing robe from a nearby chair and donned it, aware that she watched his every move.

"Becoming your mistress may not serve as a permanent answer," she said. "But it is better than nothing."

Better than nothing? His pride pricked at the thought, and he spoke without thinking.

"So I am simply a means to an end? Any man will do, as long as he offers you a modicum of protection?"

"No." She twisted her hair back into a braid with agitated fingers. "You are the only one I would approach in such a manner."

"I'm relieved to hear it. But now that your gambit has failed, what next?"

"I haven't any notion." Her words were soft. "I don't suppose I might try again."

He clenched his jaw. "You may not."

No matter how much he might want her to. He took up the candle, then motioned her to precede him into his sitting room.

"There is another coin you might use," he said. He did not like to press her, and it did not seem particularly gentlemanly to do so, but this was the perfect opportunity. "If you tell me what your uncle has been doing during your performances, that information would be valuable enough to let you stay here for a time."

She froze, the candlelight illuminating the widening of her eyes. Shadows flickered in the corners of the room.

"How could I know such a thing? I play my violin, and that is all."

He strode up to her, but she did not give way, only stared up at him. The scent, the heat of her was beyond distracting, but he forced himself to continue.

"Are you quite certain you can tell me nothing, Miss Lovell?"

"If our guardian were found guilty of some crime, what happens to me and my sister? Are you willing to shelter us indefinitely?"

Morgan shook his head. "That's a rather unreasonable request. I have no obligation toward you."

"Of course not." Her mouth twisted. "You're barely giving us one evening beneath your roof."

"Arriving on my doorstep in the middle of the night is highly irregular."

Damnation, he sounded so staid. But even though he'd refused her, tongues would wag. The best solution—for both their reputations—would be to remove the Lovell sisters from Trevethwick House posthaste.

Particularly since Jessamyn seemed determined to say nothing damaging about her guardian. And perhaps she had nothing to tell him, after all. Which put them all in a rather awkward position.

"Then I must hope that the new day offers some solution," she said. "Good night, my lord."

"Indeed." He handed her the candle. "Morning will be here all too soon. Good night."

She took the light, then turned away and slipped into the hall. He stood in his darkened doorway, watching the sphere of gold move away from him, his thoughts knotted with frustration.

She would tell him nothing, and represented a nearly impossible problem.

Now that he had seen her naked, had held her lush body close to his, he could never undo that knowledge. Or the desire for her that, he feared, had embedded itself deeply—as if she were a painful, nearly invisible sliver beneath his skin that pricked him with every movement, impossible to remove.

***

The next morning, Jessa woke when Louisa got out of bed. Her sister swept open the curtain, letting light into the room. Disorientation washed over Jessa as her eyes focused sleepily on the elegant furnishings, and then memory returned with a thud.

She had failed.

Despite her best efforts at seduction, the earl had turned her away. Her throat tightened with fear. What now?

She'd told him the truth, that she had no intention of going out and finding another man who would take her on as his mistress. It had been all she could do to gather her courage enough to try with Morgan, who, she had to admit, set her senses alight with desire. But she could not muster the will to attempt to ensnare anyone else.

Yet she might not have another choice. She had her music, and she had herself. Such little coin to spend in the uncaring streets of London.

She had come so close to telling Morgan what she knew of Mr. Burke's doings. And yet the letter promising to send Louisa to the asylum was still engraved in her memory. Even worse, Mr. Burke could still force her sister to wed, up until the point he was found guilty and his guardianship dissolved. Which would be long enough to do irreparable harm.

Her breath caught on the edge of a sob. The earl had no reason to offer them his protection, and had said as much.

Oh, if only she had been able to find proof of Mr. Burke's blackmailings! She might have been able to bargain that information in exchange for a safe haven. But her word against Mr. Burke's, lacking all proof, was far too weak. The stark fact was that their guardian still had every claim to them, and if he were taken, would do his utmost to destroy both Louisa and herself.

She could not take that risk.

"Are you awake?" Louisa jumped back onto the bed, already dressed, and gave her a bright-eyed look. "Can we go explore?"

"Not without the earl's permission."

"Can we ask him now?"

Jessa wanted to burrow back beneath the soft sheets and hide from the day—but she could not let Louisa careen unescorted about Trevethwick House.

"We will see him at breakfast." With a deep breath, Jessa sat up. "You may help me dress, and we will fix one another's hair."

It was enough of a distraction, and the time passed readily enough until the maid came to summon them to the breakfast room. She was the same girl who had taken them to their room the previous night, and gave Jessa an arch look, as if to scold her for thinking she could seduce the master of the house. Jessa sent her a rueful frown in return.

Oblivious to the undercurrents, Louisa exclaimed over the pretty vase full of peonies in the hall, the lush landscapes in ornate frames, and the thickness of the carpet beneath their feet.

"Imagine, a room only for eating breakfast in!" Louisa said, as the maid opened the white door.

"Sometimes they take tea there, as well," the maid said.

Louisa all but skipped inside, while Jessa followed more slowly. The room was filled with sunshine, and bright flowers nodded just outside the mullioned windows. A medium-sized table was set with china, and a serving board on the right side of the room held an array of covered dishes, a plate of toast, a gleaming jar of marmalade, and fresh strawberries.

The earl rose from the head of the table, his expression set in its usual severe lines. His aunt was seated on his right, wearing an emerald and scarlet robe embroidered with gold dragons. Her gray-brown hair was uncoiffed, and a trifle wild looking in the strong morning sun. She gave the sisters a curious, if not unkind, look.

"Good morning," the earl said. "Miss Jessamyn, you have already met my aunt, Lady Agatha. And this is your sister, I presume?"

"I'm Louisa," her sister said, before Jessa could make a more formal introduction. "And I'm rather hungry."

The aunt let out a snort of laughter. "An honest girl, at any rate. Pleased to make your acquaintance, my dear. Now, come sit by me and we will have the servants fill your plate posthaste. Do you take cream in your tea?"

"Yes, and lots of sugar." Louisa rounded the table and settled beside Morgan's aunt. "My sister doesn't let me suck the sugar cubes," she confided.

"It's bad for your teeth," Lady Agatha said, nodding. "But when you grow as old as I am, you may suck all the sugar cubes you like."

"Miss Lovell." The earl, still standing, gestured to the chair on his left.

Jessa hastily walked past him, then took the indicated seat. One of the hovering servant men scooted her chair in and draped a napkin across her lap. It was rather unnerving, though Louisa appeared unconcerned. Of course, her sister's nature was not one given to worry or despair, as her animated conversation with Morgan's aunt showed.

Jessa shot a glance across the table. She was relieved that Lady Agatha seemed to find Louisa charming, but that was no guarantee of their safety.

Unsmiling, Morgan motioned to the servant to fill her teacup. She nodded her thanks, then squeezed a bit of lemon into the dark brew. Unlike Louisa, she was not overfond of diluting her tea.

"I have been discussing your plight with my aunt," he said. "It's my understanding there are institutions that take in women in distress—"

"And you know precisely how I feel about such places," his aunt cut in. "I was not in favor of shuffling our guests off to one before, and I most certainly am not now. Particularly since I understand a bit more about their predicament, and Miss Louisa's sunny nature." She patted Louisa's hand. "Really, Morgan, you cannot in good conscience boot them out."

The earl leaned toward Jessamyn and lowered his voice. "Has your sister always been thus?"

"Yes. She is a lovely, simple girl." A delight and a burden all at once.

"I see how that makes things more difficult for you." He looked at Louisa, his face thoughtful. "Especially in light of your guardian's plans for her."

At least he understood that much. Jessa took a bite of toast, the marmalade sweet and tangy against her tongue. They had an ally in his aunt, but Morgan was the one who held their fate in his hands.

"I must protect her," Jessa said. "She has no one else."

His gaze returned to her, his pale eyes studying her face. "It explains much about your insistence last night."

Heat crept into her cheeks.

"It was not only for Louisa's sake," she said.

"I would hope not." His tone was dry. "Still, the question remains. What shall I do with the two of you?"

She took another bite of toast, glad to see that Louisa was heartily consuming her eggs and sausage. No matter what happened, they would have a satisfactory breakfast to carry them through the day. It might be the last good meal they ate for some time.

"A pity you're not in need of a governess, or a nursemaid," Lady Agatha said.

"Not yet—or for a long while," he said.

His aunt shook her head. "You'll be filling up a nursery soon enough, my boy. Lady Anne will be eager to bear you children."

Jessa froze, a forkful of eggs halfway to her mouth. Lady Anne. Of course. Lord Dearborn's daughter, and the girl Morgan had paid marked attention to at his musicale. Jessa had not attended closely enough to the gossip rags this past week— but she ought to have. It seemed the Earl of Silverton was on the verge of proposing to the beautiful Lady Anne.

Appetite gone, she set her fork down on the plate. No wonder he had spurned her advances. He was in love with another woman. Ah, she had been a fool.

"We will seek refuge with the Magdalenes." She forced the words out. There was no place for them here, at Trevethwick House.

"And when your dastard of a cousin comes to fetch you home, what then?" Lady Agatha asked. "He is your legal guardian, is he not?"

Mutely, Jessa nodded, her eyes fixed on the gleaming silver sugar bowl.

"Miss Louisa tells me he wishes her to marry an evil old goat," the older lady continued. "And separate the two of you. Is this correct?"

"I would not say Sir Dabbage is evil," Jessa replied. "But he did not strike me as a kind man."

"You see." Lady Agatha addressed her nephew. "The only thing to do is take them in."

134 ~ ANTHEA LAWSON

"And when their legal guardian comes, demanding their return, what then?" he asked.

"Then you boot him out on his arse!"

Louisa giggled at the profanity, but the earl firmed his lips. "We have no excuse to keep them."

"Yet." Lady Agatha tapped her cheek thoughtfully. "Give me a few days, Morgan. Let the girls stay here, and I shall see what I can do."

Jessa stared at her across the table. What could Lady Agatha possibly do?

"Oh, don't look so astonished," the older woman said, catching Jessa's gaze. "I was once very well connected, and I still have a favor or two owing."

"Aunt." The earl's voice was cold. "There must be no hint of scandal about this whatsoever."

She waved her beringed hand at him, the colorful gems sparkling in the sunshine. "You fret far too much about respectability. Leave it to me."

"I fret with reason," he said. "Promise me."

She let out a breath, but her expression became more serious. "I would not compromise what you've worked so hard for this past decade. But still, these ladies are in need of our aid."

"So, you will keep us?" Louisa asked, her lips red from biting on a strawberry.

Jessa leaned forward, hope pushing against her chest. *Please.*

The earl glanced at Louisa, then let his gaze settle on Jessa. He regarded her for a long moment. Though his face remained impassive, something stirred in his eyes—the heat of desire, and a flash of yearning.

He folded his napkin and set it aside, then rose, suddenly seeming very tall. The sunbeams gilded his hair with gold, and

Jessa was reminded of the candlelight playing over his bare skin. And the feel of his body pressed against hers.

"You may remain at Trevethwick House," he said. "For a few days more."

CHAPTER FOURTEEN

That afternoon, the maid—whom Jessa had learned was named Betts—came and knocked on their door to summon them to tea in the parlor.

"Doesn't the earl have guests at the moment?" Jessa asked.

She had spent well over an hour staring out the window, trying desperately to think of a solution, to no avail. During that time, two carriages had arrived. One with the Dearborn crest, which disgorged two fashionably dressed ladies, and another plain black one that left a blond gentleman on the doorstep.

"Yes," Betts said. "Lady Dearborn and Lady Anne are here, and milord's cousin."

"Then it's not necessary for us to attend," Jessa said, her stomach knotting at the thought. "We are hardly the kind to take tea with the lords and ladies."

Louisa set down her sketchpad, which showed an awkward drawing of a horse. "Please, Jessa? I am famished."

"Lady Agatha expressly told me your presence is desired," the maid said.

"Will there be cakes?" Louisa asked.

"Cakes, and scones with cream, and sandwiches," Betts

said. "It's a lovely tea, if I might say so."

Jessa frowned at the girl, but the maid only gave her an impish grin.

"We must go." Louisa turned to Jessa, her hands clasped. "It sounds delicious. And Lady Agatha said we were to come."

"I'll help you freshen up." Betts went to the dresser and fetched the silver-backed hairbrush that had belonged to their mother, then began fixing Louisa's hair.

Jessa let out a long breath. Surely the earl did not wish them to come to tea. He favored propriety above all things—and seating the Gypsy Violinist and her odd sister across from some of the most fashionable ladies of the *ton* was courting social disaster.

But his aunt had insisted.

At least she and Louisa had gowns that would do—though for only one event. They had just enough room in their bags to bring a single change of clothing, and each of them had selected their best gown. Tomorrow they'd be back to wearing the dark walking dresses they had arrived in.

"You look lovely," Betts said, smoothing the top of Louisa's hair. She shot a glance at Jessa. "Ready, miss?"

"I suppose I am." She tidied her own coiffure and shook out her skirts, silk striped in teal and ivory.

The dress made a soft hushing sound as they descended the stairs, but it was not enough to soothe Jessa's mind. A pall of worry settled over her the closer they came to the parlor.

Betts showed them into the room, an elegant space done up in shades of gold and apricot. The earl and his guests were seated in the center of the parlor, and upon their entrance the two gentlemen rose. Lady Agatha sprang to her feet as well, and came to take Louisa's hand.

"Here they are," she said. "The granddaughters of Viscount Trenton, whom, as I mentioned, are staying with us for a time."

Lady Anne blinked and opened her mouth, then shot a glance at her mother.

"I declare!" Lady Dearborn was not as hesitant as her daughter. "But isn't that Miss Lovell?"

Jessa gave the woman her best curtsy, and Louisa followed suit.

"Yes," Lady Agatha said. "I am pleased to introduce Miss Jessamyn and Louisa Lovell."

"Well, I…" Lady Dearborn was clearly at a loss.

"My visitors are Lady Dearborn and her daughter, Lady Anne," Morgan said smoothly, stepping into the awkward silence. "And this fellow here is my cousin, Mr. George Fielding."

"Pleased to meet you," the young man said. His eyes were alight with curiosity, but he glanced at the earl and said nothing.

"Come, sit." Lady Agatha led Louisa to the divan, and the two of them settled there cozily. There was not quite room for Jessa.

"Miss Lovell?" The earl held a chair for her, set at an angle that would allow Lady Dearborn to direct sneers at her all afternoon. But there was no help for it.

Dipping her head in thanks, she perched on the apricot silk of the wingback chair and fixed a smile upon her face. Lady Anne moved her knees away from Jessa and toward the earl's fair-haired cousin.

The conversation swirled about, and Jessa had very little to contribute except for an "ah" or a pressing together of her lips. Lady Dearborn steered the talk to the details of various events her daughter and the earl had attended recently. There were a good many: riding in Hyde Park, boating, an opera performance. It seemed the Earl of Silverton was paying quite assiduous court to the lovely Lady Anne.

Betts and another maid arrived with the tea trolley, and Lady Agatha poured out with the ease of long practice. Louisa fell gleefully upon the lemon cake and fruit tarts, which prompted a haughty eyebrow raise from Lady Dearborn.

"Your sister is rather an... enthusiastic young woman," she said to Jessa.

"She's never been one to curtail her enjoyment," Jessa replied. "I think a free and open heart is a great gift."

"I suppose. If one knows how to temper it properly." Lady Dearborn looked down her nose at Jessa. "Of course, that takes a certain amount of breeding."

Jessa felt her cheeks flush at the insult.

"Yet too much pedigree can have rather the opposite effect," Lady Agatha said. "Everyone's life should have moments of unfettered joy. I pity those who cannot feel it."

She sent the earl a look, as though she were speaking of him.

Jessa glanced at Morgan, remembering his smile gleaming in the moonlight as they galloped over the green. Remembering the passion in his kiss. She did not share Lady Agatha's opinion that the earl was entirely joyless. It was simply that he buried such emotion so deep as to be nearly undetectable.

What had made him so contained?

"I think displaying the proper amount of enjoyment is only polite," Lady Anne said. "One wouldn't want to offend."

Jessa glanced from the prim young lady to Louisa, who had a bit of jam smeared on her cheek and a look of pure contentment.

"I know which life I'd choose," she said. "Happiness is more important than respectability."

"I disagree." The earl's expression was set. "Respectability is paramount. It cannot destroy happiness, despite what my aunt thinks. While the opposite, abandoning hard-won respectability in the foolish pursuit of happiness, is all too common."

Jessa bit her lip. She wanted to argue, and yet was not her own life a result of her mother's choice to abandon respectability in the face of love? A choice that had ultimately brought only sorrow.

"Just so." Lady Dearborn gave a sharp nod.

"I believe there must be a balance," the earl's cousin said. "It shouldn't have to be one or the other."

Lady Anne smiled gently, seeming in agreement with the young man, but the earl set his teacup down firmly.

"You will learn the truth of it, Geordie. I only wish I'd been wiser at your age."

"Well," Lady Agatha cut in. "I think we might all safely enjoy a stroll in the garden without jeopardizing our reputations. Or our complexions, as I've had the maids fetch our hats. Ladies?"

She rose and gestured to the French doors that led onto the terrace—the same terrace where Jessa and the earl had shared a midnight conversation. His study must be next door.

The women donned their bonnets, and the earl offered his arm to Lady Anne. His cousin glanced at Louisa, then Lady Dearborn. Hastily, he stepped up to Jessa.

"Might I accompany you?" he asked.

She could hardly refuse, although she longed to safeguard her sister from Lady Dearborn's sharp-tongued comments. Of course, Louisa would smile blithely through them, but she was not insensible to the venom that lurked behind people's words. Jessa was relieved to see Lady Agatha put Louisa on her right side, while gesturing Lady Dearborn to her left.

The sky was strewn with clouds, the sun beaming down for a few minutes, then sliding away to hide behind the puffs of white. Canterbury bells and dame's rocket bloomed in the borders, and the lawn edging the flowerbeds lay smooth and perfectly green beneath her boots.

"So." The earl's cousin bent toward her. "What brings you and your sister to reside at Trevethwick House? It's quite outside the normal course of things, especially where Morgan is concerned."

"We are staying at Lady Agatha's behest." She hoped he would not notice that she'd sidestepped his question.

"Mother has her opinions, that's certain. She's set on shaking Morgan's principles, though he's immovable as marble."

Not nearly so cold or hard as he would have people believe, however. Jessa could not help glancing ahead, to where he escorted Lady Anne, and her heart lurched at the sight of them in close conversation.

Ah, she was a fool. There was no place for her in Morgan's life, or his bed.

"They'll announce the betrothal any day," Mr. Fielding said. "As soon as my cousin feels it's appropriate to ask her to marry him."

"Appropriate?" Jessa turned to him. "Are they not in love?"

He let out an ungentlemanly snort of laughter. "Love? My cousin's immune to such emotion. No, he has settled upon Lady Anne as the most suitable candidate to continue the Trevethwick line."

"That seems rather unfortunate for her, to be thought of as a broodmare."

"It's how things are done among the *ton*. Oh." He glanced at her. "My apologies—I forgot that you're part of the gentry."

She sent him a wry look. The earl's cousin was endearingly frank. "I might bear the bloodlines, but I've not had the upbringing. As you know."

He pressed his hand over hers. "You seem to be doing well enough. It's plain your mother brought you up to be a lady."

And her father had brought her up to be a wild Gypsy girl.

"I can perform a proper curtsy, and sew and make lace, and play the violin—"

"Clearly!"

She smiled up at him. "I confess, however, that I am not completely sure about place settings. And I never learned how to dance." Beyond the turnings and twirlings of the traditional Rom dances, which bore as much resemblance to the ballroom stylings of the *ton* as a tiger bore to a domesticated cat.

"Then we will have to teach you. You and your sister, both." He looked over to where Louisa and the older ladies strolled beside the hedge. "My mother has been rather lonely of late. It is good to see her back in Society. The spark has returned to her eyes."

"She's a delightful lady."

"If by delightful you mean dreadfully outspoken and opinionated." Despite the words, his voice was fond.

"I value such things over what one *ought* to do and say. No doubt a sad result of my upbringing." And once again a stark reminder of how ill-suited to this world she was.

Yet where *did* she fit in? She and Louisa were adrift in cold currents, belonging to no place, no people. The sun slid behind a cloud, and she shivered.

"Mother will look after you," he said. "She was always tending to strays—animal and human both—when I was a boy."

"Yes, but she doesn't usually reside here at Trevethwick House, does she?" Jessa had gathered as much at the musicale.

"Well, no." Mr. Fielding gave her an apologetic look. "But with Morgan's upcoming nuptials, I'm certain she'll stay for quite some time."

She glanced again at the older ladies, who seemed in deep discussion while Louisa watched a silver-blue butterfly hover among the flowers. No doubt they were planning details of decorations and food for the wedding. Despite herself, she let out a low sigh.

If not for Louisa, she would leave that very afternoon. Already she had embarrassed herself with the earl, and she had little taste for becoming Lady Agatha's pet charity project. But the alternatives were even worse.

"Don't fret." He patted her gloved hand. "Come, let's join Lady Anne and my cousin. He looks a bit glum."

It was true: there was a resigned look on Morgan's face, but as she and Mr. Fielding approached, his features settled back into imperviousness.

"Excellent," he said. "We were just discussing the garden party I am hosting next week."

"And here is Miss Lovell to consult with." Lady Anne gave her a cold look. "Since you will be the hired musician, where do you think the music should be—under the trellis, or by the rose garden?"

Jessa blinked. The young lady seemed determined to bring her down in Morgan's eyes, and Jessa did understand, though she did not like Lady Anne any better for it.

"How kind of you to ask," she said. "The shade of the trellis will protect my violin. And it can be rather awkward trying to perform whilst bees attempt to land on you."

As intended, Mr. Fielding chuckled, and Lady Anne's eyes widened. Morgan, of course, said nothing.

"Has that happened?" Mr. Fielding asked.

"Yes. I imagine I appeared engaged in a most peculiar dance as I sidestepped and swayed. However, I did manage to keep playing, even when a bee landed atop my bow. It stayed there for the entire piece, and finally flew away when the music stopped."

"It seems your playing entrances every listener," Mr. Fielding said. "I haven't had the opportunity to hear you, and I'm greatly looking forward to it."

Morgan sent him a sharp glance, as if in warning. It made Jessa's heart stutter briefly. But no—the earl had made his disinterest in her quite clear.

"Miss Lovell is rather talented," Lady Anne said. "We're all so very pleased that you will be able to perform at the party. Have you other upcoming hired engagements?"

"I'm currently taking a short hiatus," Jessa lied. "With the exception of the earl's party, of course."

A calculating light came into Lady Anne's eyes, and it seemed she clung harder to Morgan's arm. "Perhaps, Miss Lovell, you might be prevailed upon to play another event in the near future. A very happy one. Don't you think, my lord?"

"Certainly." The earl's voice was cool, and his cousin gave him a thoughtful look.

For her part, Jessa did not want to understand the tangle of her emotions at the thought of seeing Morgan and Lady Anne wed.

"Look, Mother is waving at us to come in," Mr. Fielding said. "Morgan, do part with Lady Anne and allow me to escort her back to the house."

"Do not fill her ears with lies about me," the earl said.

"Never." His cousin's voice was full of laughter as he extended his arm to the young lady. "We will simply pass the time in discussing your shortcomings."

"Oh, I'm sure the earl has very few of those," Lady Anne said, sliding him a glance. "You are a most exemplary gentleman, Lord Silverton."

"Then I must tell you about the summer he tricked me

into jumping, fully clothed, into the lake at the country estate," Mr. Fielding said, leading her away.

"Shall we, Miss Lovell?" The earl held out his arm.

Jessa took it, still pondering Lady Anne's naiveté. Did she truly think the earl was a paragon of virtue? Could she not see the fire lurking in his eyes, or feel the suppressed heat of his body?

It was a pity the earl insisted on maintaining such a cold façade. He would certainly gain more enjoyment from life if that shell were cracked open. Some imp seized hold of her tongue, and she looked up at him.

"Have you kissed her?" she asked.

He missed a step, then gave her a quelling glance. "That is absolutely none of your concern."

Heat stormed into her cheeks, and she studied the grass beneath their feet. "You're right. That was far too presumptuous of me. However, as you are aware, I'm no exemplar of ladylike behavior."

"And you're implying I'm not the gentleman Lady Anne thinks me to be." The coolness in his voice was marred by a warm streak of anger.

"I'd wager that midnight gallops and stolen kisses do not fall within Lady Anne's parameters of propriety."

"You are hardly one to make accusations, what with sneaking naked into a man's bedchamber and attempting to seduce him." His hand closed firmly over hers, as if preventing her from escaping.

Not that there was anywhere in the garden she might flee. Besides, she relished cracking his cool façade, welcomed the undercurrent of roughness in his usually controlled voice. It meant she still had an effect upon him.

"I was wearing my nightdress."

"As if a thin layer of cotton could conceal your..." He

146 ~ ANTHEA LAWSON

checked himself. "I am not pleased that you and your sister will be here a few days more. During the remainder of your stay, there will *not* be a repeat of last night's folly. Understood?"

She glared up at him. "You've made your position quite plain, my lord."

"Good."

Despite his words, she was almost certain he still desired her. Yet if he were determined not to act upon it, there was nothing she could do to sway him. And no matter how much she might contemplate sneaking back into his bedroom at midnight, the regret she'd feel when he turned her away again would be too much to bear.

CHAPTER FIFTEEN

The Tattler has it on good authority that the Earl of Silverton, usually an unshakeable pillar of polite society, has two most unusual houseguests. Trevethwick House now shelters the Gypsy Violinist, Jessamyn Lovell, and her sister. One cannot help but speculate as to the circumstances!
-Tilly's Mayfair Tattler, July 16

The day of the garden party dawned clear and blue. Morgan stood at his bedroom window and scowled at the azure sky, scanning it for any hint of cloud that might enable him to cancel the event. The serene arc overhead stared placidly back at him.

Blast.

He did not want to endure another afternoon of playing the attentive suitor to Lady Anne. He did not want to host the gossips of the *ton*, not with the Lovell sisters still living beneath his roof. And he most especially did not want to put Jessamyn on display and watch the gentlemen slaver over her, while giving him the wink and nod for keeping her so close.

Any man with red blood in his veins would have leaped at the chance to take her for his mistress. Half the time he cursed himself for not doing so—but he could not allow her to ruin herself. Or everything he had worked for over the past ten years. No matter how very, very tempting she was.

He had to force himself not to watch her eat strawberries at breakfast, gave her a wide berth whenever they encountered one another in the halls, and tried not to breathe in the scent of her when he entered the drawing room where she had taken to practicing.

But even when she was out of sight, her music sang through the house. Despite himself, he listened. Usually she began by playing scales, the ascending and descending tones a warning that he should either leave immediately, or become ensnared by the sound of her playing. Over the last several days, he had stopped resisting. Whenever she began to play, he sat back in his study chair and let the sound wash over him.

He did not understand why the music affected him so, but as long as he was unobserved, he accepted the siren song. It was as though the notes were a balm to his long-abraded soul. In an odd way, he felt the music understood him, though that was simple foolishness.

The music transported him to a place beyond his everyday cares, his worry over Geordie, even the thorn of Mr. Burke. Whether Jessamyn played slow and sweet melodies, or rapid and tempestuous tunes, the music slid beneath his skin. There were only patterns of notes and silence, of breath and song, and the beat of his own heart.

It was why he had not pressed Aunt Agatha yet—but he could wait no more. Despite her residence at Trevethwick House lending their guests a certain measure of propriety, he could no longer house the Lovells.

On the way to breakfast, he caught his aunt in the hall.

"Aunt, a word," he said, gesturing her to his study.

She lifted her brows, and the hem of her gaudy cobalt dressing gown, and stepped into the wood-paneled room.

"You're looking imperious this morning," she said. "Do you have last-minute instructions for the garden party?"

"Of sorts. I need this business with the Lovell sisters settled. Today." He would be able to still the gossiping tongues and parry the speculative glances if he had a firm answer to give as to why the sisters were still there. And when they were leaving.

"Can't you wait another few days?"

"You know full well I cannot." With effort, he kept his voice from rising. "How do you expect me to propose to Lady Anne with two other unmarried women living indefinitely beneath my roof?"

"I suppose that is true." His aunt smoothed the bright silk of her robe thoughtfully, but there was a glint in her eye.

"What are you scheming at? I thought you wanted to see me married and settled."

"Nothing would give me greater pleasure," she said briskly. "Except, perhaps, seeing Geordie happily settled, as well."

"Then help me in this."

"I am helping—but I do take your point. Luckily, I have come to a decision."

He braced himself for her next words. When Aunt Agatha made up her mind, she was nearly impossible to turn.

"I've so enjoyed being here, Morgan. It's helped me see that, although I was content before, I was not truly happy."

"Contentment is the same thing as happiness," he said.

She shook her head at him, her gray ringlets bobbing. "They are similar, but no. Contentment is floating down a lazy river. Happiness is being borne by a rushing current, full of sparkle and spray."

"You're quite the poet this morning. But I cannot agree with you."

"I know you cannot." She patted his arm, then glanced

about the study and out the mullioned windows at the brightly lit flowerbeds. "I wish you might understand. Well, perhaps you shall in time."

"What is your decision?"

She turned back to him and smiled. "I would like to engage Louisa Lovell as my companion."

"What? But she's—"

"She's delightful, and just what an old woman needs to bring freshness into her life. We will get on very well together. I'd like to take her on a tour of the Continent."

He stared down at her, concern foremost in his mind. "I can't help but worry that you will find her more burdensome than you think. Certainly, she is a sweet girl, but her mind is so childlike."

"Tut." Aunt Agatha swatted his arm. "I've raised three children, if you recall. I'm well aware of the amount of exertion it requires. I'd far rather be put to some small effort with the reward of Louisa's joy than sit at home embroidering pillowcases and waiting for the days to pass."

"I didn't realize you were so lonely." He ought to have visited her more often, and made Geordie do the same.

"To be frank, neither did I." She patted his hand. "Coming up to London has been very salubrious for my state of mind."

"If you're determined, it seems a fair solution. But what of her guardian, Mr. Burke? A legal wrangle in the courts would be difficult. I might be an earl, but blood is stronger than a title." He frowned at her. The arrangement was not quite satisfactory.

"I'm working on a remedy for that. Mr. Burke is not the only, or best, relative to take responsibility for the girls. Now, do I have your approval?"

Morgan firmed his mouth. "You'll go ahead whether I approve or not."

"Well, yes." Her eyes twinkled at him. "But I'd rather the earl not look quite so forbidding when I tell the girls at breakfast. Speaking of which, I'm certain our toast is growing cold."

She turned to leave, but he caught her elbow. "What about Jessamyn?" he demanded.

"Oh, I've plans for her as well." His aunt gently pulled out of his grasp and opened the door.

"Wait, Aunt. I demand you enlighten me."

"Come to breakfast, dear. Life is so much easier to bear on a full stomach." She headed down the hallway, and Morgan could swear he heard her laughing.

***

Afternoon warmth spread over the gardens of Trevethwick House. The scent of late roses and lilies drifted, mingling with the sound of conversation and laughter. Jessa played beneath the dappled shade of the wisteria trellis. A small audience occupied the chairs arranged on the lawn in front of her, but the rest of Morgan's guests strolled and chatted—or sat in the parlor, with the French doors open, drinking sherry.

Still, a handful of listeners was better than none. Although one gentleman at the front was clearly intent on ogling her body instead of listening to the music.

Ignoring him, she gave herself over to the tunes. Her own mood was sifted light and shadows, and her choice of music reflected that. A fast-paced dance let her express her joy and relief over Louisa's good fortune. She was going to be Lady Agatha's companion! Over the last week, the two had formed an undeniable bond, and Jessa felt certain that Louisa would be well cared for—perhaps even unduly spoiled—as the older lady's companion.

Yet Jessa's own fate was far murkier. It was unsettling, to have her sister's future more stable than her own. She was not accustomed to being the vulnerable one. And although she still remained beneath Morgan's roof, he'd made no assurances he would protect her.

How could he? Even now he escorted Lady Anne beside the rose garden. Had Jessa known how imminent his betrothal was, she would not have tried to seduce him. Since their conversation in the garden, she had attempted to avoid him as much as possible.

It could not be helped at mealtimes, and she felt the undercurrent of tension flowing between them. He never met her gaze directly, though he had unbent enough to assist her in navigating the cutlery correctly during the long, multi-course dinners. Once, his fingers had brushed against hers as he indicated the proper fork. She had shot him a look, only to find his expression tight, as if he found the contact unsettling.

With Louisa spending much of her day with Lady Agatha, Jessa had made use of her unexpected free time playing her violin. A quiet drawing room at the back of the house suited well enough, and the touches of red brocade pleased her eye, bright notes among the mostly blue-and-ivory hued room.

So she claimed it as her own and played, finding refuge and solace in the notes. Her fears spoke through the low rumble of a tightly-wound *sirba*, and her yearning flew free with the high, clear melodies of a love song.

A song that she played for Morgan, if he but knew it. She glimpsed him now, standing across the garden with Lady Anne at his side.

Ah, she was the worst kind of fool, that her treacherous heart should carry such an unwavering flame for him. She chased the notes high up on her violin, hoping the trembling sweetness would ease her soul. Then, when she could stand it no longer, she let the melody descend, falling like sunlight through the forest, down, down, fading, until at last there were only shadows and mossy ferns and the memory of light.

She brought her current piece to a close and made a brief bow to the applauding listeners. It was time she take a break. Lady Agatha had expressly told her not to overtax herself—as if playing were something difficult. Still, Jessa was ready to retreat to the haven of her drawing room, where she would not have to watch Lady Anne laugh up at Morgan, her arm tightly wound through his.

"Miss Lovell." The gentleman who had been leering at her stepped up, too close. "Lord Cranton at your service. I must say I *enjoyed* your performance."

His dark hair was receding from a bulbous forehead, and his lips were overlarge and fleshy. He made to take her arm, and she moved back quickly, holding up her violin.

"I am glad to hear it, my lord," she said. "Excuse me, I must put my instrument away."

"You're skilled with the violin," he said. "Are you equally skilled with the male instrument?"

She felt her eyes widen. "I beg your pardon?"

It was not the first time she had been propositioned, but it was certainly the clumsiest.

"You know what I mean." He licked his lips. "Once Silverton tires of you, pay me a visit."

Before she could move away, he set his hand on her shoulder and drew a thick finger suggestively down her arm. The touch made her shudder.

"I am not anyone's doxy," she said. "And most especially not yours. Good day, sir."

She whirled and strode out from beneath the trellis, her fingers cold around her violin. What a distasteful man. Even the scent of roses could not erase the oily smell of his cologne from her nostrils, and she felt his gaze heavy on her back all the way across the lawn.

Once she reached the house, she glanced over her shoulder, but thankfully he had not followed her. Letting out a breath of relief, she went to the back drawing room, where she had left her violin case.

The soothing colors enfolded her as she tucked her violin away. She should go find Louisa and see how her sister fared. Hopefully she was not unduly affected by the storm of gossip that her proposed role as Lady Agatha's companion had evoked. That news had deflected much of the attention from Jessa—but no doubt the sharp tongues of the *ton* would fasten back upon her soon enough.

She turned to go, then started as she caught movement from the corner of her eye. Had that odious fellow snuck in from the garden?

It was not Lord Cranton, however, who stepped from behind the door, but Mr. Burke. Panic stabbed through her, and she darted for the door.

"My dear Jessamyn," he said, blocking her path. His fingers closed hard about her upper arm. "We must have a chat, you and I."

"Let me go." She tugged, trying to free herself. "I'll scream."

"And I'll accuse you and your sister of stealing from the earl. I'm sure the trinkets stowed in your valises will support my case."

"We've done no such thing!"

"And yet I know for a fact that a number of small yet valuable items will be found in your possession."

"You are hateful." She wanted to spit upon him, rake her nails over his face.

He towed her toward the door, shut it firmly, then locked

it and pocketed the key. "My girl, you are always so impetuous, without considering the consequences."

"How did you get in?" She finally yanked free of his grasp, then shot a glance at the locked door.

No one would come to her aid. Fear slid icy fingers about her ribs.

"It's simple enough to breach the houses of the *ton*. Especially during a party. One might say it's my specialty." His expression darkened. "You were clever, I'll grant you that. I wasted nearly a week tracking down those cursed Gypsies, to find you were not with them. Ambitious of you, to take refuge with Silverton. Luckily, the gossip rags are full of useful information."

With one stride, he was upon her. He grasped her chin and glared down into her face. She was certain his fingers would leave smudged bruises upon the morrow.

"I'll have you thrown out," she said.

"Ha! I don't advise it." His oniony breath gusted over her face, and she closed her eyes.

"I'll tell the earl everything, unless you leave."

"Remember this, my girl. There's no proof, and I *will* name you my accomplice. If Scotland Yard takes me, we'll go together. And there is the little matter of your petty theft."

"With evidence *you* planted." She clawed at his fingers, finally breaking his hold, and stepped back. "At least Louisa is safe from you."

"And you owe me even more for that. Your sister might have slipped away, but I still have you." He raised his fist, and she scurried away, putting the low-backed settee between them.

"I'm not coming back," she said.

"Oh, I think you are. Silverton will put you out on the street soon enough."

Her guardian sounded so confident that a cold shiver slid

down her back.

"He wouldn't." Despite her words, however, she was unsure.

She knew the earl had little concern for her. And kind as Lady Agatha was, one Lovell sister was more than enough for her to take on.

"If that pretty nose of yours was broken, he'd lose interest." Violence humming off him, Mr. Burke rounded the settee.

Jessa sidled away, her heart beating a crazed rhythm. If she screamed, would anyone hear?

He lunged for her, and she ran to the mantel and snatched up one of the heavy silver candlesticks displayed there.

"Stay away from me." She shook the candlestick at him. Perhaps she could get one or two good whacks in before he overpowered her.

Behind her guardian, the door opened so violently the handle thudded into the wall. Mr. Burke spun about, his fists clenched. Jessa almost dropped her candlestick in relief when she saw the earl standing there, flanked by two of his footmen.

"Mr. Burke," he said, his voice icy. "You are not welcome to set foot in Trevethwick House."

"I've come to reclaim what's mine." Her guardian's voice turned oily. "I'll just take my niece and go."

He advanced upon Jessa, but she slid around the edge of the room, toward Morgan. The earl's expression was impassive, but she could see the rage blazing in his eyes.

"Miss Lovell will remain here," he said.

A sneer curled Mr. Burke's lips. "What you could want with a clumsy Gypsy maid in your bed, I've no idea. The lure of the exotic, I suppose—"

His words cut off with a garble as Morgan strode forward, took Mr. Burke's collar in one angry fist, and twisted.

"Miss Lovell is a lady, and your insinuations bore me. Leave, now, and I'll not press charges of housebreaking."

Morgan shoved Mr. Burke back a few paces, and Jessa's guardian coughed and rubbed his throat.

"She's a thief," he wheezed. "Her and her sister both, stealing from you. Go ahead and check their room. You'll see."

Jessa froze, candlestick heavy in her hand.

"I find that highly unlikely." Morgan turned to his footmen. "Escort this vermin out of the house. The entire neighborhood, in fact. Use force if necessary."

"Don't think you're immune simply because you're a lord. I'll bring you down." Hatred flared in Mr. Burke's narrowed eyes.

A muscle in Morgan's cheek twitched, but otherwise he appeared unmoved. "I brought myself down long ago. There's nothing a worm like you can do to me. And if you attempt to contact Jessamyn again, I'll have you flogged."

Mr. Burke straightened his rumpled coat and gave the earl a look filled with venom. "Just wait, Silverton."

The earl looked to his men, and they stepped forward, corralling Mr. Burke between them. As they led him from the room, Jessa's guardian glared at her.

"We're not finished," he called. "You're mine, by blood and family debt."

She waited until their footsteps faded down the hall, then slowly set the candlestick on a nearby table. She was surprised to see her hands were shaking.

"Are you all right?" Morgan took her fingers in his warm grasp and drew her close. "Did he hurt you?"

He scanned her face, and she shuddered, thinking of what might have happened.

"He did not," she said. "But he wanted to. Thank you for coming to my aid."

"I'm sorry I wasn't here sooner." His expression hardened. "Damn the man, for daring to threaten you in my very house. I'll be having words with my butler, you can be assured of that. Your guardian won't be able to enter Trevethwick House again."

"And what about when I leave these walls?" It had to be asked. "What will become of me then, my lord?"

A shadow darkened his eyes. "You cannot leave. My lady aunt has some plan, though she has not seen fit to divulge it."

"Perhaps she means to marry me off to her son." She said the words mockingly, in jest, and was not prepared for his response.

"I forbid it." His words cracked through the air.

She pulled her hands from his. "Am I so distasteful to you?" Anger pressed hotly against her throat. "Lord Cranton did not seem to share your opinion. Perhaps I ought—"

Her words were stilled by his mouth descending over hers. Morgan gathered her tightly against him, his lips hungry and demanding, and she yielded in an instant. All her anger, all her fear, swept away in the wave of desire that crashed over her. This was what she wanted—his embrace, his kisses. Nothing else mattered but the insistent beat of their two hearts, the close press of their bodies.

***

Morgan could not pull away from Jessa, though his good sense demanded he stop. He could no more stop than a man dying of thirst could keep from plunging into the pure waters of an oasis.

When he had seen Mr. Burke threatening her, red rage stormed through him. He'd barely been able to restrain himself from beating the man to a pulp. She had looked so ridiculously beautiful, clutching that candlestick, and all he had wanted in that moment was to protect her.

And then to suffer her jests about other men... The heat in his blood overrode every caution, and he pulled her into his arms. The only man he wanted to imagine her with was himself.

Her lips parted, ripe and sweet beneath his mouth, and he swept his tongue into that warm hollow, tasting. Claiming. She molded her body to him, all curves and softness, and he was lost. One hand came up to cup her breast, while the other held her against him.

She sighed, her hands clutching his shoulders. He could take two steps, and lay her down on the settee, pull her gown off her shoulders, and...

A burst of laughter from the garden finally cut through the fierce concentration of his desire. Breathing heavily, he set her at arm's length, while his body pulsed with frustration. *Take her upstairs, to his bed. See her midnight hair unbound upon his pillows, caress and taste her full breasts—*

For God's sake, he must leash himself!

She stared at him, her dark eyes bright, and he did not know what to say. There were no promises he could make her, no assurances of her future. No reason he could give for his unrestrained behavior where she was concerned.

"I beg your pardon," he finally said. The words were stiff and formal, but they were better than nothing.

Her eyebrows rose. "Are you sorry for kissing me? It does not seem like something either of us should regret."

"I am sorry for placing you in a compromising position."

Pink tinged her cheeks. "If you recall, it is a position I applied for. And one that many of your guests assume I have already taken."

"They are idiots." His fingers curled at the thought of what

Cranton might have said to her.

"For thinking me desirable?" Her voice held a bite.

Damn, she was impossible.

A soft knock came at the door, and then Lady Anne peeked inside.

"Oh, there you are, my lord," she said.

His shoulders tightened, and he moved away from Jessamyn. "I apologize for leaving you, Lady Anne. I was just fetching Miss Lovell from her intermission."

How much had Lady Anne overheard? He studied her face, but her expression was serene, no sign of mistrust in her eyes. Either she suspected nothing, or she was a consummate actress.

Jessa had turned back to her case, and was busying herself with her violin.

"I will be out shortly," she said.

"Good." He offered his arm to Lady Anne. "Shall we return to the garden?"

"Nothing would please me more. I believe the servants have brought out cakes."

Her innocent comment made her seem nearly as young at heart as Jessamyn's sister, and Morgan's conscience twisted. How could he call himself a gentleman? He had all but ravished Jessamyn in the drawing room, behind the backs of the *ton* and the sweet-natured girl to whom he was intending to propose marriage.

And that, too, was beginning to seem a less than gentlemanly endeavor—especially as the wildness he had thought purged from his soul reemerged. Could he truly inflict himself upon Lady Anne when he felt his façade of the proper earl crumbling more every day?

CHAPTER SIXTEEN

After supper, Jessa retired to her room. Earlier, with Betts's help, she had managed to return all Mr. Burke's pilfered treasures back to their proper places. Touching the items he had handled made her feel grimy, and she'd washed her hands thrice over with lavender soap before she felt cleansed of his presence. The events of the afternoon still whirled madly through her thoughts.

She closed the door firmly behind her, removed her boots, and lay across the bed. The coverlet was soft under her palms, the delicate embroidered flowers a faint texture beneath her cheek.

What should she do? Trevethwick House was not a haven—at least not for her. For once, Louisa had been the lucky one. An unexpected dart of jealousy pricked Jessa's heart. With a deep breath, she smoothed it away. Her sister's good fortune was something to celebrate, not cry over.

But still, the question remained. Where was her own place?

She had pulled Lady Agatha aside after the garden party, firstly to thank her for taking Louisa under her wing, and secondly to demand an answer to her own plight.

"Don't fret, my dear." The older lady had patted her hand. "I've something brewing for you, as well. You must be patient just a short while longer."

Even when pressed, Lady Agatha simply smiled and shook her head, her eyes glinting with a touch of mischief.

Jessa rolled onto her back and stared at the ceiling, painted a pale blue with a few puffy white clouds. Patience was not her strong suit. And every time she had trusted someone else to determine the course of her life, she had foundered on the shoals, or wrecked horribly on the rocks.

Her throat tightened with memories. Mama, before she had fallen ill, smiling as she took the girls on an outing. Papa whirling about the fire, then taking her hands and dancing with her to the wild, pulsing music. Dear Louisa, innocently believing a fairytale and stepping out into the night in search of a precarious refuge.

But Mama and Papa were gone, and Louisa was safe in her new position. Jessa must strike out on her own.

Perhaps… Perhaps she could parlay her brief fame as the Gypsy Violinist in England to a wider reception on the Continent. But she would need a manager or agent, and perhaps an accompanist—people who must be paid in advance of any concert monies she might earn.

She now had a few hundred pounds, however, tucked at the bottom of her valise. After her performance, Morgan had followed her back into the drawing room. Not, alas, to kiss her. Instead, he had paid her.

"Three hundred pounds." He'd held out a wallet. "I believe it is your usual fee."

She had shaken her head. "I can't accept it. My sister and I owe you far more than that for your hospitality."

His lips had flattened into a severe line. "I insist. You were booked for this performance before you came to Trevethwick House. This is a business matter."

There would be no swaying him, not with the unyielding light in his eye she had come to recognize. She had taken the wallet without further argument.

She would give some of the money to Louisa, so that her sister would not be wholly dependent upon Lady Agatha's generosity. And the rest, well... It was not nearly enough to finance a performance tour of Europe, but it was a start.

And she did have a connection in Italy, although if her distant cousin refused to recognize her, she could not fault him. She might, however, be able to invoke his sense of family obligation. At the very least, she could do what she had done here. Namely, appear upon his doorstep and beg his aid.

Jessa chewed her lip, sparks of possibility racing through her, hot and bright. There was a fellow who had given her his card after one of her performances earlier that year. Mr. Burke had confiscated it, but she'd read the card before he'd ripped it in pieces and tossed it in the waste bin.

The man had been an agent to some musicians of note. She pressed her fingers to her temples, trying to recall his name. Mr. Peter Widmere, that was it. If she remembered correctly, he'd mentioned he represented Master Darien Reynard and his family. And wouldn't that be a triumph, to share an agent with the most revered violinist in the world!

She sat up, hope warming her.

It was not the easiest of plans, but perhaps Lady Agatha would provide some assistance, as well. Especially if she were planning to take Louisa to the Continent. The three of them could travel there together, and Jessa could contact her viscount cousin, and somehow Mr. Widmere might be able to book some performances.

It was still all a tangle, but with enough substance that she felt lightness ease her soul. She did not need to beg for help from Morgan, or cast herself as mistress to the distasteful Lord Cranton.

Jessa tipped her face up and breathed a quick prayer of

thankfulness to the heavens. With luck, everything would come out right.

**

Warm rain greased the streets as Morgan strode into Scotland Yard. He had not met with Commissioner Rowan for nearly a fortnight, having nothing to report to the man until now.

The junior constable waved him through. Morgan entered the commissioner's office and shut the door firmly behind him.

"Lord Silverton." Commissioner Rowan stood and gave him a firm handshake over the messy expanse of his desk. "Excellent to hear from you. Take a seat."

Morgan shrugged out of his damp overcoat, then sat facing the commissioner. He drew an envelope from his pocket and handed it to Rowan.

"I'm afraid it's still not conclusive," Morgan said.

"Hm." Rowan examined the envelope. "Posted from the same busy station as all Mr. Z's correspondence."

He slid the letter from the envelope and studied it, sandy brows drawing together.

"It demands I cease sheltering Jessamyn Lovell," Morgan said, "or the facts of my 'transgressions' will be provided to the newspapers. No doubt the information I planted specifically for Mr. Burke. It must be him."

"Yes, but it's too circumstantial. The letter is unsigned." The commissioner rubbed his cheek. "We can't pull Burke in, not yet. He'd know we were on to him, and he's too slippery. Without actual proof, this kind of evidence trail is too tenuous."

"But who else would insist I remove Miss Lovell from my house?"

"I can think of a number of possibilities." Rowan folded the letter and slipped it back into the envelope, then returned it to Morgan. "Lord Dearborn, or another member of his family—they can't be pleased that you have such a lovely young woman living under your roof. Any man who hopes to make Miss Lovell his mistress by removing her from your sphere of influence and then offering his protection. A jealous competitor who would like to see the Gypsy Violinist unseated. Or—"

"Enough." Morgan frowned. "I take your point. But I'm hardly going to put Miss Lovell out on the street simply because this letter demands I do so."

"Certainly not. It's essential you keep her close. Burke will either publish the false information, in which case we will have a further lead, or try something more reckless when he doesn't get his way."

Morgan crossed his arms. "I'll not put Miss Lovell in danger."

"She's a pawn in this already." Rowan gave him a keen-eyed glance. "Have you questioned her further? Determined the depth of her involvement, found out everything she knows?"

"She's my guest." Reluctant as his hospitality might be.

"She might also be a criminal! Good gad, man, stop thinking with your nether parts, and question the girl."

Morgan clenched his jaw, but had to acknowledge the commissioner was right. He should have made her honesty a condition of remaining at Trevethwick House. Desire had clouded his thoughts—which only proved he should excise it entirely from his life.

He leaned back in the uncomfortable wooden chair. "I'll see what I can get out of her."

"Good. I've been concerned that you've lost your

commitment to this case. We could still reinstate the charges against your cousin, don't forget."

"I've been occupied recently." Morgan glared at the man.

"Ah, yes. Lady Anne seems a nice enough girl, but pray, don't let her distract from the matter at hand. Exposing Mr. Z and bringing him to justice is our top priority."

"Yours, not mine." Morgan held up a hand to still the commissioner's protests. "Yes, I understand the gravity of the situation. No need to splutter at me."

"I never splutter. And I expect you to pay me a visit in three days. With answers."

Commissioner Rowan stood, a clear signal their interview was over. Morgan donned his overcoat, and shoved the letter into one of the deep pockets.

"You do understand that you're nearly as guilty as Mr. Z?" he asked.

"I'm not extorting enormous sums of money from you," the commissioner said dryly. "Simply helping you do your duty for the greater good."

"You'll not earn my gratitude."

"Not yours, no." Rowan handed Morgan his hat. "But the rest of the *ton* will sleep easier once Mr. Z is apprehended. And perhaps the queen will give you a medal."

"Dare I hope?"

Morgan's sarcasm made Rowan's lips twitch, but the commissioner swallowed his smile. "One can always hope. But evidence is far better. I'll see you in three days."

Morgan nodded, donned his hat, and strode out of the commissioner's office. The gray skies matched his mood, and he welcomed the discomforting drizzle.

He'd been an idiot not to question Jessamyn more insistently. Why hadn't he pressed her harder?

Because he was a confounded gentleman. His decade of

exceptional behavior had clearly penetrated deep. Except when it came to leashing his desire.

Blowing out an impatient breath, he stalked down the sidewalk. Keep Jessamyn close, the commissioner had said. Yet question her relentlessly. He feared the latter contradicted the former. What, after all, would prevent her from leaving Trevethwick House in search of a new protector, since he had not offered the refuge she was seeking? Her sister was now safely employed as Aunt Agatha's companion, leaving Jessa free.

Would she actually go to that lout Cranton? His shoulders tightened at the thought.

If not Cranton, there were plenty of other men of the *ton* who would gladly take Jessamyn Lovell for their mistress, and take her innocence as well. The thought made a haze of anger mist his brain. The commissioner had put him in an impossible situation. If Morgan pressed Jessamyn too hard with questions, he had no doubt she would simply leave.

Unless…

Damn him for a black-hearted schemer, but he could see only one solution. And though the part of him that was a gentleman protested, the part of him that was simply a man approved.

Although it might send his soul to perdition, he would take Jessamyn Lovell to his bed.

CHAPTER SEVENTEEN

During supper, Jessa was aware of the brooding glances Morgan sent her way, but she could not decipher them. Between courses, Louisa and Lady Agatha talked of the Continent. Jessa gladly joined in, especially when the discussion turned to Italy.

"Of course," Lady Agatha said, with a pointed look at her nephew, "we shall have to wait until after Morgan's nuptials."

Jessa's chest burned at the thought. Oh, she understood that the earl would declare himself to Lady Anne soon, but the knowledge did not hurt any less when spoken aloud. Keeping an amiable look upon her face, she reached for her wine glass. The beverage tasted bitter, but she swallowed it back.

"In good time, Aunt," Morgan said. "I've a few matters to attend to first."

"Well, don't take forever about it," Lady Agatha said. "Lady Anne is a catch, and everyone is waiting for the announcement."

"I thought *I* was the catch." He gave his aunt a dry look. "Don't fret. Everything is under control."

Lady Agatha set her fork down. "That is *precisely* why I worry. One can't control matters of the heart."

"Not that again." He lifted his own glass and studied the garnet liquid within.

Sometimes, Jessa noticed, the earl did choose to take a glass of wine with his dinner. Tonight being one of those times.

"I think Jessa looks very pretty today," Louisa said, blithely unaware of the undercurrents. "Don't you, Lord Silver?"

Jessa had explained that the "lord" came first, but she could not persuade her sister to give the earl his full title. At least he seemed amused by it, rather than offended.

"Yes," he said, his gaze moving to Jessa. He studied her intently. "Very pretty. Is that a new dress?"

Warmth flooded her cheeks. "It is one of the gowns your aunt has so generously provided. Since, as you recall, we arrived here with very little."

"You look well in it." His eyes locked with hers, and she felt her pulse beating in her throat.

"Mine is new, as well," Louisa said.

Jessa tore her gaze from the earl's and managed a smile for her sister. "Pale rose is very becoming on you."

"And royal blue suits your strong coloring, Jessamyn," Lady Agatha said. "Now that we have suitably complimented the ladies on their new apparel, I wish to inform you of what the evening holds."

"I've no intention of going out tonight," Morgan said.

"Of course not." Lady Agatha patted his hand. "We shall be staying in. Geordie will arrive shortly, and we are going to teach the girls how to dance."

"I beg your pardon?" Jessa asked.

"I understand neither yourself nor your sister knows the steps commonly performed in the ballroom," Lady Agatha said. "I intend to remedy that situation."

"It's not necessary." Jessa tucked her napkin beside her plate, choosing her words with care. "While it's kind of you to think of us, I don't imagine Louisa or myself would ever need such a skill."

"Nonsense. Every girl needs to know how to dance."

"Jessa is a marvelous dancer," Louisa said. "She knows all the Rom dances."

"Hardly all of them, duckling. Besides, you'd never see them performed at a Society cotillion." Jessa shook her head at the image of herself performing those wild and whirling steps over an elegant marble floor instead of packed earth. And how scandalized the *ton* would be at the amount of ankle and leg exposed.

"Don't impose your mad ideas on the Lovells," Morgan said to his aunt. "While I know you mean well—"

"Oh, hush. It's only one evening. You can all indulge an old lady's whims for that long. Besides, I have been practicing the pianoforte in preparation."

"I turn the pages for her," Louisa said, nodding.

Jessa was aware that Lady Agatha played for a short while every afternoon. But she had not ascribed any ulterior motive to the sweet melodies tinkling forth from the piano.

The butler entered the dining room, closely followed by Lady Agatha's son, Geordie.

"And here he is now!" Lady Agatha rose from her chair and hurried to greet her son.

"Sorry I couldn't join you for supper," Geordie said. "But I hear we're having a private ball this evening."

He winked at Jessa, and she suspected he had shared her admission she did not know how to dance with his mother. Why else would Lady Agatha seize upon this impractical idea?

"I really don't—" Jessa began, but Louisa grabbed her hand.

"Please," she said.

Jessa studied her sister a moment. There was the possibility that, as companion to Lady Agatha, Louisa might be called upon to dance some day. As for herself, it was very unlikely— but she could not rob her sister of the opportunity.

"The ballroom has been readied, at your request," the butler said to Lady Agatha.

Morgan raised a brow at his aunt. "Excessive as ever."

"Nonsense. Where else should one learn to dance? The parlors are all too small, and the floor in there is much more suitable. As is the piano." She waved her hand at him, dismissing his concerns.

"Perhaps I should fetch my violin," Jessa said. "I will play, and Lady Agatha can take my place in the dance."

"Not with these old knees of mine," Lady Agatha said. "Now come along, all of you. Yourself as well." She pinned Morgan with her gaze.

He frowned, but made no further argument, which seemed to satisfy her. Taking her son's arm, Lady Agatha led them from the dining room. Louisa, still holding Jessa's hand, skipped down the hall behind them, and the earl followed like a dark cloud.

Why had he not simply refused to participate? Jessa felt his presence, the way one could feel imminent rain gathering in the sky above.

She supposed he was so fond of his aunt that he indulged her even at cost to himself. Much like herself with Louisa. And agreeing to dance was not so very high a price, to see both of them happy. She could manage one evening of it.

Especially if she were paired with Morgan.

A shiver of anticipation trembled through her. Although she tried, she could never, ever forget the sight of his naked chest. Or the feel of his kisses.

Oh, why had he kissed her the other day? Just when she had felt able to ignore his effect upon her senses, just when she had let go all hope that he wanted her, he must go and stir the ashes of her longing into flame again.

Yet he was intent upon marrying Lady Anne, and Jessa was not certain she would be able to bear that happy event. Far better that she go to the Continent, without waiting for Louisa and Lady Agatha.

She had written a letter to Mr. Widmere, and the butler had promised to find out his direction. Such a flimsy plan. There was every chance the man was not currently in London, and even if he were, how probable was it that he would agree to represent her musical career?

Still, she must try. If she did not hear back from him within the week, she would have to cast about for some new course of action.

Lady Agatha stepped through the wide double doors leading into the ballroom, and nodded with satisfaction. "Excellent."

Twilight sifted in through the windows lining the room, and the near end was alight with candles set in ornate silver candelabra. Empty vases, nearly five feet high, stood along the walls, and Jessa guessed they would overflow with flowers during an actual ball.

The grand piano gleamed—a much better instrument than the upright in the front parlor. A pity Jessa had no talent on the keyboard. Lady Agatha sat and played a chord that echoed into the high-ceilinged room. The acoustics were inspiring, and Jessa resolved to ask the earl if she might practice her violin in the ballroom.

Not that she would remain much longer at Trevethwick House.

Louisa laughed and spun into the middle of the room, then clapped her hands. "It's just like in a fairytale."

"And you are the princess," Geordie said.

"Oh, no." Louisa gave him a serious look. "Jessa is."

"Morgan, dance with Louisa," Lady Agatha said. "Geordie, with Jessamyn. We will begin with the most basic steps of a set dance."

Geordie made Jessa an absurdly florid bow, and she could not help but smile at him as she placed her hand in his, despite her disappointment at not being paired with his cousin.

"I apologize in advance for stepping on your toes," she said. "But it is your own fault. I suspect you had some part in suggesting this foolish idea to Lady Agatha."

"If you tread upon me, I will only feel it as a flower feels the brush of a butterfly's wing," he said. "And you wound me by thinking our endeavor tonight is folly. I only mentioned in passing to my mother that you and your sister lacked the skill of dancing."

"You knew that would be enough," Jessa said, trying to make her voice stern. "And your gentlemanly fripperies are useless on an uncultured lady such as myself."

He sobered, and gave her a serious look. "Do you truly think yourself so outside the *ton*? Miss Lovell, you do yourself a disservice. After all, you are granddaughter to a viscount."

"Not that is has done me any good, being more recently daughter to a half-Rom stablehand."

"Couples, face your partners in a small set," Lady Agatha called. "We shall teach the ladies the British Grenadier."

Geordie stepped a pace away and turned to give her a bow.

"Louisa, you are there, next to your sister," Morgan said, going to stand beside Geordie.

"In this dance, the men are on one side, facing their partners," Geordie said. "But for some sets, we go opposite—lord, lady, and so on."

Since it was unlikely she would ever need to know the difference, Jessa merely nodded.

"Walk the paces, before I begin to play," Lady Agatha said from the piano. "Geordie, do you recall it?"

"Of course. You did not waste your money on dancing masters for nothing." He grinned at Jessa. "Firstly, you must imagine we are in a line of perhaps a dozen couples. Now, you and I will walk separately down the outside of the lines—yes, like that. Turn and come back up."

"How will we know when to return?" Jessa asked, going back to her place.

"It is with four counts of the music," Lady Agatha called. "Now go again, but down the middle."

Geordie offered his arm, and he and Jessa paraded past Morgan and Louisa, and another set of imaginary couples. When it was time to turn, she went the wrong direction, and nearly collided with her partner.

"Normally, we will just turn in place," he said with a smile.

"This is a rather boring dance," Louisa said. "So far, I have done nothing but stand here."

"At least half of dancing is simply standing about, marking the time," Morgan said.

"Well, that is not dancing at all." She set her hands on her hips. "The Rom do it much better."

"Once you have danced a few sets, you'll be glad of the chance to catch your breath between figures," Geordie said, escorting Jessa back toward the front of their imaginary line. "But now, Miss Louisa, you and Morgan enter the dance."

When he and Jessa drew even with the other pair, Geordie stopped and released her arm. "Now, we cast off—Jessa, you'll take your sister's arm and turn about, so that you are now below her in the line. Here, watch as Morgan and I demonstrate."

The two gentlemen turned in time, and Jessa and Louisa did their best to emulate them.

"I still think this is the most boring dance ever invented," Louisa said.

"It is not so bad, if you are the active couple," Geordie said. "Now, extend your right hands into the middle, so that we all touch. That is a right-hand star."

Jessa's hand fell beneath Morgan's, and she suddenly realized why gloves were essential at balls. The feel of his bare palm above her fingers was too intimate, too warm and distracting.

"Walk, walk," Lady Agatha directed. "That is how you turn it about. Good, now switch hands, and directions."

They pulled their right hands out, and repeated the motion on the left. This time, Jessa was careful to place her hand on the very top, just above her sister's.

"Halt," Geordie said, once they were back to their respective places. "Now, face us again, and we will walk forward, passing right shoulders in the middle."

Louisa, who had a less-than-perfect memory of which was her left side and which her right, walked directly into Morgan. He deftly whirled her out of the collision and set her on her feet.

"That is better," she said. "I would like more twirling, and less standing."

"If you can endure this dance a bit longer," Morgan said, "perhaps Aunt Agatha will have pity and play us a waltz."

"All in good time," the older woman called. "Now, once more across, to your home places, and the figure is complete. Are you ready to begin again? I shall play an introduction."

The second time through, the dance was rather more entertaining. It certainly helped to have music guiding their steps. Partway through, Lady Agatha instructed them to change, so that Louisa and Morgan had the more active part. The sound of her sister's laughter made the entire endeavor worthwhile for Jessa.

Lady Agatha brought the music to a close, and they all took a moment to catch their breath.

"If we were at a proper ball, I'd offer to fetch you a cup of refreshment." Geordie grinned at her.

"That way, the gentlemen can remove themselves and thus appear to be unaffected by the exertion of dancing," Lady Agatha said, rising from the piano bench. "Don't think we are unaware of the subterfuge, my boy."

"I *am* thirsty," Louisa said.

"Luckily, I have prepared for such an eventuality." Lady Agatha pulled the bell rope beside the door. "Refreshments will be arriving shortly. Lemonade and ratafia for the ladies, a brandy for Geordie. And plain water for you, Morgan."

She sighed heavily, and Geordie raised an eyebrow at his cousin. "You could drink wine, you know, if you're still refusing brandy."

"Water shall suffice," the earl said. "I had wine at supper."

Jessa could not help but notice that he seemed completely recovered from the dancing. Her cheeks felt flushed, and her breath still came a little short. This life of a lady of leisure was turning her far too soft.

Another reason to leave it behind.

Betts brought in a tray of refreshments, and Louisa happily quaffed her glass of lemonade. Geordie fetched Jessa a cup of ratafia, and she gave it a dubious look.

Noticing her hesitation, Lady Agatha smiled at her and lifted her own cup of reddish-brown liquid. "My secret recipe. Wine, marc brandy, and a generous amount of almond sugar. Do try it."

Jessa raised her cup, the scent of alcohol and almonds stinging her nose. She took a sip, and the beverage warmed her mouth and throat. The flavor was not unpleasant, if one's tastes ran toward sweet liqueur.

"It is the best ratafia I have ever tasted," she said.

Lady Agatha gave a hearty laugh. "I'll wager it's the *only* ratafia you've ever tasted. Now drink up, and we shall have a waltz. Switch partners this time, for Louisa and Geordie are better matched in height."

Jessa took another swallow of Lady Agatha's brew and tried not to glance at Morgan. Half of her burned to be held again in his arms, but the wiser part of her soul protested. Every step she took toward him would make her leaving all the harder. Better she distance herself now, and not give in to the traitorous yearnings of her heart. The Earl of Silverton would never be hers, despite their midnight rides and stolen kisses.

Lady Agatha sat again before the piano and began playing a simple melody, with accompanying chords in three-quarter time. Geordie took Louisa's hands and counted aloud, showing her how to pattern her steps after his.

"Miss Lovell?" The earl held out his hand.

"I am a trifle weary," she lied. "Certainly Louisa and Geordie may dance again, but I am better suited to observe, I'm afraid. I will just finish my ratafia."

"Nonsense." The earl plucked the cup from her hand. "You will waltz with me, Jessamyn."

The sound of her given name on his tongue made heat flash through her, as though she had drunk an entire bottle of ratafia instead of half a cup. Despite her resolution to keep her distance, her feet carried her forward. Morgan took her right hand and slipped his arm about her waist. Her heart gave a tremendous thump, and she tried not to inhale too deeply of his spicy scent. Oh, she was a pitiable fool, to be so smitten with the earl.

"Put your other hand on my shoulder," he said. "Good. Begin on the right foot—now."

Before she could untangle her tongue enough to ask questions, he swept her into the dance.

Fortunately, she had seen couples waltzing before. The alternating steps—one two three, one two three—were not difficult. The turning was a bit more complicated, as she tried to anticipate which direction they were going to pivot.

She stumbled over his foot as she turned the wrong direction.

"Easy," he murmured. "Lean back into my arm, and the dance will go more smoothly."

"Why, my lord, one might think you actually desired to waltz with me." Despite her tart words, she allowed herself to relax into his embrace.

"I do desire you." This close, his voice thrummed through her as he pulled her closer.

Jessa swallowed and averted her eyes. Thank goodness the piano and the sound of Louisa's laughter masked their words from the others.

"And yet," she said, "you turned me away."

He had been right in one thing—clasped against him, it was easier to follow the shifts and turns of the waltz. Morgan spun and whirled them away from the glowing candlelight and into the boundary of the shadows. Their thighs brushed, and his bare fingers tightened over hers. Jessa blessed the dimness for hiding her blush, and the longing that was surely written in her face.

"I am beginning to regret that decision," he said. "Meet me in the library tonight, after midnight."

Startled, she met his gaze. "It is too late to change your mind. Lady Anne awaits your proposal."

"Blast the proposal." His voice held a rough edge. "Jessamyn, I…"

Lady Agatha played a loud chord, bringing the waltz to a

close, and Morgan swallowed whatever he was about to say. His gaze burned through Jessa, and she felt absurdly giddy.

She absolutely ought not to meet him in the library.

"We have both made our choices," she said, the words scalding her tongue. "Your life and mine are on different paths."

His grip on her tightened. "And what is yours? Tell me."

She could not tell him her plans, for she suspected he would try and stop her. But she must wait to hear from Mr. Widmere before she even knew if her mad dreams could become reality.

"Only to help Louisa," she said. "And wait to see what your aunt has in store for me."

"Are you quite certain?" His eyes searched hers.

"Ahem!" Lady Agatha called. "Gentlemen should not linger in the shadows with ladies once the dance has ended."

Jessa pulled out of Morgan's embrace and made him a proper curtsy. "Thank you for the dance, my lord."

"It's essential I speak privately with you," he said in a low voice. "Concerning the activities of Mr. Burke."

His words sent a jolt through her. After that first night, she'd foolishly thought herself safe from Morgan's questions. Had some new information come to light about her guardian, to raise Morgan's suspicions?

"I..." She hesitated.

"We must speak. Tonight. Your safety is at stake." His gaze was insistent.

"Very well. I will meet you in the library." Even as she said the words, she knew it would be utter folly to be alone with him.

She turned and, without waiting for him to follow, went back to the piano. To the bright circle of light cast by the candelabra, to Louisa's laughter, and Geordie's cocked eyebrow, and Lady Agatha's half smile.

She could still feel Morgan's gaze hot on her back, feel the weight of his arm about her waist as they danced out beyond the reach of the candlelight.

The shadows were full of a hopeless, bittersweet future—and midnight could not come soon enough.

CHAPTER EIGHTEEN

Morgan paced over the scarlet and amber patterned Turkish carpet in the library. The house lay quiet and still around him, but he had lit two lamps to diminish the press of night against the windows.

It was nearly half past midnight. He resisted the urge to pull his gold pocket watch out and consult it once again, but looking at the damnable timepiece wouldn't change the fact that Jessamyn Lovell was not coming.

He clenched his jaw and continued pacing, frustration firing his steps. Back and forth. Back and forth.

If only she were not sharing a room with her sister, he would go and find her. Instead he was reduced to prowling his own library like a caged lion. He'd thought she would come to him of her own accord. Indeed, she'd said she would.

He was the Earl of Silverton, and he was not accustomed to having his will thwarted. Especially not by quarter-blood Gypsy girls who haunted his dreams.

He wished he had never met Jessamyn Lovell.

He wished he had taken her to his bed when he first had the opportunity.

The watch lay heavy in his pocket, the chain gently

brushing his waistcoat every time he turned. She was not coming. He exhaled heavily, then went and extinguished one of the lamps.

When he straightened from turning down the wick, Jessamyn stood in the doorway. She wore her nightdress and one of those gaudy oriental wrappers his aunt so favored, this one featuring a bright gold dragon curled on a turquoise background. Jessamyn's hair lay in a braid over her shoulder, and her dark eyes watched him warily.

"There you are. Come in." He motioned her forward.

She entered the library and closed the door behind her. "My apologies for being late. Louisa was restless, and I could not slip out before now."

She was not flouting him, or disinterested, or angry. Relief coursed through him, and he attempted to stifle it. Jessamyn Lovell was entirely dangerous to his equilibrium.

"Sit." He pulled out one of the wingback chairs and waited for her to take a seat, then settled across from her.

She perched upon the edge of the chair and gave him an anxious look. "You wished to speak to me about Mr. Burke?"

"Yes. Jessamyn, I want the truth. You have enjoyed my hospitality for some time now. Your sister will be my aunt's companion. I deserve your honesty."

She laced her fingers tightly together, then met his gaze.

"You do," she said. "And I will tell you what I know. But you must promise me you'll protect Louisa, no matter what."

Morgan studied her intently: the worry in her face, the tension in her shoulders. "What, in particular, do you fear?"

She let out a shaky breath. "Before his scheme of marrying my sister off to that horrible man, Mr. Burke promised to send Louisa to an insane asylum should any hint of what I am going to tell you reach the constabulary's ears. I do not doubt he will do his utmost to carry out that threat."

At last—the truth. Morgan leaned forward. "Agreed. I will do everything in my considerable power to keep your sister safe."

"Well then." She unknotted her fingers and smoothed the bright turquoise silk covering her knees. "Mr. Burke has been blackmailing members of the *ton*, using information obtained during my performances."

"I knew it." Triumph flared through him. "Are you willing to testify to this in the courts?"

"It won't be enough. Some might argue I am trying to condemn him so that I might claim your protection, instead." A flush rose in her cheeks. "The fact remains he is still my legal guardian, and has the right to determine the course of my life. Also, I have no proof of his misdeeds. It would be entirely my word against his."

"Surely the letters from his victims are somewhere."

"I saw them—but only once, when I first discovered what he was doing. I did search for them, later, but everything had been removed from his desk. I don't doubt he now keeps such incriminating evidence safely tucked away."

"Damnation."

Morgan made a fist and tapped it against his leg, thinking. Without proof, it would be far more difficult to make a compelling case against Mr. Burke. And much as he hated to admit it, the defense would, indeed, take the very tactic Jessamyn feared—that she was lying in order to be free of her guardian in order to become Morgan's mistress.

"I could…" Her voice faltered, but then she continued. "I could return to him, and search his house to find the letters."

"No." Everything in Morgan recoiled from the thought of sending her back into Mr. Burke's clutches. "There is every likelihood he has removed them to another location, since he knows you've seen his correspondence. You will remain here."

184 ~ ANTHEA LAWSON
She gave him a grim smile. "Rather a different tune you're playing these days, my lord. But tell me—when I performed at your musicale, I know that my guardian prowled about Trevethwick House. I was under the impression he had found some deep, dark secret from your past."

Morgan shook his head. "There's nothing to discover, beyond the facts that all Society knows. My older brother and I were wild and careless, he died while racing his curricle, and our father was a debauched and lewd old man who drank and wenched himself to death. Sordid, but nothing I have not already made amends for."

The look on her face softened, and she reached over and took his hand. "I am sorry, Morgan."

He gripped her hand tightly for a moment, then forced himself to ease his hold. "I will do everything in my power to protect you from Mr. Burke. As you say, I have changed my tune. I don't need your condolences." He grasped her other hand. "I need you, Jessamyn—the taste of you on my lips, the feel of your skin against mine. Do you want that, as well?"

Her eyes widened, but she did not pull her hands free. "Yes," she whispered.

"Good." He stood and drew her into his arms in one smooth motion.

Every nerve flared at the feel of her against him, all curves and softness, unfettered by a corset or yards of skirts. He bent his head and pressed his mouth to hers, and she eagerly returned his kiss. She felt so right in his embrace, he nearly groaned aloud at the sensation.

His tongue explored her lips, and she opened her mouth to him. Their tongues met, and he tilted his head, the better to plunder her mouth. Heat hazed his mind, and his hands roved, weaving through her dark hair, claiming the sweet roundness of her breast.

When his thumb brushed the silk-covered peak of her taut nipple, she gasped. He forced himself to pull back from the kiss, but only so that he might run his hands over her, and watch her eyes fill with desire.

"I like this dressing gown on you," he said, caressing her through the soft silk. "But I think I would like it off you even more."

One tug of the sash, another pull, and the gaudy dragon slid away, bright turquoise cloth slipping to pool on the rug.

"I remember this nightdress," he said, fingers already going to the ties on her bodice.

"But I don't recall you being quite so formally dressed," she said, a teasing smile on her lips.

"I did remove my coat," he said, nodding to where it lay folded on the back of his chair.

She glanced at the garment. "Do you have any coats that aren't gray?"

"Of course. Black and dark blue."

"Perhaps you might consider a more daring color," she said, reaching up to tug at his neckcloth. "You ought to remove this, as well."

He untied the complicated knot his valet had made before supper, and unwound the strip of cloth.

"Better?" he asked.

"Let me see."

She leaned in and slid her hands around the back of his neck. The brush of her fingers against his skin, riffling through his hair, made desire roar to the forefront of his brain.

His neckcloth dropped from his fingers, and he pulled her against him once more. Hunger burned in his blood—years of starvation fueling his craving for her, until he could barely think. There was nothing but the taste of her mouth beneath his, the soft pulse of her breath, the curve of her hip under his hand.

After a minute, or a year, she pulled back. Her lids were heavy, and her chest rose and fell with deep breaths. His gaze fell to her breasts, and he undid the last tie of her nightdress. The inner curve of her breasts tantalized him, and his groin tightened even more. With both hands, he pushed the nightdress down off her shoulders.

The soft light illuminated her perfect breasts—lush and full, with rosy, peaked nipples.

"You are beautiful," he said. "No, don't cover yourself."

She met his gaze, and ceased trying to pull her nightdress back over one shoulder. "Very well—but it's only fair of you to bare your chest in return."

"Care to assist me?"

"Are you saying you can't undress without assistance?" She smiled at him again, while her fingers went to the buttons on his silver brocade waistcoat. "How dreadfully difficult is the life of a gentleman."

"You may help me to undress at any time."

"Any time?" She pushed aside his waistcoat and deftly began unfastening his white linen shirt. "That might prove awkward, my lord."

"You have a mischievous mind, Miss Lovell." And, despite her understandable shyness, she also seemed unafraid of the heat pulsing between them, meeting it with wit rather than fear.

Somehow, he could not imagine Lady Anne doing the same.

Jessamyn tugged his shirt free of his trousers and opened it wide. She ran her palms over his bare chest, and all thoughts of Lady Anne fled.

"Satisfied?" he asked.

"Nearly." Her gaze fell to the bulge in his trousers, and she flushed and looked away.

"Much as I would love for both of us to undress completely, I don't think my library is the ideal spot." Besides, the skin he had acquired for this eventuality was upstairs.

"Perhaps not." There was a touch of wistfulness in her tone.

To erase it, he pulled her closer. The feel of her breasts against his skin scorched him. He wove his fingers through her hair and kissed her again. God, but he wanted her under him, fully naked. He wanted to coax the flames of her arousal higher and higher, until they were a bonfire illuminating the night.

He wanted to print himself on her soul, so that she would never forget him.

But that was too disquieting a thought. He refused to ponder the end when they had barely begun. And so, he ravished her mouth, and let tomorrow slip like water through his fingers. Only now, this moment, this woman in his arms.

He broke the kiss to lower his head and stroke his tongue across the peak of her breast. She shivered, and a low moan escaped her lips. Desire rushed through him, as heady a sensation as though he'd been drinking fine brandy. His trousers were unbearably tight.

"Come upstairs," he said, his voice rough. "To my bedroom."

He would not take her here, on the library carpet, though the beast inside raged at him to do just that. No—she deserved a bed, and all the sensual consideration he could lavish upon her.

She gazed up at him, and he could see the indecision in her eyes. He wanted to kiss it away, but he could not force himself upon her. This was for her to choose.

At last, she gave him a single nod. "I will."

Pulling away, she covered her glorious breasts once more. Trying not to regret it, Morgan bent and picked up the abandoned dressing gown. The silk was cool and soft between his fingers as he settled it around her shoulders. A tendril of dark hair had come loose from her braid, and he gently tucked it behind her ear.

Quickly, he re-fastened a few shirt buttons, scooped up his coat, then lifted the lamp.

"After you," he said, holding the light high so that she might see.

She preceded him from the library, through the darkened hallway, and up the stairs to the second floor. At the door to the bedroom she shared with her sister, she paused, and Morgan's fingers tightened on the lamp.

Would she change her mind?

After a brief hesitation, she moved on, and he let out a soundless breath. Damnation, it was unsettling how badly he wanted this woman.

They neared the end of the hall, and he lengthened his stride. Another few moments, and he would have Jessamyn in his bedroom, where they would at last finish what she had started.

"Jessie?" The sleepy voice drifted down the hallway.

Morgan turned, mood already darkening. The lamp showed Louisa standing at the open door of her bedroom.

"Duckling—what are you doing out of bed?" Jessamyn took a few steps toward her sister.

"Why are you?" Louisa blinked and rubbed her eye with a fist. "Did the Silver Lord need a drink of water, too?"

"There is a pitcher and cup on the washstand," Jessamyn said.

Morgan detected the faintest edge of impatience in her tone. For himself, thwarted desire made him want to storm down the hall, lock Louisa in her bedroom, and resume his seduction of Jessamyn. He suspected that plan, however, would not sit well with either sister.

"I spilled it, and now I am thirsty again."

Jessamyn blew a breath from her nostrils. She turned to Morgan, frustration and apology clear in her expression.

"I must tend to Louisa," she said.

"Of course. Thank you for your company," he said, trying to mask his irritation. "Perhaps I might see you... later."

She glanced at her sister, then firmed her lips. "I think it unlikely, my lord. Tomorrow will be here soon enough."

He strode to where they stood, and handed Jessamyn the lamp. "We will resume this conversation tomorrow evening."

"Yes," she said.

"Then I bid you both good night."

"Good night," Jessamyn said, while her sister simply yawned.

Before he turned away, he gave her a look full of unspoken promises. The night shadows enfolded him as he stalked back to his rooms. Alone.

CHAPTER NINETEEN

The dreadful heat has sapped much of the liveliness from London events. Indeed, no less than seven ladies fainted during Lord Caversham's ball yesterday evening! Already, some members of the ton are quitting Town for the havens of their country estates.

-Tilly's Mayfair Tattler

"**I** have splendid news," Lady Agatha announced during teatime the next day.

She smiled at Jessa, then Louisa, and lastly at the earl, looking as smug as if she were a cat that had been in the cream.

Jessa was grateful for the older woman's talkative spirit. She could barely bring herself to meet Morgan's gaze. Last night, they had nearly become lovers. The thought both elated and terrified her.

"Are you going to tell us this news?" the earl asked, calmly buttering his scone. "Or are we going to play at guessing?"

He seemed his usual unemotional self, but the few times their eyes locked, she saw the fire in his gaze.

Louisa clasped her hands together. "I guess that Lady Agatha is planning to purchase a pet bird," she said, hope filling her voice.

"No birds," the older woman said. "I find their incessant chirping grates after a time. Jessamyn, do you care to venture an answer?"

Jessa studied Lady Agatha, whose eyes were most decidedly twinkling. "You've met a delightful gentleman who has sent you flowers."

Lady Agatha laughed. "Perhaps—but that's not my news this afternoon. Morgan?"

He set down his scone. "You've discovered the perfect shade of peacock blue, and are going to dye all your gowns that color."

"Intriguing... but no. I received a letter. From Italy."

"Ah." Morgan leaned forward. He sent Jessa a speculative glance, then fixed his attention once more on his aunt. "And?"

"Viscount Trenton is a kind and well-spoken gentleman, as far as I can tell. Much as I recall him from decades ago. Of course, he was not the viscount then."

"My cousin sent you a letter?" Jessa bit her lip. "Why?"

"He was replying to the one I dispatched to him," Lady Agatha said. "Concerning you and your sister's welfare."

"You might have consulted me," Jessa said, trying to keep the hurt from her tone. She was beyond weary of having other people dictate the direction of her life.

"Now, now." Lady Agatha reached across the table and patted her hand. "I did not want to get your hopes up, in case I never received a reply. I am an acquaintance of his from years ago, and was not certain he would remember, or even respond. But I shall, of course, take your wishes into consideration from this point forward."

"What does the viscount say?" Morgan asked. "Skip the pretty details about the weather in Italy and his health, if you please."

Lady Agatha gave him an impatient glance. "Not to put

too fine a point on it, Lord Trenton is happy to assume guardianship of his cousins, Jessamyn and Louisa Lovell. Furthermore, being in Italy, he is content that the earl and myself act on their behalf and see to their best interests."

Jessa leaned back in her chair, attempting to absorb the news. "You are saying Mr. Burke is no longer our guardian?"

She could not quite believe it. Almost nightly, she woke from troubled dreams that their guardian had managed to force her and Louisa back to his home. She could not imagine shedding the weight of that worry, the dread that somehow Mr. Burke would wed Louisa to Sir Dabbage, and herself to someone equally detestable.

"Let me see the letter," Morgan said. "You did bring it down to tea, I presume?"

Lady Agatha nodded and gave him the folded pages. He scanned them, then held the letter out to Jessa.

"It's true," he said. "Near the end of the page, he assumes guardianship."

She took the letter, barely breathing, and read.

...and will therefore remove the burden of Jessamyn and Louisa Lovell's guardianship from my younger brother, Mr. Edwin Burke, and place it upon myself. Which, as viscount and head of the family, ought to have been my responsibility all along...

Jessa read the lines, then drew in a great, shuddering breath. The spidery writing blurred as hot moisture gathered in the corners of her eyes. What a blessed relief.

"Splendid news, indeed," she said, just managing to keep her tears contained.

She handed the missive across the table to Lady Agatha, then took her sister's hand and squeezed. Louisa was safe. They both were. Her heart pounded out the rhythm. *Safe now, safe now.*

"Of course, the first thing the earl and I shall do is

approve Miss Louisa's new position as my companion," Lady Agatha said briskly. "And you needn't fear any longer that Mr. Burke might remove you from Trevethwick House."

"Not that I would have allowed it, in any case," Morgan said, his tone dark. "But you ladies must excuse me—I have a meeting this afternoon with my solicitor."

He rose, made them all a general bow, then strode from the room.

"It is good news, isn't it?" Louisa asked Jessa, her voice low and worried.

"Very."

"Then perhaps you oughtn't hold my hand so tightly. My fingers are going numb."

"Sorry, duckling." Jessa released her grasp. "I am so very thankful to you, Lady Agatha. Might I have Viscount Trenton's address, so I may write him, as well?"

"Of course." Lady Agatha beamed across the table at her. "And do forgive me for keeping it a secret. I truly was not at all confident this scheme would prove successful."

"It was most kind of you, to presume upon your acquaintance with the viscount on our behalf," Jessa said.

Indeed, it was remarkably generous of Morgan's aunt. Jessa and her sister were little better than orphans of an inferior social class in most people's eyes. That Lady Agatha would champion them made Jessa's heart squeeze with gratitude.

As if she could hear Jessa's thoughts, Lady Agatha gave her a keen look. "You and Louisa are members of the *ton*, whether you like it or not. I will not see you living in poverty and distress if I can help to better your situation."

"As to that," Jess said, "I must ask, have you certain plans for me, Lady Agatha? I would like to be apprised."

The older lady had the grace to look a bit sheepish. "I had thought... but no, nothing that has borne fruit, and so there's nothing to be said on that account. Let me ask you, Jessamyn. What do *you* want?"

"To marry the prince," Louisa said brightly.

"Well, of course." Lady Agatha nodded. "But what else?"

"I have been thinking." Jessa picked up her teacup, then set it back down again. The amber liquid shivered in little ripples. "I would like to make a career of performing, beyond London."

"Hm." Lady Agatha pressed her lips together thoughtfully.

"Don't go without me!" Louisa cried.

"My darling sister, you will be safe with Lady Agatha. And I will visit you often."

"But—"

"Do not fret, Louisa," Lady Agatha said. "Perhaps Jessamyn must journey on further quests. And, like all heroes, she must go alone."

Louisa pouted, but did not argue further, and Jessa shot Lady Agatha a grateful glance. Already the older woman understood Louisa and her world full of impossible tales. It portended well for their companionship.

"Although I do wish you might stay in London with us for some time longer," Lady Agatha said.

"I'm not certain I can." Jessa feared her tone was overly bleak, revealing too much of her heart. She made herself smile. "At any rate, that is just a fancy. Who knows if such a wild dream can even come to fruition?"

Lady Agatha did not smile back, and there was a sympathy in her eyes that made Jessa suspect the lady comprehended too well. But if she knew how Jessa felt, then she must certainly understand her distress at the thought of seeing Morgan wed to Lady Anne.

"I must go practice," Jessa said, setting her napkin on the table and rising. There was always one refuge she could go to.

The perfect solace of the music.

"Play well," Lady Agatha said. "Louisa and I will remain at tea until she has consumed sufficient quantities of marmalade."

"Just one more scone," Louisa said with a happy smile. "And then we will go walking in the park, don't you think?"

Already they were so comfortable together. Despite her earlier words about her ambitions to perform abroad, Jessa felt a pang as she left the room and heard Louisa and Lady Agatha laughing together.

Her sister was safe, and content, and well cared for—and where did that leave Jessa? So much of her life had been built around caring for her sister, she felt a bit lost without that underpinning.

Not that Lady Agatha would take on Louisa forever. Indeed, it might only be a handful of months, which meant that Jessa must do everything she could to establish herself in the meantime.

Which, for now, meant keeping her musical skills at their peak.

She opened the window in the back drawing room, letting the breeze come in to dance with her notes. She would begin with her drills, the scales and arpeggios that kept her fingers limber and her playing honest.

She had not struggled under the tutelage of one of the best Rom fiddlers in the land for nothing. When she skimped on her technique, she could still see Donny Faa's fierce eyes flash beneath his bushy brows.

"No!" he would yell. "Your finger is too low. You must *listen* to the instrument. Make it sing for you."

He had taught her, as he'd learned from the famous fiddler Janos Bihari during his travels. Just as he had been made to play scales, so he passed on his technique.

"Whatever is of best use, we will take," he said to Jessa

when she complained that Rom musicians shouldn't have to practice such boring *gadje* techniques. "If you want to play like mud, then do not practice what I teach. But if you want to fly like the birds, then you must learn to grow feathers on your fingertips, *rakli*. This is how."

Finally, after scales and arpeggios and bow exercises, Jessa was ready to play. And, in the way of things, that was the precise moment the butler knocked, then opened the door.

"Forgive the interruption, Miss Lovell," he said. "You have a caller."

Her heart jumped, her fingers tightening on the wood of her violin. "It's not Mr. Burke, is it?"

Had he somehow learned of the change in guardianship, and come to drag her away?

The butler shook his head, frowning. "No—the earl gave express instructions that Mr. Burke be refused entry, should he ever call again. Your visitor is a Mr. Peter Widmere. Will you receive him?"

Jessa set her violin down, relief flowing through her, while hope sparked in her chest. "Indeed I will. Send him in."

The butler left, and returned a short time later leading a sandy-haired man of middle years. He was not dressed in the height of fashion, but in well-made clothing of excellent materials—clearly a fellow of means, if not extreme gentility.

"Miss Lovell." The man bowed. "Peter Widmere at your service."

"Thank you for your visit, Mr. Widmere," she said. "Do come in and take a seat."

"Will you need anything else, miss?" the butler asked, one brow faintly raised.

She looked at him a moment, then caught his meaning. It was a breach of the proprieties for her to receive Mr. Widmere in the back drawing room, alone.

"Send Betts in with tea," she said. That ought to satisfy, although teatime had already passed.

The butler made her a very correct bow, and departed once again. Jessa went to the grouping of chairs near the hearth and settled into a blue-upholstered chair. As soon as she was seated, Mr. Widmere joined her.

"I see you've had a change in situation since we last met," he said, glancing around the richly decorated room. "I understand at the time you were living with your uncle?"

"Yes." She did not elaborate. "It's very kind of you to call upon me, when we are barely acquainted."

Indeed, it had been rather forward of her to send a note. And not quite the thing for him to pay a visit in person. Then again, neither of them was constrained by the strictures of the *ton*. No matter how much Lady Agatha seemed to cherish notions to the contrary where Jessa and Louisa were concerned.

Mr. Widmere nodded. "It is a bit irregular, perhaps, but then I believe we are both in service to the music, Miss Lovell."

"As to that." She leaned forward, hope thumping in her chest. "Are you, perchance, taking on new clients?"

"I wasn't planning to." He gave her a speculative look. "It depends on the musician."

"Might you... consider the possibility of becoming my agent, and booking performances on the Continent?"

"Hmm." He leaned back and studied her. "I might contemplate it. Are you at liberty to make such arrangements, Miss Lovell?"

"My elder cousin, Viscount Trenton, has assumed guardianship of myself and my sister. I will write to him today to discuss the matter, and the fact of my musical aspirations."

She spoke with confidence, though she'd no idea if her distant relative would truly consent. But Lady Agatha had already given her approval, and she was acting on the viscount's behalf.

"As to that..." Mr. Widmere steepled his fingers together and cleared his throat. "Do you understand that, should you embark upon a performance career, you will not always be viewed in the most, er, genteel light? Especially given your style of music."

Heat rose in her cheeks. Mr. Widmere was implying that some people would consider her a loose woman. Not that it was any change from how the Viscount Crantons of the world already saw her.

"I am aware of it, yes."

"Well then." Mr. Widmere returned to his brisk, businesslike demeanor. "I must say that, should you begin by appearing on the bill with the Reynard family, it will mitigate such assumptions. They are very well regarded."

"Of course." Her pulse sped at the thought of sharing the stage with the celebrated master violinist. "Do you think I am accomplished enough not to disappoint Master Reynard's audiences?"

Mr. Widmere studied her a long moment. "From what I heard of your playing before, I think listeners will enjoy your performances. But I see your violin is just there. Would you play something for me?"

"Certainly." She rose, nerves fluttering like cloth in the wind.

The colorful scarf brushed her fingers as she took her instrument from the case, and the feeling steadied her. She had a wealth of melodies to share with the world. And she would begin with one of her favorites—a lullaby her father used to sing to her in his deep, husky voice.

She strode to the center of the room, and Mr. Widmere turned his chair to face her. Taking a breath, she relaxed her bow arm, and began. Low and warm and comforting, the simple melody filled the air. Slowly, she began to embellish it, adding a bright spark of memory here, the fall of a teardrop there.

Betts, the maid, came to the door with the tea tray, then hesitated, listening. Jessa nodded to her to come in, then, without missing a beat, launched into a dance tune. It was a new arrangement she had been working on, where she played chords beneath the melody in a demanding interplay between solo and accompaniment, while bouncing the bow back and forth for percussive energy.

She missed one or two of the fingerings, but Mr. Widmere still tapped his foot. The maid swayed in time near the small table where she'd set the tea tray. Smiling, Jessa played the last phrase, ending with a triumphant pull of the bow across all four strings.

"Bravo, miss!" Betts cried, applauding.

Jessa made her a bow. "Thank you for listening."

"Oh, I shouldn't have—there's that much to be done. But I couldn't help it. Enjoy your tea." She bobbed a curtsy and hurried out of the room.

Jessa turned to Mr. Widmere, sure that he could see the question in her eyes.

"Excellent," he said. "The Continent will adore you."

"I'm so glad you think so."

Hope flared through her. Perhaps the future she had imagined for herself was not so impossibly far away. She put her violin away, then joined Mr. Widmere and poured out the tea.

He took a sip from his cup, then briskly set it aside. "So, Miss Lovell, to the details. I go to rejoin Master Reynard's tour shortly. We'll return from the Continent in five weeks, and then you and I can draw up the contracts."

"Oh." She laced her fingers together in her lap. "I was

hoping for sooner."

He gave her a piercing look. "Is there something I ought to know, before taking you on as a client?"

Jessa picked up her teacup and took a hasty swallow. She could hardly reveal that she was hopelessly in love with the Earl of Silverton. Who was poised to marry another woman.

"No," she said. "I am eager to embark on this next stage of my career."

"I must discuss it with Dare and his wife, before making you any promises. And he will likely want to hear you play for himself."

A lump stuck in her throat at the thought of auditioning for the most preeminent violinist in the world, but she nodded. "I understand."

"I am not trying to dissuade you," Mr. Widmere said. "From what I've heard, Dare will entirely approve your playing. The chances that you'll begin touring soon are excellent."

Jessa uncurled her fingers from where they had tightened into anxious fists.

"When do you depart London?" she asked.

"Thursday. I'll rejoin Dare in Paris, and then the tour continues into Spain. They've been through Austria and Prussia, during this first leg." He rose. "Indeed, I must take my leave of you, Miss Lovell. Already I am behind in my preparations."

She hastily stood. "Then I am even more in your debt for taking the time to call upon me today."

"Look for my correspondence soon, after I speak with Dare—though I expect it will be good news." He made her a bow. "Good day, Miss Lovell."

"Safe travels, sir." She dipped him a quick curtsy.

After he departed the drawing room, Jessa sat again, her mind whirling. It seemed almost too easy. And yet the fruition of her dreams was not yet within her grasp. Master Reynard might decline to put her on his performance bill, and Mr. Widmere might decide he'd erred in his assessment of her talent or musical appeal.

She brought a knuckle to her lips, then let out her breath against it. Well, there was little she could do, except wait. And practice.

Rising, Jessa drank back the remainder of her lukewarm tea, then took up her violin once more.

CHAPTER TWENTY

Morgan's butler met him at the door when he returned that afternoon to Trevethwick House. The man's expression was a shade more dour than usual, and Morgan gave him a curious look.

"Is anything the matter?"

"My lord," the butler said, taking his hat and overcoat. "I must inform you that Miss Jessamyn received a gentleman caller earlier today."

Possessive anger swept through Morgan like a sudden squall full of thunder and dark clouds. With effort, he kept his voice steady.

"Who was this man?"

"A Mr. Peter Widmere. He and Miss Jessamyn met for over half an hour in the back drawing room. I heard her playing her violin for him."

Morgan's hands twitched with the need to hit something. "And where might I currently find Miss Jessamyn?"

"I believe she and Miss Louisa are in your aunt's suite."

"Thank you." Morgan strode to the stairs, then took them two at a time, questions hammering through him.

Breathing a bit heavily, he rapped on the door of Aunt

Agatha's parlor, then swung it open. A riot of color and the reek of sandalwood assaulted his senses.

"Who is it? Oh—Morgan." His aunt beckoned to him from the settee, where she reclined among a pile of exotic cushions. "Come in."

He did, his gaze going to where Jessamyn sat across from his aunt. She smiled when she saw him, but her expression faltered as he stared at her.

"It's Lord Silver," Louisa said. "I am looking at pictures of monkeys."

She held up a book filled with bright illustrations. He broke off glaring at Jessamyn to give her sister a brief nod.

"Very nice."

He quickly returned his attention to Jessa, trying to determine whether her lips appeared any redder. Had the fellow kissed her?

"Goodness, Morgan," Aunt Agatha said. "What has possessed you? Such a fierce look you have."

"I would like to speak with Jessamyn. Alone."

Jessamyn began to rise, but his aunt took her arm and drew her back down again.

"Whatever you need to say, you may do so in my company," Aunt Agatha said. "Or it can wait until we have finished our game."

Belatedly, Morgan noticed the jade and marble chessboard on the table between the two ladies. He strode over and picked up one of the discarded pawns. It was carved wearing an ornate costume, but at least there was nothing lewd about it. To be sure, he glanced at the board, but all the pieces appeared decently clothed.

"Miss Lovell, I understand you had a visitor today." He set the pawn back on the table with too much force, and it clacked loudly.

"Take care," his aunt said, giving him a warning look.

Jessamyn looked up at him. "Yes, Mr. Peter Widmere came to call upon me."

"And you met with him, unchaperoned, in the drawing room." He did not care that his words were sharp.

Jessamyn furrowed her brow. Then the confusion in her eyes cleared, anger taking its place.

"Do you truly think I would entertain a lover beneath your roof? Is that what you are accusing me of, my lord?"

"Morgan!" Aunt Agatha frowned at him. "How could you suggest such a thing?"

His righteous wrath faltered, but he turned to Jessamyn once more. "You played your violin for him."

"I did. Since he is the agent for the most renowned violinist in the world, he wanted to hear me play before he decided whether he might take me on as a client."

Her unexpected answer cooled his anger somewhat. "An agent?"

"Morgan, do sit down," his aunt said. "You look a trifle unwell. Yes, take that chair."

He tossed away a brilliant orange pillow decorated with tiny mirrors, and sank into the chair. Perhaps he had come to an overly rash conclusion.

Damnation. The longer Jessamyn stayed beneath his roof, the more muddled his thinking became. He longed for the days when the proper course of action lay straight and clear before him. It might have been stultifyingly boring at times, but at least he had known precisely what to do for every occasion.

"Explain," he said.

"I was not expecting him to visit," Jessamyn said. "But I wrote Mr. Widmere last week, asking if he might be willing to represent my musical career."

"Jessamyn is considering touring on the Continent," his

aunt added.

"Why was I not informed?" He suspected he sounded peevish—but as the earl, he was accustomed to knowing, and controlling, everything that occurred within his domain.

"It only just transpired," Jessamyn said. "Though… I have been thinking of this for some time."

"You can't leave."

Aunt Agatha raised an eyebrow at him. "If Jessamyn desires to perform abroad, why would you stop her?"

He had no answer for that. Only a roaring in his soul that would not cease.

"Very well." He stood. The smell of sandalwood was driving him mad. "Have a pleasant afternoon, ladies. I shall see you at supper."

***

"Be careful," Louisa said, as Jessa brushed her sister's hair before bed.

"Careful of what, duckling?"

Louisa turned to face Jessa, her expression earnest.

"When you go tonight to see the Silver Lord. I am glad he did not devour you yesterday."

Jessa regarded her sister. "Whatever are you talking about?"

She tried to keep her voice neutral, but worry fluttered through her. How much had Louisa guessed? And had she even understood what it meant when she caught Jessa and Morgan in the hallway? She had not mentioned it until now.

"You will go see him tonight, won't you?" Louisa's question was perfectly innocent.

"Why would I do such a thing?" Jessa asked cautiously.

Certainly, she had thought of it. Aside from her meeting

with Mr. Widmere, she had thought of little else all day. In truth, her conversation with the agent had helped crystallize her decision.

She had no reason to doubt Mr. Widmere's assertion that a touring female violinist would be regarded as a fallen woman. Indeed, her small fame in London had garnered plenty of speculation, even before she had fled Mr. Burke's house to shelter beneath Morgan's roof.

If, maiden or not, people would think the worst of her, then she was determined to make a choice. And that was to lose her innocence in the arms of the man she loved.

It would change her forever. Though her heart might break from it, at least she would have that much, for as long as she possibly could.

But what of Lady Anne? her treacherous conscience whispered.

Jessa firmly shut the door on that voice.

"You must finish the quest," Louisa said. "I know you tried to last night, but I was so thirsty."

Jessa began braiding her sister's hair, avoiding her direct gaze. "And what does finishing the quest entail?"

"I believe the Silver Lord still sometimes transforms into a beast at night," Louisa said, her voice low and thoughtful. "You have to help him, and then he will give you the final talisman."

It was such an innocent notion, but then, Louisa had always made up fables to explain the things around her that she did not understand. Even though the future was not one of castles and princesses and true love, Louisa still clung to her fairytales.

"Don't you think everything is coming out well enough?" Jessa asked. "You are Lady Agatha's companion, and will have many fine adventures with her. And I will go play my violin in all the courts of Europe."

Louisa shook her head, causing a lock of dark hair to slip free of her braid. "It is not the right ending."

"Ah, duckling. It is the best ending we will have. Be happy for it." Jessa tucked the loose strand of hair back in, then tied off the end of Louisa's braid.

"Promise me you will go visit him." Louisa turned and took her hand. "I will stay quiet and in bed all night, and will not spill the water this time."

"I am not certain he will be pleased to see me."

Indeed, his manner toward her that afternoon, and through supper, had been laced with irritation. Half of her wanted to respond in kind, but the rest of her still yearned for his kisses.

"You must try," Louisa said with a decisive nod. "And that is settled."

Jessa smiled and dropped a kiss on her sister's cheek. Louisa's insistence was enough to tip her over the edge. An edge she would likely have fallen off, in any case—but this way she need not fret that Louisa might wake in the night and come in search of her.

"Very well, duckling. But I must wait a while longer."

"Tell me a story, then," Louisa said, hopping into bed. "The golden apples, please."

Jessa drew up a chair, trying to keep her nerves from shivering like leaves in a strong wind. Tonight, soon, she would go to Morgan's bedroom. She prayed that this time he would not turn her away.

CHAPTER TWENTY-ONE

An hour later, Louisa's deep breaths filled the room. Jessa watched her sister sleep for a moment, the merry eyes now closed, the smiles smoothed from Louisa's face. The single candle on its holder beside the bed swayed in a draft, and from outside the window Jessa heard the creak of a cricket.

Quietly, she rose from the chair. She ought to change into her night dress. Or, more daring yet, simply undress and don the oriental robe Lady Agatha had given her.

The thought of arriving in Morgan's room wearing only a thin silk wrapper made her heart beat faster.

If anyone saw her in the hall, they would assume the worst. Yet half the *ton* already did, and when she began touring, half the world would as well. If she were going to displease so many, she might as well please herself.

It took a bit longer than she would have liked to shed her gown and unlace her corset. But she had not wanted to change her clothing in front of Louisa. Yes, her sister had seen her in her nightdress with Morgan, but Jessa would rather preserve her innocence whenever possible. At last, she was undressed. She pulled the silk dressing gown about herself, then finished unpinning her hair.

She would go to Morgan nearly naked, with her hair unbound. Surely he could not refuse her then.

Anticipation tangled with fear as she took up the candle and slipped from the room. The hall carpet was soft beneath her bare feet, and she watched her reflection in the far window coming closer. Closer, until she stood outside the earl's door once again.

Almost, she lost her nerve. It would be easy to blow out the candle, creep back down the hall, and climb into bed next to Louisa. No one would ever know.

Yet she feared she would regret that choice for the rest of her life. Already, she had too much to be sorry for.

The flame flickered, and Morgan's door opened. He stood there barefoot, his shirt half unbuttoned and untucked from his trousers. Without a word, he took her hand and drew her into his sitting room.

Neither of them spoke until they gained his bedroom. Morgan shut the door, then took her candle and set it on the bedside table, beside the amber-shaded lamp.

"You came," he said.

"And you did not turn me away."

His eyes darkened with desire as he regarded her. "I would not make that mistake again."

"I was not certain…"

"Because I was a beast to you earlier? My apologies, Jessa." His expression was set, though she suspected it was more from annoyance at himself than her. "I could not bear the thought of you meeting another man beneath my roof."

His words sent a thrill through her. Had Morgan truly been consumed with jealousy?

"You are the only one I want," she said. It was shockingly forthright, but then, she was no lady of the *ton*, to cover her meaning with sugar and lace.

He made a low sound in his throat. Two strides forward, and he caught her up in his embrace, his firm lips descending to cover hers. Jessa leaned into him, her senses flaring. All doubt fled. This was right—to be held in his arms, to breathe one another's breath, to taste and tangle and tempt, their bodies pressed tightly together.

She slid her hands up beneath his shirt, reveling in the feel of the muscled planes of his chest, the light dusting of hair that tickled her fingertips. For his part, his hands roved over her back and hips, the silk gliding beneath his touch.

Heat flared in the wake of his touch, pooled in the center of her body. He parted the robe, and it slid off her shoulders with a soft hushing sound.

"You are so beautiful," he said.

Her face warmed at his words—but this was no time for modesty. Not tonight. Mirroring his action, she pushed his shirt down his arms. Then, with a brief hesitation, she reached for his trousers. She could not help noticing the bulge there, and anxiety flitted through her.

"Don't worry," he said. "I promise to be gentle."

"What if I don't want gentleness?" She leaned forward and nipped at his shoulder.

He caught her to him, skin on skin.

"Then I will do my best not to hurt you."

He helped her undo the flap of his trousers. They fell to the floor, and his manhood pressed up from his drawers. She untied the string, and the cloth fell away, revealing him.

His shaft was strong and straight, rising from a cluster of golden hair between his legs. She did not ask if she might touch him, but reached to stroke one finger up its length.

"You may use more force than that," he said. "It's not breakable."

"If you insist." She wrapped her hand about him, the skin

hot and satiny under her palm.

He let out a low hiss, and she closed her hand around him even more. A bead of moisture lay at the top of the shaft, and she brushed her thumb over it, curious to feel its slickness. Then she brought her finger to her mouth and tasted it. Salty, like the sea.

"You'll undo me," he said, his breathing ragged.

"Because I like the taste of you?"

"And I am starving for you."

He took her mouth again, plundering the moist hollow with his tongue. The hardness of his shaft lay against her thigh. She could not quite imagine how he would fit inside her. His hand moved to pluck at her breast, the touch sending tingles down her spine and stomach.

Slowly, he walked backward, drawing her with him until they were at the edge of the bed. She was glad, for her knees were weak with pleasure.

"Sit," he said. "Yes, just on the edge."

He gently spread her legs, making a place for himself to kneel. His head was at a level with her breasts. Giving her a heated look, he leaned forward and drew his tongue over one taut nipple.

She gasped at the sensation, nearly dizzy as he closed his mouth about the peak. His fingers played with her other nipple, and she had to close her eyes at the sharp, delicious sensation. The juncture of her legs was throbbing now, her pulse seeming to come from that place and resonate through her entire body.

Morgan left her breasts and trailed kisses lower, to her stomach and waist. Then lower still.

Half of her wanted to protest, but the other half was wound tight with anticipation. She was so very hot between her legs. Did he intend to cool her with his mouth?

It seemed so, for he lifted her ankles and set her feet on

212 ~ ANTHEA LAWSON

the bedrail. Her thighs parted even more, until her most private
place was revealed to his sight. To his touch. To his tongue.

She gasped and nearly bucked at the sensation, but quickly
dissolved into pleasure. Oh, heavens. She'd no idea.

A moan escaped her, and she let her head fall back, giving
herself up to the desire building between her legs. It was
urgent, almost painful. She shook, and he grasped her hips, his
mouth moving eagerly against her.

Lightning struck, a flash that sizzled through her entire
body. She cried out at the intensity and fell back on the bed.
Aftershocks like thunder pulsed through her. One. Two. Three.

She drew in a long, wavering breath.

"Morgan. What have you done to me?"

He came to lie beside her, his eyes dark with need, with
amusement.

"What you deserve, my lovely Gypsy girl. Have you never
touched yourself, seeking pleasure?"

She shook her head at the notion.

"Not even once?" he asked.

"Perhaps... once, while swimming in a fast stream with
the other Rom children. I found a place where the current
pushed curiously against me. I stood there for a time, but it
only remained a tingling sensation. Nothing like this."

"Then I am happy to further your education."

"Pray, educate me further." She glanced at the naked,
magnificent length of his body.

He rose to his knees and pushed the bedcovers aside, and
she scooted into the middle of the bed.

"One moment." He reached over to the bedside table, and
retrieved a curious length of material that somewhat resembled
a stocking.

Seeing the question in her eyes, he gave her a half smile.

"It's a skin," he said, drawing it over his rigid shaft. "It helps prevent conception."

"A useful device," she said.

He tied the ribbon at the base of the skin, then gave her a look filled with intense need. Jessa caught her breath at the fire in his eyes.

The bed gave slightly under his weight as he came over her and slowly lowered himself. His shaft nestled between her legs, and the feel of him pressing against her made her nearly swoon. She was grateful to be already lying down, with all that hot, hard maleness touching every inch of her.

He bent his head and kissed her, and she slid her hands up over his muscled shoulders. His hips moved against hers, and she parted her thighs. The tip of him prodded against her.

"Breathe," he said.

Taking his member in one hand, he guided himself to her entrance and pushed slowly, slowly in.

Her body tightened, and she made herself relax. Then he began stroking her down there with his other hand, and it was easy to release the fear. She wanted this. Wanted him. Push, then stroke. Tighten, then ease. She felt stretched, but not beyond bearing, as he inched his way inside.

At last, their hips touched, and Morgan lowered himself over her again.

"All right?" he asked.

She nodded, experimentally wiggling her hips. His expression clenched, and she stopped.

"Did I hurt you?"

"No." His voice was tight. "I do want to last for more than a minute, however."

"Is this... all?" Compared to the glory he had shown her before, she found the act itself curiously uninspiring.

He let out a short laugh. "No. Just, wait a moment. In the meantime..."

214 ~ ANTHEA LAWSON

His mouth touched hers, nibbling softly. Then his tongue, playfully licking at her lips. She smiled and pulled him down over her, darting her tongue into his mouth. Slowly, she became aware that he was moving over her, his shaft pulling out a few inches, then working back in. Out. In.

At first, her body did not quite know how to accommodate the motion. She drew her legs up and tilted her hips, and that seemed to help. Morgan began to thrust faster. Heat spiraled up, winding about her belly, her breasts, sparking into her brain.

Faster.

She clutched his shoulders, now lightly sheened with sweat, and tried to match her body to his. Forward and back. Smoke, then embers and then…

"Ahh," she gasped, as she caught fire.

He plunged into her twice more, then stopped. The muscles in his neck were rigid and she could feel him shuddering over her in his own pleasure.

Flames licked about them both, and her heartbeat matched his, chest to chest, thigh to thigh. Mated.

The candle flickered, sending light and shadows to dance over Morgan's chest. He held her gaze, and she felt as though she glimpsed his soul.

I love you.

The emotion shivered over her. She could never say it, but her pulse beat out the words. Instead, she smiled at him.

He let out a long, shuddering breath and levered himself to the side.

"I am sorry if I hurt you," he said.

"It did not hurt."

"Still, there might be blood."

She felt the moisture between her thighs, then lifted her hand. "Perhaps a little."

"Here." He strode to the washbasin and returned with a dampened towel.

While she cleaned herself, he removed the skin and did the same. How messy lovemaking was, though she supposed the blood was only for the first time.

"Should I go?" she asked, feeling strangely lonely.

"No. Stay."

He bent and kissed her on the lips, long and lingering, then climbed back into the bed and drew the covers over them. His body was warm as he pulled her tightly against him, exciting and comforting at the same time. Jessa let out a contented sigh.

It was done. She was no longer a maid, and she was suddenly, fiercely glad of it. She had claimed Morgan as much as he had claimed her. They had shared their bodies so deeply, how could they not be affected?

"Sleep a little," he said, kissing the top of her head. "I will wake you before the servants are stirring, to return to your room."

She was still thirsty for the touch of him, so she did not protest, merely snuggled back into his embrace and closed her eyes. At the soft edge of sleep, she thought she heard him murmur her name.

CHAPTER TWENTY-TWO

One must wonder at the behavior of certain gentlemen who have expressed an interest in marriage, yet seem reluctant to come to the point. Ladies, under such circumstances, remind your suitors that they would be wise to close the trap, 'ere their catch escapes!

-Tilly's Mayfair Tattler

Jessa slept late the next morning since, for once, Louisa was careful not to rouse her. She woke smiling, and stretched, reveling in the luxurious softness of the sheets. Almost, she laughed aloud. She felt transformed and yet, in a curious contradiction, somehow more herself than ever.

And hungry, as well. Her stomach grumbled, and she rolled out of bed, dressed, and went in search of breakfast.

The service was cleared away, but Betts promised to bring her a plate of sausages, a crumpet, and a cup of tea.

"I'll be in the drawing room," Jessa told the maid.

She could not express her emotions to anyone. Except Morgan, and then only in the privacy of the night. But she could play the feelings surging through her, give them voice with her violin. Quickly, she unpacked her instrument and ran through her warm up exercises.

Betts came in with her breakfast, and Jessa ate, then brushed the crumbs from her hands and resumed playing. The music danced and sang, full of happy leaps and trills. Bright sunshine streamed in through the windows, picking out the glints of gold embroidery in the scarlet cushions and shining off the polished tabletop.

It was foolish, this giddiness—but she could not help it. Despite the soreness between her legs, she felt amazingly alive, her entire body awake. No regrets. And no lingering worries that she might bear a child, since Morgan had considered the risks ahead of time.

She slowed the tune, the notes growing wistful. Not that she did not want a child. Or several. But to bring Morgan's bastard into the world would be a terrible thing for all of them. It would destroy the reputation he had worked so hard to restore. It would ruin her, of course, and the child would suffer the ache of abandonment. An ache she knew all too well.

When she was nine, her father had decided he could no longer live penned between four walls. He'd left, and taken half her heart and most of the happiness in the world with him.

Yes, he would fetch her in the summers, and for three glorious months she'd live with him among the Rom. The pain of missing her mother and Louisa was greatly eased by the adventures of traveling from town to town, the freedom to run barefoot and not brush her hair for weeks on end.

Even though the clan was often met with distrust, and sometimes outright hatred, she was sheltered from it. The Rom world was a place apart, full of mystery and laughter, color and music.

Then the rain would come, and the darkening days, and her father would take her home to the shabby Oxford neighborhood. Hot tears ran, bitter, down her face every time she stepped through the door of their dingy two-room rental.

But however much she pleaded to go with him, he left her there.

"Your mother needs you," he said. "I will come back again. I always do."

And so she tatted lace to help with their meager living, and later, played her violin on the streets for coin during festivals and holidays.

True to his word, her father would make an appearance every now and then, promising to return for her in the spring.

With a deep breath, Jessa set her violin down. This melancholy turn had led her fingers into sad, winding tunes that she had no heart for.

"Miss?" Betts rapped at the door, then came into the room. "A message for you."

The maid held out a folded paper. Perhaps it was a correspondence from Mr. Widmere. Her nerves leaped, but it was far too soon to hear from him. He had not even left London yet.

"Who sent it?"

"A boy delivered it to the servants' entrance, just now." Betts gave her the note, along with a narrow-eyed look. "You're not seeing another gentleman on the sly, miss?"

"Of course not. How could you think such a thing?"

The maid had the grace to look abashed. "Just wanting to make sure. The earl's rather partial to you—we all know it."

"Yes." Jessa's cheeks heated.

She had no doubt the servants were aware of everything that transpired beneath the roof of Trevethwick House. Hopefully, their loyalty to the earl would keep them discreet.

The paper was closed with a clot of red sealing wax. Jessa picked at it with her nail until the paper parted from the wax. She unfolded the note and read, her breath tightening with every word.

Miss Lovell,

Your benefactor is not the gentleman you think him. Read the letters in his study from a Miss Abigail Smith if you do not believe me.

Return to Mr. Burke in the next twenty-four hours and he will not punish you for leaving.

-A concerned party

No. She stared at the note, heart thumping in her chest.

Morgan told her he had nothing hidden in his past. Whoever sent this note—and certainly it was Mr. Burke—must surely be mistaken.

"Bad news, miss?" Betts asked.

Jessa swallowed and hastily folded the paper in half. "An old acquaintance of mine has taken ill."

"That's a pity. Can I bring you more tea?"

"Yes, thank you."

As soon as the maid left the room, Jessa sank down on one of the chairs, her thoughts careening.

She should show Morgan the note and ask him directly what Mr. Burke meant. But... what if Morgan *had* lied to her? What would keep him from doing so again? Even though they had shared their bodies, she did not know what was in his mind. And the Earl of Silverton was adept at hiding his thoughts.

She doubted his transgressions were all that terrible. Despite the fact that her guardian thought that whatever she learned would send her fleeing back to him.

Betts returned with a steaming cup of tea, and Jessa took it gratefully.

"Is the earl at home today?" she asked.

"No." Betts made a face. "He went to pay a very special visit, or so I hear."

Jessa's ribs squeezed in another notch. "Not... to Lady Anne?"

"Aye." Betts nodded. "He took an enormous bouquet of flowers. Red roses, and jasmine blossoms from the conservatory. Reckon we know well enough what that means."

"Yes." Her mouth dry as parchment, Jessa took a hasty sip of her tea, scalding her tongue. "It means he is going to propose marriage to her."

Sorrow, equally mixed with hot rage, pushed up from her chest. *This* was her reward for giving herself, body and heart, to the Earl of Silverton. She was such a besotted idiot.

Betts gave her a sympathetic look. "Not as if it's unexpected. He did wait rather a long while, too."

Long enough to seduce Jessa.

Had taking her to his bed been the final act that propelled him toward Lady Anne? Jessa suspected Morgan's sense of honor had been strained nearly to the breaking point by their liaison. Perhaps he thought he would repair it by rushing off to make Lady Anne his betrothed.

Not that Jessa had any sort of a future with him—but she had hoped for a little more time. She blinked back the tears threatening to spill from the corners of her eyes.

"Well, miss, I must tend to my duties," Betts said.

"Of course," Jessa managed.

"Here." The maid handed her a mended handkerchief.

Jessa nodded her thanks, then turned away as the first drop slid down her cheek. The door closed quietly behind Betts, and the storm broke.

A rain of tears first, quickly followed by hard anger. How dare Morgan use her so! What a cad, to make love with her, and then flee the very next day to ask another woman to be his wife.

Jessa tucked away the damp kerchief and picked up her teacup. It would be so easy to break the delicate china, patterned with roses. She nearly flung it into the hearth. But the earl would not even notice, and Betts or one of the other maids would have to clean up the mess.

So. If Morgan was not at home, she would take this opportunity to search his study for the mysterious letters. Surely nothing she discovered could shake her more than the fact of his imminent betrothal. And it served him right, having her pry into his secrets.

Morgan's study smelled of leather and ink as Jessa slipped inside and quietly shut the door. She stood for a moment, trying not to feel as though she had invaded his privacy.

As if she should be concerned. He had taken her innocence, after all.

Slowly, she turned. His desk dominated the room—the most likely place to begin. She rounded it and sat in the chair, then studied the drawers. Three on either side, and one in the front. Although she doubted she would find any letters there, she pulled the center drawer open.

To her surprise, it held a hodgepodge of items: a chipped blue marble, an old Roman coin, a key, a piece of string, a sketch of an Irish Retriever. It was a glimpse into Morgan's past, a reminder that he had once been just a boy and not the controlled man he was now.

S almost softened—shut the drawer, and left the study.

But anger still sparked through her, and a mounting curiosity. Was there, in fact, anything in his study for her to discover, or had the note been a ploy from Mr. Burke to sow discord and suspicion? Jessa slid the drawer closed on Morgan's childhood treasures, and opened the top left-hand drawer.

Ten minutes of searching yielded only dry account books and notes from the manager of Morgan's country estate. Fingers slightly smudged with ink, Jessa opened the next drawer down. A packet of letters peeked from behind another stack of ledgers.

Tension prickling through her, she fetched them out and set them before her on the smooth mahogany desktop. They were bound with twine. Before undoing the knot, Jessa studied the packet. She would want to replicate it as closely as possible when she put the letters away.

Once she had fixed the placement of the string firmly in her mind, she untied the packet. Her fingers trembled as she unfolded the top letter.

April, 1827

My dearest Morgan, how my heart yearns to see you once again. The hours that we have spent together are precious to me...

Jessa scanned the letter, which seemed to consist mostly of declarations of love. It was signed Abigail Smith. The name the anonymous note had specified.

A love letter a dozen years old was not particularly damning, but it was only the top of the stack. Jessa set it aside and took up the next one.

At the third letter, she found the first hint of calamity.

... I fear I am increasing, however, it is still early. If we were to wed soon, no one would be the wiser...

The fourth letter made her heart plummet to her toes. The paper was marked with round water stains, as though from tears.

Morgan, how could you be so cruel? I thought you loved me! You promised to care for me forever, not cast me aside like a soiled garment. I bear your child, and can hide the fact no longer...

Jessa squeezed her eyes shut for a moment, her head filled with the pounding of her pulse. Please, let this not lead where she suspected.

The fifth letter was exceedingly short.

February, 1828.

Morgan, you have a daughter.

No.

Jessa pushed the letter away and leaned back in the chair. According to the damning evidence before her, Morgan had an eleven-year-old bastard daughter. And he'd told her he had no secrets!

Stifling a sob, she reached for the remainder of the packet. Skimming the letters, for she could not bear to read more deeply, certain lines leaped out at her.

Her name is Rosemary. I received your money, and we have settled into the cottage...

... has begun to walk. She has your bright hair. My lord, will you ever come to visit us?

It was kind of you to provide a pony for her fifth birthday. She often asks if she will ever meet her papa.

... now eight years of age. The villagers are not unkind, but they will never welcome us completely. Will you please bring us up to London?

Rosemary broke her arm falling from a tree, but is otherwise well. The dress you sent for her tenth birthday is too small, as she is growing apace.

The last, most recent letter, was dated May 14th, a mere three months prior. It held the same tone of resignation, another thank-you for sending money, and a snippet of information about Rosemary, whose feet were apparently now as large as her mother's.

Jessa shut her eyes, despair washing through her. How could she have been so wrong about Morgan's character? She had lost her heart to a man who thought nothing of abandoning his own child. She had welcomed him into her body, and her soul.

She carefully reassembled the packet and tied the twine. Her heart was filled with ashes. Moving as though her bones were brittle twigs, she replaced the letters in the drawer, then left the study.

The corridor leading to her bedroom seemed infinitely

long, and sorrow pressed against her chest with such weight that she could scarcely breathe. She gained the sanctuary of her room, grateful beyond measure to find that Louisa was not within. Jessa flung herself onto the bed and wept until her soul was wrung dry.

Finally she rose, pulled the curtains closed, and donned her nightdress. Although it was barely three in the afternoon, she was going to bed. She was sick at heart, and could not bear to see or speak to anyone. Especially not Morgan.

Tomorrow, she would rise, and plaster her heart, and carry on. But for now, she would close her eyes and let sleep drag her into blessed darkness.

CHAPTER TWENTY-THREE

Music aficionados rejoice! Maestro Reynard and his family will be returning to Paris to perform at the Conservatoire—a concert not to be missed by any person of refined tastes.

-l'Assemblee

The next morning, Jessa woke when Louisa cracked the curtains. A sliver of bright sunshine crept into the room, and Louisa came to stand beside the bed.

"Are you feeling better?" she asked, dark eyes full of concern.

Not particularly. Jessa was not certain her heart would ever mend. But she could not spend the rest of her life abed in a darkened room. Slowly, she sat up.

"I will do," she said.

And her resolution had crystallized. She would leave Trevethwick House at once. She could not bear to remain near Morgan, not with the double anguish of his betrothal and betrayal. At least Jessa had known her father, despite his frequent absences. Morgan's daughter had been raised completely bereft—abandoned in a backwater village, an illegitimate child of an uncaring lord. Her stomach twisted.

"Good!" Louisa clapped her hands. "Supper yesterday was so quiet, without you and the Silver Lord here."

"The earl was not at supper?"

"No. Lady Agatha said he went away."

"What? Where has he gone?"

Jessa slid out of bed and began to dress. It was unexpected but welcome news. If Morgan was not due home for a handful of days, it would give her time to lay her plans and depart. Better if she never saw him again. Her heart twisted with bitter despair.

"Lady Agatha said he went to his country estate. It's called Farthingwood." Louisa tilted her head thoughtfully. "I wonder if there are ponies. And a lake."

"You will have to ask Lady Agatha, for I've no idea." And did not care to know.

Settling before the mirror, Jessa pinned up her hair. The reflection in the glass stared back: wan, with red-rimmed eyes.

Today was Wednesday. Tomorrow, Mr. Widmere would be departing for the Continent. She must arrange to travel with him, and she would need a maid to go with her. It was prudent to behave as properly as possible, no matter the reality of her changed situation.

"Are you ready to come to breakfast?" Louisa asked, opening the door to the hallway. "I'm famished."

Jessa tucked up a stray lock of hair, then joined her sister. She had no appetite herself, but a cup of tea would not come amiss.

Sunshine streamed into the breakfast room, making the silver gleam. Lady Agatha was already in her usual place, wearing a pensive expression.

"Good morning, ladies," she said. "Jessa, I trust you are feeling somewhat recovered?"

"Adequately." Jessa took her seat across from Morgan's

aunt, and Louisa sat beside her, clearly sensing that Jessa needed her close.

Ah, how she would miss Louisa—the brightest thing in her universe.

"Has Louisa told you of Morgan's absence?" Lady Agatha asked.

"She mentioned it, yes. How long will he be away?"

Lady Agatha firmed her lips. "He did not say. What a vexing man."

Jessa made no comment, merely squeezed lemon into her tea. After a fortifying sip, she spoke.

"Louisa, Lady Agatha, I have come to a decision. I intend to depart London tomorrow."

"Jessie!" Louisa grabbed her hand.

Lady Agatha gave her an unhappy look. "I suspected you might be leaving us imminently, and I am sorry to hear it. But I will not entreat you to stay, and neither will Louisa."

"What if I want her to stay?" Louisa asked, her tone plaintive.

"I must go, duckling." Jessa leaned over to embrace her sister about the shoulders.

"Don't fret, Louisa," Lady Agatha said. "As soon as Morgan is wed, we will go visit your sister. Jessamyn, I presume you are going to the Continent?"

"Yes. I shall impose upon Mr. Widmere to let me accompany him. Also, I am in need of a maid to travel with me. Have you any recommendations on such short notice?"

"Hm." Lady Agatha frowned thoughtfully. "As a matter of fact, I do. It has come to my attention that one of the girls here has a difficult family situation. I'll inquire whether she would like to leave it, and join you instead. And I believe her salary is paid for the remainder of the year, so you would not need to bear that expense just yet."

Jessa narrowed her eyes. It would be true to Lady Agatha's generous nature to pay the girl in advance, but Jessa did not want to argue the matter. Truly, it would be a boon to her own limited finances.

"Do ask her," Jessa said. "If she is agreeable, perhaps she might help me begin to pack."

"I've a spare steamer trunk," Lady Agatha said. "Please make use of it. And take the gowns. You'll need to be properly garbed."

"Thank you for your generosity." Jessa's voice caught on the edge of tears, and she busied herself with buttering a piece of toast she had no intention of eating.

"I only wish you were leaving under happier circumstances," Lady Agatha said.

"You should not be leaving at all." Louisa crossed her arms. "The story isn't supposed to end this way. You're supposed to get the talisman, and live happily ever after."

"Life is full of things that don't turn out quite as we wish them to," Jessa said. "Don't worry, love. Before you know it, you'll be attending one of my concerts. In Spain, perhaps."

She spoke with a confidence she did not feel. There was still no guarantee Master Reynard would agree to put her on his program. But no matter the difficulties, she must go forward into that bleak, unknown future.

CHAPTER TWENTY-FOUR

In a shocking turn of events, it transpires that the Earl of Silverton does not intend to offer for Lady Anne Percival! Three days ago, he reportedly paid her a call where he apologized profusely for leading her to expect something he could not offer, then immediately departed London for his country estate. What a sorry state of affairs, to see how low certain gentlemen of the ton have fallen.

-Tilly's Mayfair Tattler

Morgan cantered over the morning fields. The steady rocking of Sterling's smooth pace and the sweet early air, scented with clover, soothed his exhausted thoughts. Since leaving London three days prior, he had slept poorly. He'd spent far too many restless hours in Farthingwood Manor's library, casting aside one book after another in search of something to distract his mind. Searching for answers to the turmoil within.

But there was no distraction from the perturbation of his thoughts, and the dusty philosophers offered no wisdom. So he was left to fight his demons alone.

The sun behind his shoulders cast long, spiky shadows over the fallow grasses, and the dirt road was still dark with dew. He'd forgotten how much he liked the country. It was too easy to remain mewed up in London, tending to the endless details of the earldom and ensuring he continued to represent the Trevethwick name with honor and propriety.

And how well that had turned out!

He urged Sterling into a hard gallop, trying to shake off the self-hatred that had driven him from Trevethwick House. It was no use. The stark fact remained that he had taken Jessamyn Lovell's innocence.

Jessamyn. A hot pain went through his heart. She deserved better than to be the castoff mistress of a blind and arrogant lord.

Over and over the memories played. Making love to her, his soul consumed with fire. Then waking the next morning, nothing but bleakness in his heart.

He had lain in bed, staring blankly up at the canopy, his thoughts tangled like moldering roots snarled and twisted in the dark ground.

The night before, he'd made Jessamyn Lovell a fallen woman. The fact that she had wanted him did not mitigate the blame.

How could he even call himself a gentleman, after what he'd done?

Who was he?

The façade of the earl cracked then, that shell breaking away to reveal the shallow, pleasure-seeking boy he'd been before his brother's death. Trev. Useless, foolish Trev, who could not see the destruction he sowed in his wake.

Bile in his mouth, Morgan rose. He dressed, his thoughts still battering his brain. When he stepped out the door, would the servants see the Earl of Silverton, or, his true nature revealed, would they avert their eyes and scurry from him?

It was too early for breakfast to be laid out, and at any rate he wanted to keep to his rooms. He felt as though he were stained with dishonor. There were no amends he might make.

As he paced through his sitting room, his eye fell upon one of the pretty notes Lady Anne had sent him, lying open on his desk.

Lady Anne. Ice crept up his spine. For God's sake—there was another woman he'd wronged. How had he come to this despicable pass? He stared at her note as though it were a venomous snake, ready to rise up and sink its fangs into his hand.

What would the earl do? Not the sniveling boy he had descended to, but the upright Lord Silverton?

Morgan drew in a deep, shuddering breath, then rang for his footman.

Within two minutes, Thaddeus arrived at his door.

"Fetch me a cup of tea," Morgan said. "And ask one of the maids to gather a bouquet. Have her..." He cleared his throat. "Have her include red roses and a spray of jasmine. Then saddle Sterling for me."

Thaddeus's eyes widened, but he made Morgan a precise bow. "Very good, my lord."

The hour was too early to pay a call upon Lady Anne, but Morgan could not remain within the walls of Trevethwick House. Not where Jessamyn still slumbered.

She would wake, and realize what he had done. Realize what an imposter of a man he was.

Bitterness rising in his chest, Morgan gulped back his tea, took the bouquet, and rode Sterling out into the streets of Mayfair.

He did not ponder upon his destination, but without thinking ended up at Green Park. Mist rose from the manicured lawn. Sterling pricked his ears up, but Morgan had no heart for anything faster than the measured paces of a walk.

His pulse throbbed, echoing through his head and pounding against his temples.

The scent of jasmine nearly turned his stomach, even though the bouquet was tucked away in the saddlebag, a wad of dampened paper keeping the flowers fresh. But no matter how fast he rode, there was no escaping the smell. Or the weight of his obligation to Lady Anne.

With a growl, Morgan pointed his mount away from the park, and into the streets leading toward the river. Perhaps the stench of the Thames would drive the pungent sweetness of jasmine from his nose.

Morning sunshine sparked off the water, and the cries of vendors punctuated the air as Morgan rode beside the river. The bells of Westminster struck. He counted them, surprised to find the hour was rising eleven.

Late enough to pay a visit to Lady Anne Percival. Yet he did not turn his horse from riding south along the Thames. Mayfair lay behind him, and it could wait a while more.

A woman with dark hair stood on the side of the street. For a moment, she resembled Jessamyn, and Morgan drew Sterling to a halt, breath freezing. But no, this was a stranger.

The woman smiled as a man in worker's garb strode toward her. Regardless of who might be watching, she flung her arms around him and kissed him on the lips. The sight made memory flare through him: Jessa's soft lips against his, her strong-willed determination, the joy and brightness surrounding her.

He could not put Jessamyn Lovell out of his life forever.

And he could not marry Lady Anne. Though it made a mockery of his upstanding reputation, he could not bring himself to propose to Lord Dearborn's daughter.

Morgan wrenched the bouquet from his saddlebag. He urged Sterling to the water's edge and, with a shout, flung the flowers into the river.

The bouquet floated, red and white upon the gray water, twirling as the current bore it away. He watched the flowers drift out of sight, his stomach churning. What a horrible excuse for a gentleman he had turned out to be. Nothing more than a hollow shell full of lies. Perhaps the world would be better off if he followed the bouquet into the noisome waters.

But no. Dreadfully flawed though he was, he still carried the weight of family upon his shoulders. He would not leave Geordie with such a distasteful legacy. But he could not remain in London a moment longer than he must.

He would go apologize to Lady Anne, and then retreat to the country—to Farthingwood Manor, where he would attempt to piece together the fragments of his shattered honor.

Now, three days later, he remained trapped in the swamp of his own soul. Still, one thing had become clear. It was an utter relief to have freed himself from the expectation of marrying Dearborn's daughter. Morgan's impulsive folly of telling her as much seemed, in retrospect, to have been the best course.

Only bitterness and eventual hatred would have followed in the wake of Lady Anne's expectations, and her dawning realization that she had not, in fact, married a true and worthy gentleman. They were both better out of that trap.

A bachelor earl could keep a mistress. It was what Jessamyn had proposed from the first.

As for the family name, Morgan would work with Geordie, and begin to hand over a few of the responsibilities of running the earldom. He'd be a fine heir with a little training—and no doubt it would please Aunt Agatha. Morgan was certain his aunt would have some choice words for him, but he would find understanding there. And perhaps some wisdom, too, if he listened.

Morgan took a deep breath of the fresh air, and turned Sterling back toward Farthingwood. Tomorrow he would return to London to seek Aunt Agatha's counsel. And beg Jessamyn's forgiveness.

***

"What do you mean she departed on Thursday for Paris?" Morgan demanded.

His fingers curled into fists as he stared at Aunt Agatha. How could she recline so calmly on her settee when the world was crashing into calamity?

"Calm yourself," she said. "Jessamyn had the wonderful opportunity to tour with Master Reynard, and she took it. Certainly there was no reason for her to remain here." Her last words held a bite.

"Are you saying it's my fault she left?" He began pacing over the garish red, orange, and blue carpet.

"It is," Louisa said. "You did not give her the last talisman."

Morgan shot her a glance, then returned his attention to his aunt. "I came back to apologize to her." And ask her to stay with him. To be his mistress.

Aunt Agatha's brows rose, as if she could hear what he was thinking. "I believe you owe her more than that."

"I don't know." He ran a hand through his hair, his thoughts careening about the walls of his mind. "I just…"

His aunt must have seen the confusion on his face, for her expression softened. "Take some time. Jessamyn is safe and well, and will be returning in a few weeks. Perhaps matters will seem clearer to you then."

They did not seem particularly clear the next morning, but a message arrived that proved a welcome distraction from his turmoil whenever he thought of Jessa.

Silverton – I will be calling upon you this afternoon at three to discuss a very important matter of mutual interest. Ensure that your butler and footmen permit me admittance.

–Burke

At last. If Morgan was in a quandary over what to do about Jessa, at least he knew exactly how to deal with her former guardian. He dispatched an urgent summons to Commissioner Rowan.

The commissioner arrived promptly at two, and the butler showed him into Morgan's study.

"Rowan." Morgan rose and shook the commissioner's hand. He could not suppress his flare of satisfaction that Commissioner Rowan was attending *him*, for once. "Please, take a seat."

"Do you truly think Burke is coming to threaten you?" Rowan asked, settling into the armchair across from Morgan.

"Yes. Something has set the man off, and I strongly suspect he'll be showing his hand this afternoon."

"I hope so." Rowan frowned. "I brought two of my men to take him in. Your butler installed them in the back parlor room."

"I'll meet Burke in the drawing room. There's a connecting door we can leave ajar. Listen, and as soon as he condemns himself, come in and take him."

"I hope you're right."

Morgan glanced at his pocket watch. "We'll know within the hour. In the meantime, would you and the lads care for some refreshment?"

"Something stronger than tea, please."

"Ale, then. Let me show you to the parlor, and I'll have the maid bring your drinks." Morgan stood and ushered Rowan from his study.

"I hear you've changed your mind about Lady Anne," the commissioner said. "Rather unexpected of you, Silverton. Are you still sheltering the Lovell girls?"

"Only one of them," Morgan said shortly. "Here's the drawing room. And the parlor. I'll just go over and ensure the connecting door is unlocked."

Rowan gave him a thoughtful look, but asked no more prying questions. With a brief nod of farewell, Morgan left him with his two burly companions. He unlocked the door between the two rooms and left it open a crack. Without close inspection, it was difficult to tell the door stood ajar.

It was no use going back to his study. It had been hard to concentrate on the account books earlier, and he absolutely would not be able to now. He hailed one of the maids and asked her take the men some ale, then found his steps taking him to the back drawing room. But there were too many echoes of Jessa's presence there. Firming his lips, he strode toward the front of the house, just as the sound of the knocker echoed down the hall.

He arrived at the door as the butler pulled it open. As expected, Mr. Burke stood on the step. He wore a beaver top hat and a smug look, but anger burned in his brown eyes.

"Silverton. How kind of you to meet me yourself," he said.

"My lord?" The butler gave him an anxious look.

Morgan waved him off. "I will show Mr. Burke to the parlor," he said. "See that we're not disturbed."

"Not going to offer me tea and biscuits?" Mr. Burke asked, stripping off his gloves as he followed Morgan down the hall. "How inhospitable of you."

"You should be grateful I agreed to see you at all." Morgan held open the drawing room door and let the detestable man precede him into the room.

"Rather the opposite, my lord," Burke said. "After you

hear what I'm about to say, you'll be glad you deigned to meet with me."

"Well then." Morgan folded his arms. "Out with it."

"So blunt you are with those you consider your inferiors. I hope my dear wards haven't suffered too much during their stay with you. Oh, wait." Mr. Burke affected a look of surprise. "My meddling older brother has decided to take them under his wing, instead! A pity the mail from Italy travels so slowly."

"Then you know that I and my aunt are acting on their behalf. And whatever brought you here today has no hope of success."

Mr. Burke let out a mirthless laugh. "On the contrary, their time beneath your roof is coming to an end. It shouldn't take them long to pack, once we are done speaking. I look forward to taking them back home."

Morgan burned to punch the smirk off Mr. Burke's face. Instead, he forced his anger to the side. Fighting the man would not achieve the results he and Rowan were hoping for.

"My patience is nearly at an end." He spoke through gritted teeth.

"Mine has been gone for three weeks," Mr. Burke spat back. "Listen well, Silverton. If you don't give the Lovell girls back to me, I'll make sure that news of your bastard daughter is smeared across every gossip rag in England. Your precious reputation will never recover."

"I haven't the faintest notion what you are speaking about." Morgan kept his tone haughty, though triumph flashed through him.

"Don't play the innocent." Burke bared his teeth. "It's a tawdry, yet common tale. A pity yours will be brought to light."

Morgan's hands tightened, though not from fear, as Mr. Burke surely thought. This was the trap he had laid, and he must ensure that Burke ensnared himself fully.

"How did you hear of this?" Morgan asked. "It's not generally known."

He bit the inside of his cheek to keep any hint of a smile from his face.

"I have copies of the letters from your spurned mistress," Burke said. "I'm sure she'll come forward once the sordid details are revealed. Especially if I offer a reward."

"Let me understand." Morgan raised his voice. "You are threatening to expose my previous affair and bastard child, unless I agree to release the Lovells back into your custody?"

"Precisely. And a few hundred pounds won't come amiss, either."

Morgan strode forward and took Burke's arm in a tight grip. "What if I refuse?"

"Ha!" Mr. Burke's stale breath washed over him. "This information is also in the hands of a friend. Should anything happen to me, be assured he will spread the tale far and wide."

"Then you leave me no choice." Morgan let his fingers sink painfully into Burke's upper arm. "Rowan, I believe I have your man," he called.

"What?" Burke twisted in his grasp as the door slammed open and the commissioner and his men burst through. "Let me go!"

He bent and sank his teeth into Morgan's forearm. With a yell, Morgan released his grip.

"Catch him!" he cried as Burke darted for the hallway.

Luckily, the commissioner's men were faster than they looked. One leaped forward and grabbed Burke's shoulder, while the other got his arm around Burke's neck.

"Mr. Z, I presume." Commissioner Rowan came to stand before Burke.

"I've never heard that name before," Burke wheezed, his eyes darting wildly about the room.

"Deny it all you like," Rowan said. "Mr. Alfred Burke, you are charged with blackmail, not only of the Earl of Silverton, but many other members of the *ton* as well. By the time of your trial, I'm sure we'll have more than ample proof." He turned to Morgan, "Silverton, thank you for your assistance. Your part in this has been invaluable."

"You'll be sorry once I'm free," Burke said, hatred shining in his eyes.

Morgan did not bother to reply, and Rowan simply nodded to his men. "Take him away."

They watched silently as Burke was removed from Trevethwick House. Then the commissioner held out his hand to Morgan.

"Well done," he said, his handshake firm. "You'll be needed as a witness, but probably not for another month, I'd imagine."

"Of course. It would be my pleasure. Good day, commissioner."

"It has been already." Rowan gave him a smile. "We'll be in contact when we need you."

He retrieved his hat from the butler, then hurried out the door to catch up with his men. And their quarry, bagged at last.

Morgan took a deep breath and slipped his hands in his pockets, enjoying the warm satisfaction settling over him.

Sadly, the feeling was short-lived. Finally, Mr. Burke was dealt with—but whatever was Morgan to do about Jessamyn Lovell?

CHAPTER TWENTY-FIVE

Listeners were treated to a surprise at Maestro Reynard's concert on Friday. Debut musical sensation Mlle. Jessamyn Lovell, oft called the Gypsy Violinist, took the stage early in the evening to perform a selection of sad and beautiful melodies. She then raised the mood by playing a medley of fiery dance tunes that set toes tapping. An excellent addition to the bill!

- l'Assemblee

Jessa played. In Paris and Chartres, in Madrid and Seville, she lifted her violin before the anonymous audiences and played her entire soul. Her violin was her wordless cry into the world. Sorrow, always sorrow first, until she became known for eliciting tears with her sweet, yearning melodies.

Mindful of her obligation—to her listeners, to Master Reynard and his wife, who had so graciously added her to their performance schedule—she always ended her portion of the concert with something happy. Well, as happy as she could muster with a broken heart.

In the three weeks she had been gone from England, she'd been very careful to avoid reading the *London Times*, or any of the news out of Town. She had perused papers aplenty, as Mr.

Widmere liked to bring her notices of the praise she was garnering. But never the *Times*. She could not bear to hear of Morgan's betrothal and the no-doubt-imminent wedding of the Earl of Silverton to Lady Anne Percival.

She had received one letter from Louisa, posted the day after she left, but Mr. Widmere had told her that most of her correspondence would be waiting for her when they returned to Paris. It was too difficult to rely upon the mails to stay reliably on schedule as the tour moved so rapidly from place to place.

And so, she played. And traveled in the Reynard family's shadow. And spoke very little, but wrote long, descriptive letters to Louisa, full of amusing anecdotes of her travel and avoiding all mention of her emotional state.

She'd found an unexpected friend in Darien and Clara's eight-year-old daughter, Annabel. After the first night Jessa performed, Annabel had marched into Jessa's suite of rooms in the Paris hotel, carrying her own small violin case.

"Teach me those songs you played," she said, regarding Jessa from determined blue eyes.

Jessa gave her a curious look. "Isn't it your bedtime, Miss Reynard?"

"My parents let me stay up as late as I like, as long as I'm playing music." She set her case on the table and began unpacking the instrument. "And you may call me Annie."

Annie proved to be a quick learner, and before long she was playing the Rom melodies as though she'd learned them in the cradle. Her sweet nature and delight in the music helped ease the wretched ache in Jessa's soul. Once or twice, she even made Jessa laugh with one of her childishly forthright observations.

This evening, the concert tour took them to the Teatro Nacional in Lisbon. Jessa waited in the hushed shadows of the wings, her violin tucked beneath her arm. Five rows of balconies rose to the ornately painted ceiling. Directly facing the stage was an elaborate box, columned and gilded with gold paint. Tonight, Queen Maria and King Consort Ferdinand were in attendance.

Two weeks ago, the prospect of playing before royalty had made her sick with nerves. But with a few concerts, and the kind support of Master Reynard's composer wife, Clara, Jessa was able to steady herself and perform without undue panic. Though her pulse still fluttered at the thought.

The lights along the balconies were extinguished, and the hum of anticipation rose. In a few moments, the concert would begin.

Jessa took a deep breath. Her portion of the performance would be over in fifteen minutes. Before she went on stage, it seemed an eternity, but once she started to play, the time sped.

And now the manager was announcing her.

Trying not to blink at the brightness of the stage lights, Jessa strode forward. Applause washed about her, but not loudly. Some members of the audience continued to converse. They were here to see Darien Reynard and Clara Becker, not some unknown Gypsy girl.

Jessa had become accustomed to the lack of interest. It was a challenge, to woo the listeners until they fell silent beneath the spell of her playing. Some nights she was more successful than others.

The air in the Teatro was warm, and the scent of perfumes swirled about the stage. Jessa bowed to the audience and, without waiting for their silence, began to play.

Strangely, she had found that beginning quietly hushed her listeners more quickly than if she thrust the music at them with force and volume.

The first notes crept into the air, curling like faint tendrils of smoke after a candle is blown out. Jessa let the sound twist and dissipate, almost coming into silence. The audience stilled.

She did not smile—not outwardly. But she felt that moment when the attention in the room shifted to her. Jessamyn Lovell. A woman in an emerald satin dress, playing the violin. Slowly, she increased the pace of the music.

The notes swirled and flurried, no longer smoke but fallen leaves. Dancing, even in decay, bright against the ominous clouds of winter. She danced with them, swaying as the tune rose and fell, until it ended in a gust, and blew all the leaves away.

The applause was far more enthusiastic this time.

"*Obrigado*," she said. "Now, I will play for you a selection of Rom songs, dedicated to love, and sorrow."

She had often wondered why so many of the Rom love songs were sad. Now she knew, to the depths of her heart. The two emotions were intertwined, just as shadows could not exist without light. At least in the music she could sob and wail, and give voice to everything she had lost.

Morgan.

His name was a burning coal lodged inside her chest, painful and bright.

When the aching sadness became too much, Jessa segued into the dance tunes. They still carried the echo of melancholy in the minor modes, but the tempos were jaunty. She stepped the pace up, and then again, driving the beat forward with her bow, driving all memory from her mind as her fingers flew.

At the end of the final tune, she pulled the bow across all four strings in a full, triumphant chord. It rang up to the ceiling, and the crowd applauded madly.

Jessa bowed, but declined the cries for an encore. Her part of the concert was over.

A few flowers were flung on stage, and a nimble stagehand

scrambled to pick them up. He handed them to Jessa, who waved them at the audience as she headed for the shelter of the proscenium curtain.

"Well done, Jessamyn!" Clara Becker Reynard stood in the wings beside her husband, her fair hair glowing in the reflected stage lights.

"Indeed." Master Reynard gave her a nod of approval. "Your performances grow stronger with every concert."

"I cannot thank you both enough," she said.

Clara sent her a sympathetic smile. Though Jessa had not spoken of why she left England, Master Reynard's wife seemed to have guessed that it had something to do with unfortunate love.

"Come, my dear." Master Reynard held out his free arm to his wife. "They are clamoring for us."

"Play well," Jessa said.

They always did, of course, with an ease and brilliance that continued to astound her. There was a wordless interplay between them that added such depth to the music, the weave of violin and piano into one voice as the couple performed Clara's compositions.

Jessa was fortunate to hear them perform so often. Her musician's soul delighted in the small variations and changes they made during each performance, keeping the pieces fresh and vital.

They strode on stage to deafening applause, and Jessa made for her dressing room. She would put her violin away, place her flowers in the vase provided, then return to listen to the rest of the concert.

As she passed the Reynards' dressing room, she heard Annie laughing at her little brother, and the calm voice of their nanny in response. The sound cheered her, in a bittersweet fashion. Would she ever have children of her own?

Sighing, she pushed open the door of her dressing room, then froze in shock. A man stood there—a tall, blond-haired fellow. He turned, but she already knew who he was.

Morgan. Her lips shaped his name, but she could not speak it aloud.

Joy crashed over her, followed by bleakness that froze her to the bone.

"Jessa," he said. "You sounded marvelous."

"What are you doing here?" She forced herself to walk past him.

With trembling fingers, she set her violin in its case. The flowers she set on the table to wither. Her suddenly numb hands would not be able to jam them into the vase.

"I came to find you," he said, as if that were explanation enough.

"And you have. Now you may depart again." She knew her voice was cold, and she did not care. Inside, her heart careened wildly.

He took her hand, and she pulled it away, then folded her arms.

"I suppose I deserve your scorn," he said with a wry look. "And you deserve my apology in full measure."

"Your apology?" She clutched her arms close to her body. "Did your new wife send you on this mission, so that you might return to her with a clear conscience? What else did you bring—gold to buy my silence, so that your reputation may remain unsullied?"

He took a step back, a wounded light flashing through his gray eyes. "No. And I am not married."

"Yet."

"Yet." He ran a hand through his hair. "You are making this damnably difficult, Jessa."

"You may take your leave of me at any time." Her body

trembled with the need to touch him, but she forced herself to remain still. "Did Lady Anne accompany you to Lisbon? No doubt she is curious about your absence."

"I'm not going to marry Lady Anne!" He strode forward and took her elbows. "I want to marry *you*."

She blinked at him, the room suddenly tipping at the corners of her vision. Surely he had not just spoken those words. Her pulse beat loudly in her chest.

"I... beg your pardon?"

He stared into her eyes. "Jessamyn Lovell, will you marry me?"

It must be a cruel joke, yet his expression was completely serious. Pleading, even, if one knew how to read his face. Which, to her sorrow, she did—all too well.

"But you took her a bouquet." She feared her replies were making her sound as simple as Louisa, yet she could make no sense of his words.

"To perdition with the bouquet. I threw it in the Thames, then told Lady Anne I could not fulfill her expectations."

The truth in his voice pierced her. He had not married Lady Anne. He had come to Portugal to find her. But no matter how the embers in her heart burst to full flame at the thought, she could not be his ruin.

"Morgan, you cannot marry me. What of your name, your reputation—"

"Blast the reputation. My aunt was right, though it took me far too long to see it. A proper life is no good, if one is desperately unhappy all the way to death's door. My brother..." He swallowed, then continued. "It was not a love of life that killed him. I tried to make myself believe it, though. I thought if I shut away that part of my soul, I would be safe. But you stormed into my life with your music and passion, and I was lost."

She gazed at him, noticing that he wore a new coat in a deep moss-green color. Had Morgan truly broken free of his prison of respectability? Her chest expanded with ridiculous hope. Then the breath crushed out of her as she remembered the other reason she had fled.

"I still cannot marry you," she said, her voice low and miserable.

"Why not? I told you, I don't care what the *ton* thinks. We can go live in the country when you are not performing. Society can gossip all it likes, but it will not matter one whit."

"You should have realized that a dozen years ago! What about Abigail, and Rosemary?"

He looked at her blankly, and she wanted to slap his face.

"Rosemary?" he asked.

What a blackguard he was, lacking all human decency. To think she had misjudged him so badly. She'd foolishly given her heart to a man who deserved to rot in hell.

"Your bastard daughter," she said bitterly. "Or did you forget?"

To her shock, he threw his head back and laughed. She raised her hand then, to slap him in truth, but he caught her wrist.

"Wait. Wait." His expression sobered. "You read the letters in my study?"

"To my everlasting regret."

"What a tangle. I should have burned them."

She could scarcely look at him. "You would consign Rosemary's entire history to the fire?"

"Jessa, listen to me." He moved his hands to her shoulders, his gaze clear. "There is no bastard daughter, no lover from the past. Those letters were a ruse, planted the night of the musicale for Mr. Burke to find."

She swayed, and he steadied her.

"Is this the truth?" Her heart trembled violently with fear, with hope.

"I swear it. You can ask Commissioner Rowan of Scotland Yard if you won't take my word for it. We laid the trap for your guardian." His voice took on an exultant note. "When he came to threaten exposure, the constables were waiting in the next room. He's in custody now, awaiting trial—and he named his accomplice, a Mr. Dabbage. He tried to pull you into it as well, but I told the commissioner to have none of that."

"I must sit." She felt as though she were about to collapse from the waves of revelations crashing over her.

Morgan drew the single chair over and settled her in it. Without asking, he fetched a glass of water. When she took it, the water shivered from the trembling of her hand.

"I am a bit disappointed." A touch of the old coolness returned to his voice. "You believed those letters. Do you really take me for that kind of man?"

"No." She took a sip of water, the coolness soothing in her mouth. "I could not believe it, although the proof lay there, before my eyes. At first I was going to ask you about them, once you returned home. But then…"

She paused to swallow back the lump of tears in her throat.

"Then you discovered I had gone to propose to Lady Anne." He knelt on the carpet, heedless of his dignity, and took her hand.

"It was too much," she said. "I could not bear to see you married, and the letters were yet another reason for me to go. Thinking you heartless allowed me to leave you. Morgan, I am so terribly sorry."

"Not as sorry as I am." He shook his head. "We both behaved like idiots."

"You, more than me."

She meant it in truth, but also in jest. By the wry light in his eyes, he understood both her meanings.

"I believe you owe me an answer," he said.

"Why do you want to marry me?"

"Ah. I believe I've neglected the most important part. I desire you. I need you." Holding her gaze, he brought the back of her hand up to his mouth and kissed it. "I love you."

Her pulse jolted, as though she had just landed from leaping a great distance.

"If I agree, it won't be easy." Slowly, slowly, her heart was opening, cracked apart by the blaze within.

"I'm weary of spending my life working so hard for no joy." He gave her a rueful look. "I'd far rather put that effort toward happiness. And so I'll ask you yet again—and I'll keep asking until you tell me yes. Will you marry me, Jessamyn Lovell?"

She stared at him a moment, nearly blinded with emotion, and the sheer unbelievability of his question. He cocked his eyebrow, and she leaned forward, slipping her arms about his neck.

"Yes," she said softly. "I love you."

She kissed him, their mouths meeting like a chord of music, like sparks and benediction. Like truth. Heat ran from her head to her toes, a rush of wildfire. If they were not in a dressing room during a performance, she would have begun unbuttoning his shirt, taken down her hair, and shared her body with his in a blaze of passion.

But they would have time, and more time, to give in to that yearning desire.

When the kiss ended, they both were breathing heavily. She did not care that a tear or two had slipped down her cheek. He blotted them with the back of his hand.

"I have something for you." He reached into his pocket

and drew out a small, round box.

He undid the small hook and opened the box to reveal a diamond ring shining against black velvet. One large oval stone was mounted on a gold base, surrounded by smaller diamonds. It glittered like a flower made of stars.

"It's beautiful," she said as he slipped the ring on the finger of her left hand. "And it fits perfectly."

"Louisa helped me choose it. She told me to size it to her finger, and then it would fit you. She called it the last talisman, and was utterly confident you would accept my proposal. Her faith in that happy ending is one of the reasons I am here now."

Jessa glanced at him. "My sister knows of this?"

"Yes, and my aunt as well. They came with me to Portugal, and are in the audience even now. Louisa begged to come back to your dressing room with me, but I would not allow it."

"They are here?" Jessa rose, happiness filling her so that she could scarcely draw a breath.

He stood, too, keeping her hand in his own. "When they learned I was going in pursuit of you, they insisted on coming along. Either to celebrate with or to comfort you, as need be. I'm unspeakably grateful that it is to be celebration."

"So am I." She shook her head. "I cannot quite believe this is not a dream."

"If it is, then we can dream it together. But come. It's intermission, and your sister will be overjoyed to see you."

Any more joy and Jessa was certain she would rise up into the air. Perhaps float up to the painted ceiling of the Teatro Nacional. She smiled at the image of herself bobbing above the crowd, then laced her arm through Morgan's. Her true and honorable love. He would keep her from floating away.

EPILOGUE

Earl of Silverton shocks!
After years of nothing but the most proper behavior, Lord Silverton
astounded Society with his announcement that he is going to wed the Gypsy
Violinist, Miss Jessamyn Lovell. Our most sincere condolences to Lady
Anne Percival, and felicitations to the earl and his next intended. One
hopes there will not be a third!
-Tilly's Mayfair Tattler, September 1839

Jessa sat stiffly in the carriage bearing them to St. George's Church. She did not want to crease the organdy of her wedding gown, or disturb the wreath of orange blossoms in her hair. Luckily, the church was in Mayfair, a short distance from Trevethwick House, otherwise she would arrive at her own wedding with a crimp in her neck.

"Now you are the princess," Louisa said, nearly bouncing on the seat with excitement. "I knew the Silver Lord would give you the third talisman, and everything would come out right."

Jessa held up her hand, and the diamonds in her ring caught the morning sunlight, sending sparks of rainbow across the carriage's interior.

Across from them, Lady Agatha smiled. "I cannot tell you

252 ~ ANTHEA LAWSON

how happy I am that this day came about. Ever since you came to us, seeking shelter and protection, I'd hoped Morgan would see what a perfect match you were."

"A Gypsy girl and an upright lord." Jessa shook her head at Lady Agatha, though she could not erase the smile from her own face. "Certainly, ideal in every way."

"Hmph. You needed one another, that much was plain to anyone with eyes to see."

"We are there!" Louisa cried, sticking her head out the window.

The church was not an imposing edifice, and for that Jessa was grateful. She had tried to convince Morgan to hold a private ceremony at his country estate, but he refused.

"I'll not have it said that I'm ashamed to wed you, and snuck away to Farthingwood to do the deed in secret. No, we may have a small ceremony if you wish, but it will be held in the heart of Mayfair."

The carriage drew up at the columned portico of the church. The door swung open, and Louisa hopped out before the footman could assist her. Jessa followed, glad of Thaddeus's steadying hand.

"I wish you a very happy day, miss," the footman said. "And no matter what some people say, I'm pleased as punch that you're going to wed Lord Silverton."

"Thank you."

Indeed, all the servants had been kind. Betts had thrown her apron over her head in excitement upon hearing the news, and insisted she come along when Jessa and Morgan removed to Farthingwood after their wedding.

A wedding that was now upon Jessa. Before she had scarcely drawn breath, Viscount Trenton was at her elbow, ready to escort her up the aisle.

He had come from Italy when he had heard of her

betrothal, and seemed delighted to be back in London after such a long absence. He and Aunt Agatha had struck up a lively friendship, and were often in one another's company.

"I do not mind that she is busy," Louisa had confided. "For I get to see more of you. I missed you terribly when you were away."

"I will be away for a portion of every year, duckling."

To her amazement, Master Reynard had offered her a permanent position on his concert bill. Luckily, the Reynards did not have an overly punishing schedule, due to traveling with their children. Two months in the summer were devoted to concertizing, mostly on the Continent. Jessa could not have asked for a more satisfactory timetable.

"I know," Louisa had said. "But you will come back."

"Yes, love." Jessa had kissed the top of her sister's head. "I will always come back."

The interior of the church was plain, with a spacious nave and a purple velvet canopy over the pulpit. Tall pillar candles scented the air with wax, and the wreath of white flowers on her head added a waft of sweetness everywhere she walked. The distance to the altar seemed miles, and Jessa gripped the viscount's elbow a bit more tightly.

"Steady on," he said, patting her hand.

She gave him a grateful glance, relieved at how little he resembled his younger brother. Viscount Trenton was nearly completely bald. He and Mr. Burke had the same brown eyes, but where her former guardian's were the color of dried molasses, the viscount's held a humorous sparkle.

Viscount Trenton had also come in time to attend his brother's trial and sentencing. Morgan's planted evidence had been the key. Once Mr. Burke understood he was well and truly caught, he had not hesitated to expose Mr. Dabbage and confess everything, in return for a lighter sentence:

transportation for life to Van Diemen's Land.

"He always was a fretful, unhappy child," Viscount Trenton had said, shaking his head sadly at the verdict. "I should never have let him assume your guardianship, Jessamyn, and for that you have my profound apologies."

But Jessa refused to let the thought of Mr. Burke blight her day. Already he was a bad memory, fading in the light of her newfound happiness.

And the center of that joy lay ahead, watching her approach with a smile in his eyes. When she was three paces away, the smile settled upon his lips. He stepped forward and extended his arm.

Viscount Trenton handed her to Morgan with a slight incline of his head, and her beloved led her to stand before the altar. The minister called the assembled to prayer, and Jessa bowed her head, letting the words of benediction wash over her. She could hear Lady Agatha already sniffling slightly in the front row. By the end of the ceremony, she would likely have gone through several handkerchiefs.

When it came time to say the vows, Morgan spoke the words clear and true. He held her gaze, and she felt each promise ring through her like the chime of a bell. It was easy to say the words back to him, to admit the depth of her love before the handful of guests, the minister, and God.

"The ring," the minister said.

Morgan slipped a plain gold band onto her finger. It was warm from his touch. Hidden against her skin, their names were engraved, and the date. *Morgan & Jessamyn Trevethwick, 20-9-39.* The truest talisman of all.

And then it was done, and the church bells pealed, and Morgan kissed her, holding her in his embrace a touch longer than propriety would allow.

"My lord," she said, pretending outrage. "You are

scandalous."

"Just for that, I will kiss you again, Lady Silverton."

He did, until the minister cleared his throat loudly. "If you will follow me, we may sign the license."

Morgan escorted her to the side of the nave, where they signed the documents legally pronouncing them man and wife. Jessa's hand was steady as she penned her name.

Then Louisa and Lady Agatha, laughing and crying both, came to embrace her. Geordie looked on, grinning, and the other guests applauded.

"Is it time for the wedding breakfast now?" Louisa asked. "There is a splendid cake. And gifts."

"The carriage awaits," Lady Agatha said.

Morgan took Jessa's arm once more and escorted her down the aisle. "I have a particular gift for you. I hope you don't mind."

They stepped out of the church into the autumn sunshine. There, next to the carriage, Morgan's head groom stood holding a pair of horses. Sterling snorted and bobbed his head as his master approached. The chestnut beside him was decked with white flowers braided into his mane.

"I would like to give you Mayberry," Morgan said. "The two of you got on very well together, as I recall."

Jessa smiled up at him, delight bubbling up from her chest. "Thank you. I hope you will join me for a post-wedding ride."

"Nothing would make me happier."

Though she was ridiculously encumbered by her wedding gown, Jessa did not care. She handed her bouquet of white roses to Louisa and, with assistance from both Morgan and the groom, managed to mount Mayberry and hook her leg over the pommel.

Her skirts spread over the horse's withers and rump, and she nearly laughed aloud at the impracticality of it.

"Are you secure enough?" Morgan asked.

"I am." She leaned forward and back, finding her seat surprisingly stable.

"Excellent." He mounted Sterling and, amid good-natured cries of farewell from the guests, they rode away.

Jessa was still not particularly conversant with Mayfair's streets, but as Morgan turned them down St. George Street, she gave him a curious glance.

"Isn't Trevethwick House more to the west?" she asked.

"We are taking a short detour. Nothing that will delay our wedding breakfast overlong, however."

Ahead, she caught a glimpse of trees and shrubbery. Not Green Park, for that was too far out of their way.

"Berkeley Square?" she guessed.

"Indeed. I hope it is not too crowded for a good canter."

She tipped her head back and laughed, and his lips turned up in the faintest of smiles.

"You continue to shock, Lord Silverton."

"What good is life if one can't enjoy it?" He reached over and grasped her gloved hand, giving it a tight squeeze.

The horses' ears pricked up as they stepped from stone to grass. The greensward ahead lay mostly empty, and although the far side of the park was a short distance away, Jessa leaned forward and gave Mayberry a nudge with her heel.

He needed no further prompting, but strode out into a trot, then a canter. Jessa gripped the saddle tightly as her skirts blew in the wind of their passage, but she was in no danger of falling. She laughed again, filled with more happiness than she knew how to contain. Behind her, she heard the thud of Sterling's hooves.

Morgan drew up beside her when she halted at the end of park. Uncaring of the faces turned their way, he leaned over and kissed her soundly. The wind stirred the remaining leaves overhead. A scattering swirled down, dancing and turning under the cloud-flecked September sky.

Smiling, Jessa drew back, and side by side they rode toward Trevethwick House and their waiting guests.

Toward a happier future than they'd ever dared to dream.

THANK YOU!

Thank you for reading MISTRESS of MELODY! If you enjoyed it, please consider helping other readers find this book:

1. Lend this book to a friend!

2. Leave a review on Amazon, Goodreads, or any other site of your choice. It makes a difference, and is greatly appreciated!

3. Request that your local library purchase a print copy, so that other readers can discover Anthea's romances.

Be the first to know about new releases and reader perks by subscribing to Anthea's newsletter at tinyletter.com/AntheaLawson.

ACKNOWLEDGEMENTS

This book was partially inspired by all the talented folk fiddlers I've had the pleasure of playing and studying with over the years. Thank you to so many musicians for continuing the vitality of diverse musical traditions, in particular: Martin Hayes, Bruce Molsky, Alasdair Fraser, Arkaitz Miner, Lunasa, and the Festival of American Fiddle Tunes.

The novel itself was greatly improved by the input of my critique partners Chassily and Matt, my editor Laurie Temple, my proofreader Ginger, and the always excellent copy-editing skills of Arran Nichols at Editing 720.

Once again, Kim Killion proves her talent in cover design. Many thanks for a gorgeous cover, and thanks also to the fine models at Period Images and the Killion Group.

ABOUT THE AUTHOR

Anthea Lawson's first two novels were co-written by Anthea and Lawson, a husband and wife creative team living in the Pacific Northwest. Their first novel, *Passionate*, was released from Kensington books in October 2008, and was a finalist for the prestigious RWA RITA award for Best First Book. Booklist has named Anthea one of the "new stars of historical romance."

Since 2010, Anthea has branched out solo, continuing to write historical romance and hitting the *USA Today* bestseller list. She also pens award-winning YA urban fantasy as Anthea Sharp. Anthea is still happily married and living in the Northwest with her husband and daughter, where the rainy days and excellent coffee fuel her writing.

Discover more at anthealawson.com and on Facebook/AntheaLawson. To find out about Anthea's upcoming releases, please subscribe to her mailing list at www.tinyletter.com/AntheaLawson. Thank you!

Made in the USA
Lexington, KY
21 May 2015